"I have discovered I no longer find solitude agreeable," Giles said hoarsely.

"My lord, I fear . . ."

"You have nothing to fear, Caroline. I will not hurt you. Just stay a moment, thus so," he whispered huskily, drawing her into his arms. He held her gently, pressing her head to rest against his shoulder. "Let us hold one another for a moment to take away the loneliness."

His breath fanned the hair at her temple. "You must sense the rightness in this, Caroline. I cannot be alone in my feelings."

Caroline stood quietly, drawing comfort from his solid strength. Giles was right. The loneliness that lingered dropped away and she was at peace for the first time since her father's death.

Lord Castleton stroked her back from shoulder to waist. It was a touch meant to comfort, not inflame. She instinctively burrowed deeper into his arms, until the touch of his lips against her temple forced her back to reality.

Caroline stepped out of his grasp, wanting nothing more than to remain in the secure haven of his arms. "I'm sorry, my lord," she whispered, reason slowly reasserting itself. "We have been over this before and you know it will not do. I pray you excuse me." She turned and disappeared, leaving a frustrated man staring after her. . . .

Love In Disguise

Alana Clayton

ZEBRA BOOKS
KENSINGTON PUBLISHING CORP.

To my mother,
Cova E. Ward,
with love and appreciation
for her unswerving faith

ZEBRA BOOKS are published by

Kensington Publishing Corp.
475 Park Avenue South
New York, NY 10016

First Printing: February, 1994

Printed in the United States of America

One

Lord Giles Anthony Griffin, seventh Earl of Castleton, was foxed. He sat elegantly sprawled in a rickety chair, booted legs stretched toward the ill-drawing fireplace of the local inn.

Raking his fingers through already-rumpled hair, he surveyed the dark, low-ceilinged room of the Laughing Drake, finding nothing commendable about it. The air was stale from spilled ale and sour wine. Guttering tallow candles added their smoke to the stifling atmosphere, compelling him to loosen his cravat and release the top button of his fine lawn shirt. Despite the meager blaze before him, dampness from the spring rains had seeped into the room, reminding him too much of Spain's insufferable experiences for comfort.

A few locals gathered at the bar drinking cheap ale and exchanging gossip to pass the time of day. They slanted curious glances in his direction, but he was too far above their reach to be drawn into conversation. Heartily disappointed with the lack of entertainment, Lord Castleton nonetheless lingered, unwilling to return to the emptiness of the manor house. He now regretted his hasty decision to repair to the country alone, temporarily forgetting he had been just as dissatisfied in the crush of London. Irritated anew at his restlessness, the earl reached for the solace of his drink. The table shifted under his elbow, tilting on a short leg, as he emptied his tankard and replaced it carefully.

Searching out the barmaid, his dark gaze raked over the narrow-waisted, buxom figure, knowing most men looking for a diversion would rate her a prime article. Though a comely enough wench, she had just enough coarseness to remind him of the camp followers on the Peninsula. There he had elected celibacy rather than sharing a woman, and probable disease, with others.

Noticing his empty tankard, the maid approached with a swish of overripe hips. "Can I get you another, milord?" she asked eyeing the black coat molded expertly across broad shoulders, before leaning over to display a glimpse of her generous bosom.

Uninterested in the view offered repeatedly that afternoon, he waved her away without a word. "Jeb!" he called to the young lad sweeping the hearth. "See my horse is brought around."

"Yes, milord, but there's a powerful big storm ready to bust loose," the boy advised.

"Then the more reason to hurry," the earl responded, flipping him a coin.

"Yes, sir!" Jeb agreed with alacrity, and loped off toward the stable.

A moment later, hearing the clatter of iron-shod hooves, Lord Castleton tossed several coins on the ta-

6

ble and trod carefully to the door. Taking the reins from Jeb, he mounted the imposing chestnut with a precision undeterred by drink, turning toward his country estate of Castleton.

Clouds had massed, dark and heavy, since his arrival at the tavern, and the spring storm, once a dark spot in the morning sky, was now upon him. Intent on remaining dry, the earl left the main road, guiding his mount onto a sparsely traveled shortcut through the home woods. He had ridden the trail many times over the years and felt no apprehension as the gloomy copse closed in around him.

Touching his heels to Palisades, he invited the stallion to stretch his legs after the morning's inactivity. The horse leaped ahead, muscles bunching, welcoming the challenge to outrun the storm chasing at their heels. Barely discernible in the Stygian darkness, the trail was hazardous to any but the most expert rider. Tree limbs, long untrimmed, hung low, forcing Lord Castleton to hug the neck of his mount. While the thick forest protected them from the main force of the wind, it further darkened the day, and the earl prayed Palisades's eyesight proved better than his own.

Suddenly, the stallion stumbled in a deep rut, and the earl struggled to help the horse keep his legs beneath him. Before the animal could regain his stride, an enormous thunderclap rolled across the sky, followed by a jagged streak of lightning that illuminated the woods around them, striking nearby. Too late, Lord Castleton glimpsed a figure on the path ahead and uttered a startled oath when Palisades swerved, then lurched from the impact. A scream ceased abruptly as they swept by.

7

For once unmindful of his horse's mouth, the earl hauled on the reins. Palisades reared and whirled on his hindquarters with a quickness that had served them well in battle. Retracing their steps, Lord Castleton jumped from the chestnut's back close to where the lightning had struck. The odor of burnt wood was thick around him, but he knew the approaching rain would soon extinguish any smoldering embers. Dropping his reins to the ground, he stepped into the edge of the woods.

The dense thicket that swallowed him obscured the woman until he was directly upon her. Her features were vague and still in the dim light, but her breasts, rising and falling lightly beneath a green dress, testified to her life.

Kneeling, he followed a habit left over from war and expertly searched her arms for breaks or swellings. Faltering only slightly, he lifted her skirts and continued his examination. His hands traveled over her slim, shapely legs from ankle to knee before moving upward to her thighs, stroking the warm skin above her stockings. Relieved he had found no obvious injuries, Lord Castleton studied the woman lying defenseless before him. Her delicate build was far more enticing than the overblown barmaid's could ever hope to be, and for one short moment as the fury of the storm broke about them, the urge to possess her raced through his blood. A sudden spattering of cold spring rain cleared the last vestige of liquor from his head. Straightening her dress, he went in search of Palisades.

Returning a short time later with a cart and his man, he found the forest empty. Rain had already washed away every sign of the accident, and it was as if she had never been.

Caroline adjusted the black poke bonnet over her hair and stared at the somber figure reflected in the mirror. The black did not stop at the top of her head, but bound itself around her throat in the form of a high-necked black bombazine dress, spilling down her slight figure, leaving only small unadorned hands peeping out from beneath black buttoned cuffs.

"What do you think, Madeline? Will I do?" she asked dubiously.

"I'll tell you what I think!" The short, gray-clad figure puffed up like a ruffled hen. "I should never have mentioned Mrs. Davies' accident to you. Then you wouldn't have this misbegotten notice of filling her position at Castleton. Mark my words, it can only bring you trouble."

Having been born and raised nearby, Madeline had served at Cresthill long before Caroline arrived. And while Caroline valued her opinions, she unfortunately could not afford to follow them.

"The trouble will begin if I'm not hired," corrected Caroline. "You know I must find employment as soon as possible." The reply was not a plea for sympathy, but rather a simple statement of fact.

"I know," Madeline grumbled in reluctant agreement, plucking at the worn skirt of her work dress in agitation. "But it isn't fitting . . . a young woman like you in a single man's household."

"Don't forget, I'm a widow with a child," Caroline reasoned, as if that answered Madeline's doubts.

"That doesn't make you any less appealing, only more available, in a man's eyes. Even wearing that horrible bonnet and dress, you can't disguise your attractions." Madeline had seen too many looks cast Caroline's way to think she was mistaken. "How long do you think you can hide beneath that garb before the earl finds you out?"

"Long enough to be hired as housekeeper, I hope," came the saucy reply. "I have it on good authority, Madeline, that a man as sought after as Lord Castleton will not ravish me at first glance. Perhaps the second or third, but definitely not the first."

Madeline snorted with disbelief at her levity. "And after that? Remember, the earl's just returned from living in a near womanless world. If anything can make a man sniff out an attractive female, that will do it. Then where will all your fancy ideas of disguise leave you?"

Caroline turned first one way then another, viewing her reflection. In two more years she could reclaim her inheritance and her place in society; she would never be compelled to masquerade again. "I'll handle that situation when and if it arises," she insisted, her gaiety already a thing of the past. "The earl is a nobleman and has his honor to take into account. He wouldn't force himself on a lady."

"That may have been true when you were considered a lady," Madeline countered bluntly, seeking to shock her into reconsidering her plan. "But now you're a paid employee and the rules have changed. You're fair game. Do you think the men who have come here haven't noticed you? It was only the viscountess's presence that held their baser instincts in check."

Caroline flinched at her plain speaking, and some of the uncertainty she had been holding at bay came crowding back. "I know you're right," she confessed with slight trepidation. "However, that doesn't change my situation in the least. I'd rather face one man here in familiar surroundings than take my chances in London with strangers. The viscountess hired me because she knew my mother, but that was an exception to the rule. I won't have such an easy time again."

She glanced across the room where Lucinda sat playing with her dolls and knew she had made the right decision three years ago. Determined to avoid the scandal a fatherless child would bring, Caroline's stepmother had made arrangements to send the infant away at birth. Just as determined to save the child from the orphanage, Caroline had taken Lucy and fled Birchwood, her family home. She had felt safe with the viscountess, but now that sanctuary had vanished, leaving her more insecure than she dared admit.

Since her stepmother preferred city life, living in the countryside greatly decreased the chance of the two being discovered and separated. At twenty-five, Caroline could claim her inheritance and return to Birchwood her own mistress. Until then, she and the child must contrive to survive quietly.

But enough! It was far too late to lament her situation. She had chosen her path at Lucinda's birth and would not deviate from it now.

Reaching up to tug the detested bonnet further over her face, Caroline winced at a fresh stab of pain.

"That should remind you of the danger a woman can find herself in," admonished Madeline, noticing her discomfort.

"Nonsense. It's only a bruised shoulder," she protested, mindful that long after the bruise had faded, she would remember the great horse bearing down on her, its rider bent low over its neck.

"It could have been much more if John Coachman hadn't stumbled across you. You could have lain there in the rain and died of consumption. Or that madman who rode you down could have come back!"

"But none of that happened," soothed Caroline. "I'm fine except for a few bruises, and the salve I concocted is quickly taking care of those."

"It just shows you never can tell," pressed Madeline inanely. "I wish you'd change your mind about going to Castleton," she implored, abruptly returning to their previous subject. "It's said the earl is a changed man since he returned from the war."

Caroline considered the older woman's comments before answering. "The viscountess always spoke highly of him, and I respected her opinion. I know war can twist lives, and he might have changed since she last saw him, but I believe I'll seek an interview. I can always say no," she concluded confidently, unaware the words would come back to haunt her.

Caroline again critically studied her image. Fortunately, the drab confection she adjusted in the mirror covered her fiery auburn hair and subdued her green eyes. She must not appear too colorful or too young

12

to her prospective employer. Resolved to procrastinate no longer, she took one last appraising look, militantly straightened her shoulders, and swept down the stairs to the awaiting carriage.

Lord Castleton sat in silence, scowling down the long mahogany table. His fingers beat an impatient tatoo on the dull wood as he considered the negligence manifest throughout the residence.

Nothing was going right since his return from the Peninsula. In London, he had quickly tired of the ton's frenzied social whirl, and the silent or simpering misses thrust at his title and fortune.

Turning his back on polite society, he invaded the gambling halls and private clubs of the city's dark side. While his rakish excesses caused tongues to wag, they did not wipe the war's grisly images from his mind.

Thoroughly discontent, he abandoned the city and retreated to his country estate. Arriving unexpectedly, he found Mrs. Davies, Castleton's housekeeper of many years, abed with a badly broken leg. What was left of the staff had grown slovenly without guidance, and the cook had quit in disgust.

Complicating matters further, the earl, oblivious to the chaos that reigned at Castleton, had issued invitations for a house party at the end of the social season. It was apparent Mrs. Davies could not resume her duties by then, and there was no one to oversee the comfort of his guests in the interim. The inedible luncheon staring up at him confirmed his decision to postpone the party until his domestic crises could be righted.

Chagrined by his inability to entertain in his own home, the earl was indulging in an unusual bout of self-pity, until a loud crash followed by a stifled shriek interrupted his ruminations.

"What now!" he bellowed, slamming a flattened palm on the table. Rising to his feet, he strode impatiently across the room. "Can a man have no peace?" he growled, more than ready to vent his frustration on something concrete. Throwing open the hall door, he winced as the unoiled hinges screeched in protest.

An overturned scrub bucket blocked his way, rocking in a spreading puddle of water. The source of the scream was draped over a gilded hall chair. A nicely turned ankle, he observed with masculine appreciation, extended from black bombazine draperies, searching for solid footing on the wet floor.

Skirting the brackish suds, he reached down to pull the woman upright, his hands nearly spanning her waist. As he lifted her, she gave a push from the chair, propelling a softly rounded derriere against him. Wrapping his arms around her to keep them upright, he steadied her as she regained her balance. She was all softness beneath the black, and his irritation slipped away, replaced by the pleasure of holding this small bundle of femininity. If this was the new maid, she was certainly an improvement over the chit who last wielded the mop.

Two

"Madam, if you're here to mop the floor, could you please do it with a little less vigor?" Lord Castleton drawled, attempting to reduce their situation to commonplace.

Tripping over the offending bucket in the gloomy hall had shattered Caroline's carefully maintained composure, leaving her in no mood to accept satiric comments. Bruised shoulder forgotten, she jerked her arm free and regally drew herself up to her full height, which was still considerably less than the man looming over her.

Scraping together the remnants of her dignity, she met his amused gaze. "I'm not here to mop the floor, sir. Although I must agree it could use the attention. However, if this is your usual manner of address," she continued, deciding to give as good as she got, "I can very well see why the maid left without notice."

"A valuable observation, ma'am," he agreed smoothly, a spark of curiosity revitalizing him. "Perhaps I could just toss the scrub bucket into the servants' quarters and all the inadequate help would flee screaming. It would certainly save the unpleasantness of turning them off."

He stood expectantly, awaiting her answering barb, pleased to have found a temporary diversion from his problems.

Determined to gain the housekeeper's position, Caroline had elected beforehand to appear as subservient as need be. She now regretted her heedless remarks, particularly since it was very likely the gentleman to whom they had been directed was the earl.

No majordomo would be dressed as fine as the figure before her. A bottle-green riding coat spread across broad shoulders, then narrowed to a trim waist, where creaseless buff breeches extended down long muscled thighs before dipping into black Hessians.

The past four years spent at the edge of society had left Caroline ill equipped to deal with the closeness of his formidable masculinity. The easy give-and-take at which she had once been so adept vanished in his presence, and she struggled for composure.

Ultimately achieving a passable measure of decorum, she replied calmly, "I apologize for intruding, but the front door was standing open. I knocked and waited for some time before entering."

Disappointed with such a conventional response, Lord Castleton stared intently at the figure wearing the drab, unrelieved black. Intrigued by her cultured tone, which indicated she was Quality, he wondered what brought her to his doorstep.

Concentration deepened the scowl on his gaunt, sun-bronzed face, where prominent cheekbones

16

pierced the skin above lean cheeks. Eyes as black as his hair glittered dangerously in the shadowy hall as he considered the feeling of familiarity she stirred.

Caroline nervously cleared her throat and spoke again to break the lengthening silence. "There was no one on duty in the hall, and at first I thought the house was empty."

"It might as well be," he uttered harshly, rousing himself from his contemplation. "But that's neither here nor there. You've found someone at last. Perhaps I can help you."

"I'm looking for Lord Castleton," she replied hesitantly, almost as though if she delayed the question, the answer would not be as she feared.

"And you've found him." What passed for a smile curved the stern lips as he perceived the consternation that forced her hands into small, tight fists. "I apologize for the laxness of my household. But, as you might have guessed, all is not smooth-running at the moment. Please, step into the dining room," he invited, moving aside to allow her passage. "It's the most comfortable room in the house at present, which isn't saying much, but at least the holland covers are off."

Embarrassed by their unorthodox meeting, Caroline elected to carry on the interview with as much propriety as possible and allowed him to usher her into the room.

The dining room, hung with green watered silk, was a striking background for the mahogany table and pedestal sideboards furnishing it. The dimensions were spacious, with a high carved ceiling and a wall of French windows opening onto a terrace.

17

Caroline approved the beautiful pastoral vistas adorning the walls, grateful that no paintings of dead game or brutal hunting spectacles were displayed there. The vogue to hang such scenes in the dining room had long been a mystery to her, for once observed, they succeeded in completely eliminating her appetite. Cleaned and aired, the room would gratify even the greatest stickler, she reflected, mentally adding a centerpiece of fresh flowers to the table and additional vases on the sideboards.

"I'm Caroline Alveston," she began after they were seated at the table, which could easily accommodate twenty. "I've been companion and housekeeper to the Viscountess Darcy at Cresthill for over three years. You may not be aware the viscountess died several weeks ago."

"Her grandson told me before I left London," the earl replied, noting her tone of genuine sorrow. He mutely questioned whether the remnants of his own staff would mourn his passing or rejoice in relief, after the last few stormy days. "Charles and I are lifelong friends," he continued. "The viscountess was a favorite of mine."

The black bonnet nodded in agreement. "So she told me, my lord. She was always very complimentary toward you."

"I'm pleased. I assure you, she saw me through enough scrapes to think otherwise." The sharp angles of his face softened in remembrance of his childhood escapades.

"Yes, I do seem to remember something about very old eggs in a very new footman's wig." Laughter warmed Caroline's voice.

18

Her humorous tone, so at odds with her appearance, piqued his curiosity about the woman hidden beneath the uncomely black. From their brief encounter in the hall, he surmised her body would be one that could satisfy a gentleman's discriminating taste. Whether her countenance matched, he couldn't judge, since the outsized bonnet overshadowed her entire face, except for a small pointed chin.

"How may I help you?" he belatedly asked, surprised to be offering his services when he had more than enough problems of his own.

"I've come to make you an offer, my lord, which I hope will benefit us both," she replied, clutching her reticule uneasily in her hands.

Giles thought himself awake to every rig. But this was the first time a termagant had invaded his home, rung a peal over his head, then sat down to bargain with him. Curiosity compelled him to play out this farce to the end.

"And what is this equally advantageous proposal?" he questioned, not attempting to hide his skepticism as he toyed with the wineglass beside his plate.

Caroline was momentarily captured by the stark contrast of his strong, brown fingers against the fragile crystal stem. The movement ceased, and feeling his attention focus on her, she rushed into speech. "Cresthill is reduced to a caretaker staff until the estate is settled," she explained, "which means my job is at an end. I've heard your housekeeper is injured."

She paused, looking at him for affirmation. At his nod, she continued. "I thought to offer my services until she is well. Not only would it solve your problems, but it would give me time to find a permanent position to my liking."

The earl's face remained impassive as he observed her from beneath brooding lids. In her ill-fitting dress she looked smaller than average, and he wondered how such a delicate-looking creature could possibly hold sway over a manor house. Castleton needed an amazon who could browbeat the remainder of his staff back into some semblance of order, not this small slip of a woman of indeterminate ability.

"I have excellent references from the viscountess," interjected Caroline, nervous from his extended silence.

What could he lose? thought Giles, rubbing a weary hand across his eyes. Even a marginally adequate hand at the helm was better than none at all. Perhaps luck might be with him this time. It would certainly be a change from the disorder that continued to plague his domestic life, first in London and now at Castleton.

"You might be the answer to my problems, Mrs. Alveston. As you can see, the house is in shambles, my cook has quit, and even the door hinges are complaining of neglect. I'm reduced to hoping I'll be invited out this evening just to have a decent meal." He looked down at the congealed mass on his plate with distaste.

"There's something more you should know," she said, with a casualness that belied her inner turmoil.

He looked up, suspicion clouding his eyes. "I knew this sounded too good to be true. What is it, madam?"

"I have a daughter, my lord, not quite three years

20

old," she began apprehensively. "Her father was killed in the war. The viscountess allowed Lucinda to stay with me, but most employers would not want a child about. That's why I need extra time to find a place for the two of us."

So the black was not just a concession to her position, he reflected with interest, but also the mourning weeds of a widow.

"I wouldn't expect to bring her here," she continued, breaking in on his thoughts. "I know several trustworthy families in the neighborhood with whom I can board her. But I felt you should be aware of the situation."

The thinly disguised concern evident in her rigid posture and tremorous voice penetrated the indifference that had dominated his feelings since returning home.

In the city, he had been surrounded by people thinking solely of their own selfish pleasure. This woman's solicitude was at odds in a society that relegated children to a servant's care at birth, then shipped them off to schools as soon as their age would allow. Did she truly think him hardhearted enough to refuse shelter to a child? If so, his countenance must indeed be darker than he thought.

He could not separate mother and child, knowing only too well the feeling of loneliness. What was one more distraction in his chaotic household when balanced against a worse alternative? Besides, it would only be until Mrs. Davies recovered.

"There's no need for you to board your daughter out, Mrs. Alveston. Castleton has more than enough room to accommodate another small body. If you can

21

contrive to give me something edible for lunch, you may bring six children if you wish."

Caroline breathed an inaudible sigh of relief. "One will do nicely, my lord," she said, a radiant smile peeping out beneath the black brim. "Please remove his lordship's plate," she instructed the footman, "and pour another glass of wine. I shall return very shortly, sir, if you'll direct me to the kitchen."

Gesturing toward the connecting door, Lord Castleton settled back to sip the light wine he had ordered to offset the unpalatable food. Now his stomach grumbled, anticipating something finally worth digesting.

A short time later Caroline returned carrying a silver-domed plate. She had done her best on such brief notice, but wondered whether he would be satisfied with the modest results. Still wearing the ugly bonnet, she was thankful the earl was too distracted by the promise of food to give her more than a cursory glance.

Caroline lifted the cover, and a wonderful aroma of herbs and spices assailed Lord Castleton's senses. A golden omelette filled with mushrooms and garnished with sprigs of fresh mint graced the plate. Jervis conveyed a serving dish of steamed asparagus with cheese sauce. Day-old bread had been toasted to hide its staleness and spread with butter that had somehow survived the overall disorder in the kitchen.

"I'm afraid this will be a simple meal," she remarked as he eagerly picked up his fork. "There's a fresh fruit cup for desert. But if you're at home this evening, I assure you dinner will be more substantial."

The earl attacked his food with a vengeance, gratification clearly showing on his face. "This is wonderful, Mrs. Alveston," he exclaimed, closing his eyes momentarily to fully savor the exquisite flavor. "Just a short time ago I was facing death by starvation. Now the aroma alone has revived me." Lifting his lids, he eyed her appreciatively. "I hope you can settle in this afternoon." The hideous black bonnet still shadowed her face and he felt at a disadvantage not being able to read her expression.

"I'm sure I can manage, my lord. I've been packed to leave Cresthill for days. I need only to send for my trunks and my child. If you will excuse me, I'll ask John Coachman to return immediately." She turned, black skirts swirling around the trim ankles he had recently admired, but paused before reaching the door. "May I make one other suggestion, my lord?" she asked, crossing her fingers in the folds of her skirt.

"Of course, Mrs. Alveston." Laying aside the heavy silver fork, he gave her his full attention.

"Since the house is being closed, the viscountess's cook has also been given notice. I wonder if you would consider hiring her? She's a local woman and anxious to stay in the neighborhood." Caroline prayed his generosity would extend to include Madeline in his household. The cook was a familiar part of her and Lucy's lives, and she desperately wanted to retain a sense of continuity for her daughter.

"If she cooks like this, by all means send for her,"

he immediately agreed. "I can tolerate dull tables," he declared, indicating the surface before him, "much better than dull food."

"Your table will be shiny and your food will be tolerable this evening, my lord," she promised with a light heart before making her way through the creaking door.

Closing the dining room door behind her, Caroline stepped around the bucket still blocking the hallway, remembering the earl's arms as he held her against his solid length. Tentatively, she placed her hands over the imprint of his. Though the fabric was cool, his touch still warmed her skin, causing unusually disturbing sensations to wash over her. Pushing aside her unnerving thoughts, she quickly penned a note to Madeline and hurried toward the carriage waiting at the door.

By the time the coach returned bringing Lucy, the trunks, and Madeline, the servants were giving the kitchen and dining room a good turning out. The odor of lemon oil and beeswax permeated the air as the mahogany table was shined to a mirror surface. The sideboards, supported by carved chimeras, were getting their share of attention as well, with the carved bronzed enrichments and galleries glowing from the polishing cloth.

Madeline observed the flurry of activity as she stepped into her new domain. "I see you've not wasted time setting things right."

"Madeline!" Caroline exclaimed, clasping the

cook's hands in joy and relief. "I knew you wouldn't fail me, despite your warning."

"That's why I'm here. If I'm any judge, you're going to need all the help you can get," she proclaimed ominously.

"You can't pretend to be unhappy about a new job," Caroline scolded teasingly. "There's so much to do. Everything was at sixes and sevens, so I thought you wouldn't mind if I began before you arrived," she continued, quickly changing the subject.

"Indeed no," replied the cook, releasing her hold to step deeper into the large kitchen. "I only hope I'll be able to please his lordship until it's organized to my liking."

"I'm sure you can contrive an excellent dinner," Caroline assured her confidently. "Lord Castleton was extremely content with my simple efforts at lunch, but he'll be overwhelmed with your culinary talent."

"I'm already here, so you needn't flatter me so shamelessly," Madeline replied, her voice gruff with embarrassment at Caroline's praise.

"You know it isn't flummery, but rightly deserved fact," Caroline insisted. "But where's Lucy?" she asked anxiously.

"I left her in the carriage," answered Madeline, grateful for the change of subject. "Don't worry. John is keeping an eye on her. I'll need to know where our trunks should go."

"Staff quarters are in the east wing. Let's get Lucinda and I'll direct you." Caroline led the way toward the back entrance with a sprightly step.

"I've also met Mrs. Davies," Caroline continued as

they traversed the hall. "She doesn't seem to resent my intrusion at all and offered to have Lucy with her during the day."

"How will she manage? She's bedfast, isn't she?" asked Madeline, remembering the neighborhood gossip.

"Yes, but one of the maids is in and out of the room constantly. She said if Lucy is biddable, it would lighten her days to have company."

"It seems everything's working out exactly as you wished." The older woman paused and faced her companion before opening the outside door. "But you haven't yet mentioned his lordship."

Caroline deliberated a moment, her finely arched brows drawn together in concentration. "I'll admit I first thought him a forbidding individual. But considering the disorder in his household, I can't condemn his countenance. I'm sure after one of your dinners, he'll be a changed man," she teased, happiness evident in her voice.

Caroline instructed John Coachman as to the disposition of the trunks, before turning to the little girl who was clamoring for attention from the carriage door.

Lucinda, a blond-haired, blue-eyed beauty, was every mother's dream. Each time the small, warm arms wrapped around Caroline's neck, it reaffirmed the rightness of her decision.

Warning Lucy to be very quiet in case Mrs. Davies was napping, they peeped into the housekeeper's room, only to find her awake and eager for a diversion from her enforced solitude.

"Come in, Mrs. Alveston," invited the older woman. "And bring the little one with you."

"We didn't want to disturb you," protested Caroline.

"You can't bother me enough. I've had more sleep since my accident than is good for a body," Mrs. Davies replied in a disgruntled tone.

"A sure sign you're improving," allowed Caroline, leading Lucy into the room. The little girl hung behind, peeking around her skirts.

"Mrs. Davies, this is Lucy. She may seem a bit bashful now, but in a short time you may be regretting your generous offer."

"She reminds me a bit of my youngest grandchild. I wonder if she likes kittens just as much?" Mrs. Davies waved toward a box in the corner, where a scratching sound could be heard. Approaching cautiously, Lucy reached over the edge and lifted out a ball of calico fur, scarcely noticing when Caroline left the room.

After settling Lucy with Mrs. Davies, Caroline and Madeline conferred on their first dinner at Castleton.

Caroline took pride in the recipes inherited from her mother, particularly the ones that came from her family's French cook. Madeline could make the most mundane food taste delicious without Caroline's advice, but together they created dishes that had brought raves of delight from the viscountess's friends. Although the supplies were not as complete as she liked, Caroline was sure they could prepare a dinner the earl would appreciate.

* * *

Lord Castleton scraped mud from his boots at the back entrance of the manor house. *A lot of good this will do,* he thought. *I could most likely shovel dirt through the door and no one would notice the difference.*

He had spent the afternoon inspecting the tenant farms with Burton, his estate manager, temporarily pushing the disorganized household from his mind.

Fortunately, the neglect of the house had not spread to the estate. Burton, originally retained by the last earl while Giles was still in leading strings, took a personal interest in the efficient running and maintenance of the farms. The only repairs and improvements currently needed involved large expenditures, which Burton would not endorse without approval from his employer. Well pleased with the condition of the land, the earl wished everything had run as smoothly in his absence.

Lord Castleton's stomach gave a hollow roar, complaining of its empty status. Luncheon, while delicious and filling at the time, had burned off long ago. During the war and throughout his stay in London, food had not been first on his list of priorities. It would take a prolonged period of nourishment to satisfy the needs of his body.

Placing his hand against his still-rumbling stomach, he wondered if his angel of mercy had prepared another delicious repast, or whether she was just a lingering figment of the dreams he had cherished during the war. Dreams of home and a welcome that had proved to be no more than illusions of his mind.

The aroma of fresh baking filled the hallway. Casting aside his dissatisfaction, he followed the drift of delicious odors to the huge kitchen. The room had been transformed in his absence. It was now clean and alive with activity, the air redolent with a delectable blend of the perfumed scent of cooked fruit, fresh herbs, and hot savory breads.

An orderly flurry surrounded a short, substantial woman dressed in gray, wearing a white cap over hair the same shade. Since she was the hub of activity, the earl assumed he was observing his new cook. And if actions signified culinary skill, there was considerable grounds for encouragement for his neglected stomach. Under her direction, neatly dressed kitchen maids scurried about, kneading, chopping, and mixing, lifting lids and checking ovens.

Still unnoticed in the bustle, Giles selected a fruit-topped bun from a pan set out to cool. Mouth watering from anticipation, he bit into the light pastry, expressing his pleasure with an appreciative rumble.

"I'm glad you approve, my lord," said a voice from behind him. "But I had planned on serving you tea seated in the library rather than standing at a kitchen table."

Three

Lord Castleton turned to see a smiling countenance lifted to him. No bonnet now hid the glorious auburn hair, and as it wisped around her heat-flushed face, Caroline displayed a much different appearance than she had that morning. So much so that he found himself staring, hunger forgotten for the moment, before he realized she was waiting for a reply.

"I couldn't help myself, Mrs. Alveston. These were just too tempting." Her familiarity continued to baffle him. He knew this woman but was perplexed when his memory failed to place her. "Usually I'm not so demanding," he continued, still staring, "but I fear my stomach has had a long drought between life-giving rains."

"I question whether cook will be flattered by having her delicacies compared with rainwater," she countered dryly, "but I will accept it as a compliment."

Considering his housekeeper with renewed interest, the earl examined the oval face, retroussé nose, and tempting mouth, which had been hidden in their earlier interview. Her eyes caught and held his gaze, great pools of green, sparkling with amusement at catching a lord of the realm filching a pastry.

Caroline looked up past a powerful set of shoulders, to find the earl's dark eyes studying her intently.

Although still lean from his war experiences, his well-proportioned body exuded a commanding force. His eyes, framed in thick ebony lashes, softened the elegant ridge of cheekbones and emphasized a firm but sensuous mouth.

Nonplussed, she swept a tendril of hair from her face, leaving a streak of flour behind. "I hope you're not speculating your decision this morning was in error, my lord. Perhaps due to befuddlement brought on by hunger?"

Giles had just decided he would rather nibble her full, almost pouting lower lip than the pastry, when he was called on to gather his errant thoughts. "Not at all. In truth, I was attempting to guess what delectable treats are in store for me." He smiled, enjoying the secret of his double entendre. "I see you've wasted no time in putting the ovens to work."

"You're right," she agreed. "If you'd like to taste as well as smell the results, I'll carry through on my plans and serve your tea in the library. Sitting down, of course."

"An excellent suggestion, Mrs. Alveston." The earl automatically reached out to brush the flour from her cheek, touching skin softer than he had known for some time. His fingers lingered a moment in appreciation. Their gazes met momentarily, then broke as he reluctantly dropped his hand.

"I'll wash off the grime of the stables and see you

in the library," he said, the heavy beating of his heart revealing he craved more than tea. "This should hold me over till then." Popping the remainder of the bun in his mouth, he departed the kitchen with a satisfied expression on his face.

Left alone, Caroline also smiled with satisfaction as she prepared the tea tray. The earl had become a changed man with the assurance of a good meal and a well-run household. He was far more handsome than she had supposed that morning when intent on convincing him to hire her, his overwhelming masculinity had seemed threatening. Surprised she now deemed him so attractive, she determined her bonnet must have obscured her sight as well as her features.

Recalling the contact of his hardened hand on her cheek, she paused, amazed that such a slight caress could cause confusion to course through her, drying her mouth to ashes. She resolutely cleared her head, quickly finished filling the tray, and preceded a tea-laden Jervis out of the kitchen.

Lord Castleton arrived in the library and found Caroline arranging dishes on a Pembroke table. Her hair, though pulled into a knot at the nape of her neck, gleamed with shadows of deep red. His fingers itched to remove the pins and see the luxurious strands tumble about her shoulders. Remembering the delicate body his hands had held that morning stirred an immediate physical response. He smiled wryly, blaming the inadequacy of the local entertainment.

Settling into his favorite wingback chair, he accepted a cup of tea. "You seem extremely competent for one so young, Mrs. Alveston."

"I'm not as young as you might think," said Caroline, passing a plate to the earl. "I'm just past three and twenty."

Giles smiled surreptitiously into his teacup, quickly calculating the nine years that separated them. He wondered if she would think him ancient, and then why it mattered whether she did or not.

"This is an excellent tea," he pronounced, enjoying the sound of her voice and craving to hear more.

"They're my own recipes." She glowed with pride, offering another selection of pastries set attractively on a silver dish. "A few I baked personally, since I promised my mother they would remain secret. She always said the way to win a war and a man was by serving good food." Caroline innocently recited the phrase she had heard countless times.

"And which is your objective?" the earl questioned blandly, helping himself to another bun.

Caroline turned a becoming pink and commenced rearranging the tray to cover her embarrassment. "Neither, my lord. Unless you call bringing your household back into order a war." She kept her voice firm, determined not to be put out of countenance by their exchange.

"It could very well be," he rejoined ironically, remembering only too well his arrival at Castleton and his initial rage at the neglect that had greeted him. "But after seeing you in action, I feel you're equal to the task." *And if not, you'll be a most beautiful failure, my dear,* he thought to himself.

"I'll leave you then to enjoy your tea." Caroline

checked the table one last time to insure the plates were adequately filled.

The earl watched her move gracefully toward the door, regretting the loss of the first real conversation he had had in days.

"Will you be dining in this evening?" she inquired, standing poised at the threshold.

"Prinny himself could not move me from my dining room tonight," he promised. "I can hardly wait to see what else you will conjure up from your secret recipes."

Caroline nodded and left the library, pleased with the day thus far.

Watching the sway of her hips as she departed, the earl remembered the soft curves pressed against him that morning. Rekindled desire flooded through him and he shifted uncomfortably in his chair. He could not recall such an immediate reaction to a woman since first discovering the opposite sex.

He finished his tea with Caroline Alveston's charms dominating his thoughts, deciding he must accept the Laughing Drake's diversions before he forgot himself with a housekeeper he could ill afford to lose.

Despite his admonitions, the earl found himself comparing the feel of the delicate china to her flour-dusted face. He concluded that the china, although fragile, could not compete with the softness of her skin. Though she tried to hide it, her beauty was unquestionable. She had the manners and bearing of a lady of Quality, and she conducted herself with dignity despite the position she had assumed. Quite a mystery. Perhaps his boredom would be alleviated in its solving.

Lord Castleton surveyed his apartments as he dressed for dinner. The Chippendale furniture had been purchased at the 1804 bankruptcy auction of Thomas Chippendale, the younger. Having long been an admirer of the Chippendale talent, the earl's father had taken the opportunity to gain perhaps the last products of the famed furniture maker.

Although Denton kept his rooms neat, they had lacked the finishing touches. But now the four-poster bed, with its tall, carved posts and footed bases, was waxed to a high sheen. Even the grooves of the spiral-twisted colonnettes on the bow-fronted chest of drawers were free from dust, a minor miracle in itself. He breathed deeply, pleased with the scent of fresh flowers instead of the musty smell pervading since his arrival.

The earl was struck by his new housekeeper's intuitiveness toward the masculine viewpoint. Flowers had never before decorated his personal suite. However, this arrangement was no namby-pamby delicate bowl of fragile blossoms, but large blooms and bold colors. An arrangement one did not have to tiptoe around, but could touch and smell without fear of destroying its symmetry.

Giles tested the theory by running his finger over the softness of one of the cattails that accented the display. He had never seen the plant used in decorating, but it had long since been his favorite. As a child, he would wave the top-heavy wands in the warm summer air, scattering the light downy material and watching it being born aloft on the winds around the pond.

The same intuitiveness had been evident in the deliciously substantial tea served that afternoon. Now, some four hours later, he was again exceedingly sharp-set and his stomach cried out for more of this unusually pleasurable fare.

"It will be but a moment more, Major," said Denton, helping his master into the snugly fitted blue coat.

The valet was a slight man of indeterminate age, with gray liberally streaking his brown hair. His face was creased with lines, attesting either to a life spent out of doors or in smoke-filled rooms. Denton had not offered information as to which was the case nor had Giles asked. The earl had been too relieved to find someone trustworthy to travel to the war-torn Peninsula with him, and Denton had more than justified his faith.

He had been a dedicated batman during combat, suffering the same hardship as Lord Castleton. Giles had come to rely on Denton and was pleased when he transferred his loyalty to peacetime.

"I assure you, Denton, I will not faint from undernourishment. If you remember, we've sometimes gone several days without eating and survived."

"That's so, my lord," the valet replied, remembering his master's new address. "But then we had no choice. The talk below stairs is that you now have a housekeeper and cook which would do the finest London establishment proud."

Denton smoothed the superfine cloth across Lord

Castleton's broad shoulders and stood back to observe the effect. Although the earl dispensed with the usual intricately folded cravat when dining alone, his midnight-blue coat offset by a white shirt and waistcoat stood out starkly against his sun-browned skin. Light breeches fit snugly over well-muscled thighs that were the envy of many a London rake.

"Your evaluation may prove true," he agreed, as the valet brushed nonexistent lint from an immaculate sleeve. Giles had learned to live with this idiosyncrasy of Denton's, and he sometimes found it comforting that whatever else might change, there would always be lint on his coat.

"It might not be a bad idea to hold for after Mrs. Davies recovers," continued the earl, joining Denton in solemn regard of his image in the cheval glass. "My London establishment is sadly lacking since we returned, and I'll need a good staff if I'm to entertain properly in town." The ritual completed, he turned toward the door. "Now I had best go down before my hunger announces itself again."

When the earl entered the dining room, he stopped a moment in silent appreciation. His grandmother's silver epergne, with flowers artfully spilling over the sides, graced the center of the table, flanked by three-pronged silver candelabra. Sevres china and Waterford crystal were arranged in precise order at the head of the table.

The chandeliers, prisms recently cleaned, flashed with brilliance, dispelling the previously depressed dimness of the room. A fragrance of roses wafted through the French windows from the garden beyond. Even the door hinges were oiled and did not protest when opened.

"Well, Jervis, I must say you look better than when I last saw you," he remarked to the footman.

Jervis straightened with pride in his fresh livery of blue and gold. "Thank you, my lord. I feel much better now I'm done up proper."

Lord Castleton noted the new sense of self-esteem in the man's voice. Jervis was another who had watched over him as he grew to manhood, and the earl was grateful for his loyalty despite the difficulties since the death of his parents.

"Are you ready to be served, my lord?" asked Jervis, interrupting his musings.

"I'm more than ready," he replied, reaching for the embroidered crested napkin resting beside his plate. His stomach, for once that day, silently agreed.

Fully sated, Lord Castleton repaired to the library for his after-dinner brandy. At least he assumed the highly efficient Mrs. Alveston would have searched out an appropriate bottle from the well-stocked cellar.

His housekeeper had not appeared during dinner, but he knew from the smooth service of the delicious meal that she was orchestrating the action, and the earl felt his first full measure of contentment since his return.

While there were not the twenty-five removes that heralded a grand London affair, the dishes were tasty and, more surprising, served hot instead of lukewarm to cold, as was the case in even the best-run houses.

A delicious mulligatawny soup first sharpened his appetite as he breathed in the spicy steam. Next came trout, served with a savory tomato sauce. Beef and glazed ham followed, along with chicken breasts coated with egg and seasoned bread crumbs, fried to perfection in butter. These were accompanied by fresh peas in cream sauce and stewed mushrooms. Delicately browned, braised potatoes replaced that ubiquitous staple of the English dinner table, the boiled potato. Rolls straight from the oven filled the air with a hot, yeasty smell, melting the freshly churned butter turned from decorative molds onto a silver plate. Dessert consisted of a lightly raised chocolate soufflé and creamy rich charlotte russe.

No matter whether Mrs. Alveston's hiring had originated from instinct or desperation, Lord Castleton was thankful for the impulse that had driven him to accept her proposal.

He had no sooner settled himself comfortably when Caroline appeared. Directing Jervis to place the brandy tray at the earl's elbow, she dismissed the footman.

"Mrs. Alveston, will you keep me company for a time?" Although the request was stated casually, Giles involuntarily tensed awaiting her reply.

"It would not be proper, my lord, since I'm only your housekeeper," she replied, wishing it were otherwise.

The earl poured a generous amount of brandy into a snifter and leaned back in his chair, considering another approach. "Do not belittle yourself, ma'am. Today you've been my savior. Besides, you'd be doing a favor for someone who yearns for conversation on a subject other than yield-per-acre." A slightly comical grimace crossed his features. "I find no fault with my bailiff's dedication, but I do have a saturation point as far as new farming methods are concerned."

Caroline laughed with appreciation at his predicament. "You almost convince me to put aside propriety, my lord. For I, too, am overwhelmed with beeswax and baking."

Black eyes met green in shared amusement. He was mesmerized for a moment before renewing his efforts to detain her. "Let me persist. Consider this tête-à-tête part of your employment, not an impropriety," he urged. "Occasionally, we must speak of household matters. What better time than now, when our duties are over for the day?" he asked, his voice softly persuasive.

Although Caroline's duties were indeed not finished, she allowed herself to be convinced. Calmly seating herself, she arranged the dull skirt around her as if it were of the finest silk. She had spent four years sitting meekly in the background. Surely a few minutes conversation with Lord Castleton would not ruin her.

Listening to the rustle of her dress, the earl realized he had missed the presence of a woman in his home. This was the first time he had been to Castleton without his family, and the house seemed cold and empty, echoing with his meaningless wanderings. Now it felt warm and embracing again, responding to this woman just as he was.

"How was your first day at Castleton, Mrs. Alveston?" he inquired, eager to hear her dulcet tones again.

"Perhaps the pertinent question, my lord, is how you found my first day at Castleton," she replied spontaneously.

The earl threw his head back with a laugh and raised his glass in a silent salute. "I found it extremely pleasurable, ma'am. If you'd done nothing but serve a palatable meal, I would have termed it a success. But the inroads you've made on bringing the house back to order are near miraculous."

"First I'm your savior and now my deeds are miracles. If your compliments continue, I'll begin to think I'm not of this earth." Feeling more confident in pleasing the earl, Caroline allowed herself to relax in his company.

Warming the brandy snifter between his hands, Lord Castleton appreciatively inhaled the aroma. "And where are your earthly origins, Mrs. Alveston?"

Dark lashes obscured her eyes and a stiffness of manner replaced the comfortable ease she had exhibited a moment earlier.

Sensing her withdrawal, he added coolly, "I only ask in the spirit of becoming acquainted, ma'am. Do not feel compelled to answer."

Caroline recoiled from his detached tone. Relaxing her guard had been a mistake. She did not want to offend her new employer, yet to protect herself and Lucy, their background must remain a secret. "I meant no offense, sir. It's just that I've grown unaccustomed to anyone taking a personal interest in my history," she replied in a stilted voice.

"I'm from the north," she continued after a small silence. "A village which I'm sure is unknown to you. My mother had a slight acquaintance with the viscountess, who learned I was alone in the world and offered me a position as companion. When her housekeeper retired, I took over those duties also."

Recognizing her unease, Lord Castleton sought to mitigate it. "Whatever your origins, Mrs. Alveston, I'm indeed fortunate you appeared this morning."

Relieved, Caroline breathed a silent prayer of thanks and leaned back into her chair, immediately jerking forward again with an indrawn breath.

"What is it?" he asked, noting the paleness of her face.

"Nothing, my lord. Just a slightly bruised shoulder," she explained.

"The look on your face wasn't caused by anything slight," he judged, rising from the chair and swiftly closing the distance between them.

"I assure you . . ."

Before she knew it Caroline was standing, with the earl undoing the tiny buttons down her back. A melting warmth ran through her as his fingers brushed her neck. "My lord, you mustn't . . ." she began in a tone that lacked conviction even to her own ears.

"Now don't go all missish on me, ma'am," he commanded in a no-nonsense voice. "I know a little about contusions. You probably suffered it in your fall this morning, and I feel responsible for that mishap."

"There's really no need, Lord Castleton. It happened some days ago and is almost well." Her thought processes ground to a halt as his warm fingers brushed against her again, and she did nothing to stop him from completing his task.

Her skin cooled as he gently pulled back the side of her dress. "A minor bruise? I'm surprised you accomplished anything at all today, Mrs. Alveston."

Standing behind her, viewing the bruised alabaster skin and the delicacy of her bones, he was reminded just how fragile a woman she was. Her spirited responses imbued her with a strength beyond her physical limitations. He would not allow her to suffer again, he vowed as he observed the purple discoloration covering her left shoulder and back, disappearing into the starkness of her chemise. "How far does this extend?" he asked, angry she was marked so.

"My lord, you wouldn't," she gasped, though making no move to draw away.

"No, I wouldn't," he agreed wryly. "I'm merely trying to ascertain the extent of your injury." .

A strange lassitude overtook her as his breath fanned her neck. "Just past my waist. I was fortunate it was only a glancing blow."

He again scrutinized the discolored skin. "A glancing blow?" he questioned incredulously. "From what size object, ma'am?"

"A horse, my lord."

Four

"A horse," he echoed disbelievingly, stepping in front of her to meet her gaze.

"To be specific, a very large, fast-moving horse," she expounded drolly, attempting to remove the scowl from his visage.

The source of her familiarity was now evident. The darkness of the forest had obscured her features, but his hands had not forgotten the shape of her body, nor his ears the sound of her cry.

"Will you tell me what happened, Mrs. Alveston?" he requested grimly.

"Certainly," she agreed, comprehending the seriousness on his face would remain until he heard it all. "I was helping John Coachman look for one of Cresthill's mares during the storm last week. The thunder and lightning had caused her to bolt, so John and I were searching the woods between the estates. There's a path there, you know."

"Yes, I do," he admitted, remembering his recklessness when urging Palisades forward.

"I was following it, thinking she might have taken

the easy way instead of breaking through the under-brush. I suppose the thunder covered the hoofbeats coming from behind, for the horse and rider were upon me before I could do little more than scream.

The earl's eyes closed for a moment. He had re-called that one short cry many times over the last few days, wondering what damage it portended.

"I remember nothing else until awakening in the rain with John bending over me. He helped me back to Cresthill, and that's really all there is to tell."

Making an agitated tour of the room, he paused in front of her again. "Mrs. Alveston, it seems I owe you for more than my increased comfort today."

"You owe me nothing, my lord. I'm just doing my job," she replied, his remark confusing her.

"Perhaps you won't want to continue with it once I've revealed the truth to you," he warned, his face a forbidding mask.

"I don't understand." The bewilderment in her voice increased.

Lord Castleton took a deep breath. "Turn around and let me redo your buttons. I don't want you run-ning out of here in disarray. What I've already done to you is bad enough."

The rebuttoning was accomplished in silence, and they soon faced one another again. "Mrs. Alveston, there's no other way to say it. I'm responsible for your injuries. I ran you down in the woods."

The blunt statement caught Caroline unawares and she remained silent, staring uncomprehendingly.

"It was an accident," he continued stiffly, guilt making him appear unrepentant. "I was returning to Castleton and was upon you before I knew it. I could blame the storm, the darkness, the liquor, but it doesn't change the facts. I could have killed you."

Understanding finally washed over her. "You? You left me lying there?"

He met her censorious gaze squarely. "Yes. At the moment I had no choice. I . . ."

"I cannot credit it. Despite warnings of your changed attitude, I would never have believed you capable of this." She pushed past him toward the door.

"Mrs. Alveston . . ." He reached out for her arm, releasing it with a heartfelt "Damn" as she closed her eyes in pain.

Caroline hurried toward the staff quarters, searching for Madeline. She found her sitting and darning a stocking, next to Lucinda, who was tucked in and fast asleep. Caroline took a deep breath, forcing herself to speak quietly. "Madeline, I know who ran me down in the woods," she exclaimed incredulously.

The cook looked up from her mending. "So do I."

Like a condemned man, the earl was met with an uncommonly good breakfast the next morning. He sat for some time, ignoring the cup of coffee growing cold before him.

His thoughts still centered on last night's episode with his housekeeper. Most probably his ex-housekeeper now. Knowing she would not be responsive to useless platitudes, which was all he had to offer, he had controlled his desire to follow her from the room. After a guilt-ridden night of restless tossing, he still had no solution as to how to make amends if offered the chance.

Hearing the door from the kitchen swing open, he spoke without raising his eyes. "I need nothing else, Jervis."

"You could require another cook if you continue sending your meals back untouched, my lord. Madeline is very sensitive when her reputation is at stake," warned Caroline lightly.

He started at her voice, rising to his feet to face her. She was composed but relaxed. A slight smile curved the lips he had dreamed about during the long night, and there was a softness in her eyes he never expected to see under the circumstances.

"You're still here," he said, then flushed from the absurdity of his remark.

Evidence of a restless night reflected in his face, and Caroline felt a pang of regret she hadn't sought him out the evening before. "Obviously," she acknowledged, amused at his discomfiture. "But neither Madeline nor I will be earning our wages unless you have breakfast." She waved a hand, indicating his empty plate.

His eyes searched hers inquiringly, seeing no censure in the clear, steadfast gaze that met his.

"I learned of your actions," she said, answering his silent question. "I should have allowed you to finish the story. It made a great deal of difference."

"Not to me," he replied, his grip tightening on the napkin he held clutched in his hand. "You were still injured and it was my fault."

"It was an accident," she insisted. "You said so yourself. I understand you looked after me as best

47

you could, then went for help, afraid to move me otherwise. When you returned and found me gone, you searched every inch of the woods. At least that's what the servants say. Those are not the deeds of an uncaring man," she finished softly.

He felt unworthy of the conviction in her eyes. "That doesn't alter the facts," he insisted stiffly, lips twisting with self-contempt.

"No, but it does change the circumstances surrounding them," she replied with compassion. "Whether or not the accident could have been avoided is no longer important. I should not have been in the path, you should not have been going fast, the woods should not have been so dark. Shall I go on?"

The earl smiled slightly, shaking his head.

She returned his smile with one of complete forgiveness. "Your actions after the accident were more than could be expected. As you can see, no lasting harm was done. Now there's no more to be said," she concluded briskly, "except to tell Madeline what you'd like for breakfast."

A week later, another spring storm was lashing Castleton. Hands clasped behind his back, the earl paced before the library windows, watching the driving rain beat against the glass.

Distracted from his brown study by the door opening behind him, he turned as Caroline and Lucinda entered the library.

"Lord Castleton. We didn't mean to interrupt you," said Caroline, perturbed at the unexpected meeting.

Still unable to reconcile the feelings he stirred within her, she avoided him whenever possible.

"Any diversion is welcome, Mrs. Alveston, especially when it's two lovely ladies." He smiled charmingly at Lucy as he stooped nearer her level to wrap a golden curl around his finger. She was clad in a lovely white dress trimmed in blue ribbons, with matching blue bows securing tiny slippers to her busy feet.

"I've seen little of you in the past days," he went on, straightening again. "I never knew this house was omnivorous, but I swear, it swallows you completely."

"I seem to remember several instances we've met," she replied, guilt rendering her objection weak.

"Yes, now that you mention it, I have spoken to my housekeeper about Castleton. But occasionally I'd prefer to see the woman who's shown an inclination toward wit and conversation." He looked at her inquiringly.

Ignoring the warm, tingling sensation that began in her stomach and spiraled through her body, Caroline searched for an innocuous subject. "You were watching the storm when we came in. Do you enjoy the rainy weather?"

"Hardly," he answered with a harsh bark of laughter. "I had more than enough of this on the Peninsula. During the campaign, my men and I shared shelters with goats, horses, cows; anyplace for relief from the wet. At times, it seemed we would never pull free from the clinging mud or be dry again." His eyes were focused on things she could not see.

"You lived with horses?" asked Lucy, speaking for the first time.

"Well, not exactly lived with them," he replied, reaching down and lifting the child in his arms, smiling into her large blue eyes. "They allowed us to come in out of the rain on occasion."

"I like horses," the child pronounced gravely.

"Do you? Then I have several I'd like you to meet someday when it's sunny," he said, chucking her under the chin.

"I like you, too," replied Lucinda, tiny hands bestowing soft baby pats to his cheeks.

Lord, the man could charm little children and probably snakes, thought Caroline ungraciously.

"Come, Lucy. We mustn't take up any more of his lordship's time." She reached out for the little girl, who clung stubbornly to the earl's lapels. "Lucinda, you will wrinkle Lord Castleton's coat," she explained in exasperation.

"And well worth it," chuckled Giles, retaining his hold on Lucy.

"Mrs. Davies said there were children's games stored here," Caroline remarked abruptly, hoping to distract Lucy. "We thought they would be diverting, since we can't go out today," she explained, restoring some semblance of formality to the situation.

"If Mrs. Davies says they are here, then they must be. Shall we look?" he suggested cheerfully.

They began rummaging through the library cabinets, finding a wealth of puzzles, games, and books. All packed away carefully for the future generations at Castleton.

Caroline drew the heavy drapes against the violent

storm, shutting out the weather and its unsettling memories. With the warm glow of candles surrounding them, the earl's restlessness seemed calmed for the time being.

Lucy was totally charmed by the man who lived with horses, and he, of course, found her adorable. Sitting unceremoniously on the floor, a lock of dark hair falling carelessly over his forehead, the earl helped Lucy fit together a brightly colored wooden puzzle.

As she watched the earl with Lucy, Caroline realized he would make a wonderful father, bringing to mind the full import of what she and the child were missing. There would be no husband for her to grow old with, no brothers and sisters for Lucinda, no family circle to embrace them. Her sadness drove her to her feet.

"As pleasant as this is, I have duties, my lord. You do not pay me to play games." Caroline spoke more brusquely than she intended, to cover her emotions.

He rose, taking her hand. "Thank you for sharing the afternoon with me. I've never experienced this feeling of belonging before."

His sincerity compelled her to respond in kind. "Nor have I," she admitted candidly.

"Not even with your husband?" he asked, the intimacy of the afternoon overriding conventional politeness.

"No. He was gone before Lucy was born. Since then we've been alone." A hint of melancholy entered her voice.

"That's not a good way to be," he stated emphatically, thumb rubbing unconsciously over the back of her hand. "You were very young to be left with a child," he murmured softly, so as not to break the spell surrounding them.

His touch was unsettling, but she forced herself to respond to his remarks. "We survived. In truth, I count myself fortunate to be as well situated as I am. Others are not faring nearly as well."

"You have much to offer," he murmured, his expression clearly showing he was not thinking of her housekeeping abilities.

Fighting an overwhelming desire to lean into his strength, Caroline knew she must leave before blurting out more than she should. "If you'll excuse us, I'll return Lucy to Mrs. Davies," she said, withdrawing from his grasp.

Checking his impulse to retain her hand, Giles released her. He looked down at the little girl whose lip pouted remarkably like Caroline's, thinking of the future young men whose hearts would beat faster at the sight.

"Why don't you leave Lucy here? I'll attend her until you return," he offered. "It will take my mind off the weather."

Unable to resist the appeal in the two pairs of eyes turned toward her, Caroline left them, heads bent over the puzzle. Returning some time later, she found Lucy asleep on the settee, clutching a battered clown. The earl, a look of contentment on his face, was reading in a nearby chair. His previously impeccable brown coat was now wrinkled and a bit worse for wear after an afternoon with Lucy.

"I didn't think it would hurt to let her nap here," he whispered, an indulgent smile on his face.

"It won't," she assured him. "Children are remarkably resilient. My back would be broken from sleeping in that position."

The familiar scowl appeared on his face again, plowing twin furrows between his brows. "How is your injury, Mrs. Alveston?"

Too late, Caroline was aware her thoughtless remark had reminded him of the accident. "I hardly think of it, my lord."

"I cannot credit that," he disputed, amiability forgotten. "I should have overridden your objections and summoned the doctor," he growled.

"The salve I concoct is as effective as anything he would have recommended," she asserted. "I have used it for years and it has always served me well. I really am much better," Caroline assured him, desiring to erase the frown from his forehead.

"I'll never forgive myself for what happened." His eyes held hers intently as a surge of protectiveness swept over him.

"Please do not dwell on it any longer. It distresses me that you do so," she replied, willing her heart to cease beating in such an erratic manner.

"Will you grant me a favor?" he asked, a smile reluctantly lifting one corner of his mouth.

"If I can, my lord," she said, wondering if she could refuse him anything for long.

"Then join me after dinner tonight. I would appreciate the company on such a dreary day as this. It will convince me I'm truly forgiven." A devilish glint appeared in his eye. "I promise, I have no other confessions to make."

Despite his earlier explanation of their need to discuss household matters, Caroline knew sitting with him in private flouted proper behavior. Yet, as she studied the strong planes of his face, resentment rose strong and bitter within her that choosing to protect an innocent child had pushed her beyond the fringes of acceptability.

Under ordinary circumstances, she would be free to welcome his overtures. Not a solitary meeting in his library, of course, but under the aegis of society's strictures she could examine the curious feelings he inspired without damaging her reputation. Now, no matter how much it rankled, she had no choice but to refuse.

Thoroughly convinced she had vanquished her rebellion, her eyes widened in surprise when she heard herself say, "Of course, my lord, I shall be pleased to join you for a short time."

After riding his fields one morning, the earl returned to find Caroline standing inside the front door intently surveying the entrance hall. Satisfaction invaded him as he imagined she waited there to welcome him home.

At his invitation, she had joined him in the library several evenings during the past week, and contentment had filled him as it had the first time. But while their conversation had ranged from the Frost Fair on the Thames to the Duchess of Oldenburg's visit, she avoided touching on anything personal.

It was obvious to his experienced eye that Caroline felt the attraction between them, and he wondered why she fought it so hard. His curiosity was heightened by her evasion, and he was even more determined to ferret out the secret she held so tightly.

The earl had accepted the endless black Caroline wore, having even come to think that in a well-cut gown black would become her. But seeing her hair severely pulled back into an unattractive knot made him wonder anew about her penchant for appearing dowdy. Though he realized she could not go about her work with hair flowing to her waist, he wished she would affect a more becoming style.

"Is something wrong, Mrs. Alveston?" he finally asked, startling her out of her intense scrutiny. "Pray don't tell me the ceiling is ready to fall."

Clad in a blue riding coat, light breeches, and Wellington boots, the earl looked unusually rakish this morning. Caroline's heart beat faster as she admired his well-muscled, broad shoulders and dark, wind-rumpled hair.

"No, my lord," said Caroline. "I'm attempting to judge the entrance hall through unprejudiced eyes. However, I fear that like one's children, it's hard to find fault with something this dear."

Absurdly glad she liked his home, he followed her gaze around the hall. Since her installation as housekeeper, its appearance had greatly changed. The glowing wood paneling and gleaming marble floors were a far cry from the dusty, mud-splattered foyer that had first greeted him.

Two imposing William and Mary chairs with high carved backs flanked a table with graceful curved legs and a decorative frieze from the same period. On its gleaming surface was an arrangement of flowers in a cut glass vase, along with a silver calling card tray. A mirror, richly and intricately carved with flowers and leaves, hung on the wall over the table. Dating from the reign of George I, an improbable likeness of the king was centered at the top of the frame.

A wide staircase rose gracefully from the center of the hall to the second floor, and a chandelier large enough to rival the famed lights of Astley's Royal Amphitheatre hung waiting for its moment of sparkling glory.

"I know what you mean. I even find myself admiring a field now and then," he said with a wry smile. "Do you think it's something in the air?"

"Just a fondness for home, I believe. Although this is not my home," she hastened to add, "I feel there was once a great deal of love lavished on it."

He was slow to answer. "Yes, my mother and father were very happy here. This is my first visit since their deaths." The raw pain of loss was etched in his face and threaded through his voice.

"They were killed in a carriage accident while I was away," he continued after a silence filled with memories. "I received a letter written on their last morning. They spoke of their love and pride in me. That's one of my most valued possessions."

"I know somewhat how you feel," commiserated Caroline. "Although I was with my father when he died, I still feel his loss sharply."

The sadness in her eyes cut him to the quick, but without her complete confidences, he could do nothing to dispel it. "If you'd like to visit your family, my coach is at your disposal," he offered, thinking homesickness might have brought about her dejection.

"Thank you, my lord, but nothing is left for me there at present." Her words dropped with cold precision from inflexible lips.

"You have no family, then?" he queried, hoping to draw her out.

"No. My mother died when I was young, and I was an only child. So there's no one close," she answered briefly, shifting uneasily at his questioning.

"Except for Lucy," he prodded gently.

"That's true, but she's more than enough." Caroline's expression glowed with love and a tender smile curved her lips.

Lord Castleton was unexpectedly annoyed that the smile was not for him, but he knew that feeling was ridiculous.

"Perhaps you'd like to visit your husband's family, then," he suggested, unwilling to acquiesce so easily. "I'm sure they'd like to see Lucy."

Caroline moved away from him to the hall table. "Unfortunately, John had no family, either. Life might have been much different if he had," she concluded dispassionately, her slim hands making minute adjustments to the flower arrangement.

It disturbed him that Caroline and Lucy were alone in the world. "Surely, your father's heir would give shelter to his daughter and grandchild."

For a moment, the caution guarding her feelings slipped away. "Oh, yes, my lord, but the price is too high. I would rather deal with the devil," she stated defiantly. "I will go back someday, but on my own terms." The light of battle turned her eyes to emeralds.

Her unexpected disclosure disturbed him. "You aren't planning on deserting me anytime soon, are you?"

"I promised to stay until Mrs. Davies is well, and I will," she assured him, regaining her composure. "In fact, it will be some time before I can return, so there's no need to worry about your house party."

"That's the least of my worries, Mrs. Alveston," he replied, her obscure remarks stirring his curiosity even more. Most women would like nothing better than to pour out their troubles to a sympathetic listener, but she could not be drawn out. Perhaps, with time, she would come to confide in him.

The next afternoon, the earl made his way across the sun-dappled park spread invitingly around the manor. As he passed the summer house, he heard laughter just before a body careened around a tree directly into him. Joining in her amusement, he grasped Caroline's upper arms and held her away from him, not wanting to embarrass her by his instant response to her soft curves molding intimately to his hard planes.

Having already brought her enough trouble, he was determined to ignore his housekeeper's allure. The woman was under his protection and he was honor-bound as a gentleman to assure her safety. But his good intentions wavered as he looked down into her vivacious face and surveyed the mass of auburn hair around her shoulders. His resolve further weakened

when he discovered Caroline had undone the top buttons of her dress in concession to the afternoon heat.
Unabashed, he traced the narrow strip of creamy skin
until it disappeared into the shadowy cleft of her
bosom.

Five

"My lord, I'm sorry," Caroline cried, holding his forearms to steady herself. The earl was looking extremely handsome in a dark blue coat, cut square at the waist, with flat silver buttons. His collar was moderate but his cravat was tied in an intricate style, lending an air of formality to his dark features. Buff breeches fit without a wrinkle, disappearing into Wellington boots.

"I didn't know you were going to be in the park this afternoon, or we would have left you undisturbed," she whispered, looking back over her shoulder. "Lucy and I are playing hide-and-seek," she explained.

It would take more than staying out of the park to give him peace, he surmised, as her touch burned through the superfine of his coat. Matching his voice to hers, he replied, "I'm only here seeking you, Mrs. Alveston."

"I hope nothing is amiss," she said, a frown knitting her brow.

"No, there's nothing wrong," he stated, pulling her

behind a shrub as the child began her search. "I received a letter today from Charles Dalton, the heir to Cresthill. You'll recall I've spoken of our friendship."

"Yes, I do," she agreed. "Unfortunately, I never met him while I was with the viscountess." The earl's possessive grasp was making it difficult for her to think rationally.

"It seems that oversight will soon be remedied," he continued, rubbing her upper arms as if to warm them. "Charles writes he'll be arriving at Castleton in advance of the house party. He was wounded on the Peninsula and was still recuperating when I left London. I'm afraid he gave no date for his arrival," the earl finished absentmindedly, distracted by the pulse fluttering at the base of her throat, yearning to feel it beneath his lips.

"I'll return immediately and make sure all is ready," she said, reluctantly beginning to pull away.

"That won't be necessary, Mrs. Alveston." Drawing her closer, he lowered his voice even further as Lucy approached their hiding place. "I doubt even Charles could arrive so quickly. It could be tomorrow or a fortnight before we see him, but I wanted you to know since I'll be gone for a day or so on business."

Surprised by the announcement of his departure, Caroline met his compelling gaze. Suddenly, the air seemed too thick to breathe, and her lips parted breathlessly beneath his searching look.

Giles studied her changed appearance. She was beyond everything lovely, with sun-kissed cheeks and lips half opened in artless invitation. To his dismay, he found himself leaning toward her, wanting nothing more than to explore her mouth and the passion it promised. Recalling his good intentions, he jerked away, abruptly saying his goodbyes and briskly heading back toward the stables, with Lucy's cries of "I found you" ringing in his ears.

Caroline hugged the little girl close, agreeing she was very clever indeed, all the while watching Lord Castleton's long, soldierly stride take him away from her. The precision of his military bearing, which was still so much a part of him, was a far cry from the man who bent over her moments earlier. Then his soft gaze had been fixed intently on her lips, and she had been undeniably disappointed when he drew back. Madeline had been right about problems but wrong about the source. She must guard against herself as much as the earl.

Lord Castleton's two days in London had not accomplished what he wished. While transacting his business, he fully intended to release the frustration Caroline had roused in him. Expecting to be entertained by the ladies he had met on his last sojourn, he found their false airs and patent admiration stale and predictable, and had no wish to join any of them between the sheets. Bidding them a courteous good evening, he left to hushed murmurs of sorrow that the war had ruined such a virile gentleman. As soon as his business was completed, he set out for Castleton with an eagerness far different from the reluctant journey made several weeks earlier.

Now he strolled through the gardens at the back of the house, ostensibly to check on the progress of the new gardeners. Truth to tell, he was looking forward to seeing his housekeeper again after a two-day absence. It was common knowledge she and Lucy visited the garden when the weather allowed, and he hoped to encounter them on their walk. The emptiness of his London experience, contrasting with memories of the stormy afternoon in the library, made him anxious to feel a bond of genuine companionship again.

Pausing at two intersecting paths, he heard splashing and little girl laughter coming from the direction of the fountain. Recognizing Lucy's voice, he smiled and followed the sound.

The fountain, set in the center of a circular stone pool, came into sight, and he was rewarded with the same delectable perspective as when he first met Caroline in the hall. But the view now was even more enticing, since the black bombazine had been replaced with a thin muslin gown clinging seductively to her curves.

"Mrs. Alveston, I'd recognize you anywhere," he said wickedly, white smile flashing.

"My lord," gasped Caroline from her position hanging over the pool. "Please help me. I can't let go."

"I wouldn't want you to, ma'am," he replied, standing back to relish the view.

Lucy was enjoying herself immensely in the water, as Caroline clung doggedly to the child's soaked skirts.

Since the pool was shallow and no harm was coming to either of them, the earl did not immediately rush forward. Caroline's contortions were much too easy on the eye to end them so quickly.

"Am I to always be rescuing you from a watery fate?" he quipped, dark eyes sparkling with an amusement she could not presently reciprocate.

"I would appreciate a hand," she pleaded, ignoring his remark.

"My pleasure," he responded gallantly, attempting to decide on which delightful spot to place it. Stepping to her side, he slid his arm around her waist.

"Not me! Lucinda!" she yelped peevishly, slipping a little farther over the stone edge.

No longer able to tease her, he reached out and easily plucked the child from the water.

Lucy patted him excitedly on the face, clamoring, "Fish! Big yellow fish!"

"Yes. They're goldfish," he explained, pleased by her enjoyment.

"I'll take home to Madeline," she said, leaning back toward the pool.

By the time he explained that she and Madeline must visit the fish at the fountain, Caroline was again standing upright, wringing water from her skirts.

She could not face Lord Castleton until her emotions were under control. The past few days had seemed endless without the earl in residence. When she arose in the mornings she found no purpose to her days, and Caroline acknowledged what she could no longer deny: Her life now centered around the powerful man by her side.

Willing her expression not to betray her, she met his eyes, stunned by the fire she saw burning in their

64

depths. "We must go back and change," she declared in a shaky voice, reaching for Lucy.

"I'll carry her," he offered helpfully. "There doesn't seem to be any damage done, except for a little dampness." His eyes roved over her again. "You are charmingly dressed for a day in the garden," he commented.

"Thank you, my lord. I felt it would not be unseemly to wear colors on my free time."

"Your dedication is to be commended. Many young widows would have put it aside completely before now." He wondered if she was also ready to consider accepting a man in her life.

"I am still convinced the austerity of black brings about more respect from the staff. I could never gain their serious regard dressed like this," she remarked earnestly, indicating her damp skirt.

"You have certainly convinced me, Mrs. Alveston, that it would not be at all appropriate." He turned his head to hide the smile curving his full mouth.

His tone was suspect, but she could find no evidence of ridicule in his face. "You haven't escaped undamaged yourself, my lord," she observed, a mischievous expression lighting her face as they made their way to the back of the house.

Smiling at the dripping bundle in his arms, he shrugged, answering casually. "It will give Denton something to do. He grows lazy in such a tame atmosphere." The earl paused to pick a yellow rose and tuck it behind Lucy's ear. "Has all gone well in my absence?" he inquired.

"Up until a few minutes ago," she said wryly, holding her sodden skirts before her. "Another few days and the extra help will be finished. I know you'll be glad for that."

"I don't begrudge their use. It's just that I'm always tripping over someone who's polishing or scrubbing, but the results are worth it," he added hastily.

"I'm glad you think so, my lord. By the end of the week you won't have to worry about where you step," she assured him. "And your trip," she asked courteously, "was it successful?"

"Not entirely, but I think I'll soon be able to settle matters satisfactorily, now that I've discovered the problem." His gaze returned repeatedly to the woman by his side as they wended their way to the rear entrance, speaking of inconsequential matters.

Reaching the herb garden, Lord Castleton stopped, turning toward her. "You had best take Lucy now," he suggested.

At her quizzical look, he continued. "I think you'll cause less of a stir when you enter." His gaze fell to the front of her dress, soaked through and clinging revealingly to her slender form.

Chagrined, Caroline grabbed Lucy and held her close. "You should have told me," she ground out, turning a fiery red.

"And destroy such a pleasant view?" he said, his easy tone belying the heat in his eyes. "Besides, she's too big for you to carry so far, and had you known you would have insisted."

"You are no gentleman," she snapped.

He yearned to soothe her temper with a caress, but with the child between them, he could only give a low chuckle and reply, "You're right. I'm still too much a soldier."

A heightened awareness surrounded Caroline and Lord Castleton after what Lucy prosaically, and unromantically, labeled Goldfish Day. The earl unconsciously adopted a subtle proprietorial air toward his housekeeper, while Caroline, though embarrassed, could not deny the excitement she had felt under his admiring gaze.

Shaken by the experience, she was more determined than ever to continue on the unremarkable course of being the perfect housekeeper and no more. Since Mrs. Davies and Jervis continually bemoaned the fact the earl was at least a half stone underweight, she quizzed them about his favorite foods. Then she and Madeline prepared meals to tempt his appetite.

Luncheons and dinners were combinations of old favorites and innovative dishes from Caroline's recipes. Assured by both her advisors that Lord Castleton preferred a country breakfast, she did not tamper with the early fare.

A few mornings later, while reviewing the day's menus with Madeline, Jervis approached, nervously clearing his throat to gain Caroline's attention.

"Yes, Jervis?" she said, looking up from the list before her.

"Mrs. Alveston," began Jervis, eyes trained somewhere above her head, "Lord Castleton has made a special request for breakfast this morning. I'm sorry to interrupt, but I believe you're the only one who can fulfill it."

"Really, Jervis." Caroline's eyes widened in surprise. "And just what is it his lordship desires?"

"An omelette, ma'am. Your special omelette. And I must say he was rather grumpy about it," answered the footman with an injured air.

Caroline smothered a giggle. "Grumpy?"

"Yes, ma'am," the footman declared affirmatively. "He said he was tired of the same thing every morning, while his other meals were culinary delights. Those were his exact words. Then he refused everything I offered. He finally sent me to fetch an omelette like the one you fixed the first day you were here. The undercook has no idea how to go about it, so I felt I should come to you."

"You were right to do so, Jervis," Caroline said, trying to console the nettled retainer. "Please take his lordship some hot coffee and cook's muffins. Perhaps that will keep him satisfied until his omelette arrives.

"No, Madeline," said Caroline, holding out a detaining hand as the older woman began to rise, "I'll take care of this myself."

Madeline sat back and watched Caroline hurry into the kitchen. She shook her head, hoping this was not the beginning of the trouble she had predicted. When a woman such as Caroline cooked something special for a man like the earl, there was usually more than a hunger-induced appetite involved.

Caroline quickly prepared the omelette and slid it onto a warmed plate. Waving Jervis aside, she picked up the silver tray. "I'll deliver this myself. I don't want you to suffer for my lack of imagination," she added placatingly.

The footman held open the door and she floated through with a satisfied smile on her face, ridiculously pleased the earl had remembered the omelette she had fixed for him.

"Good morning, my lord," Caroline said, the now-familiar warmth flooding her.

"Mrs. Alveston," he exclaimed, beginning to rise from his seat at the head of the table.

"Please remain seated, my lord. It's only your housekeeper," she said, regaining enough control to put him in his place.

Uncertain whether to frown or smile at her sally, he decided she was, surprisingly, mocking propriety and settled on the latter. Sketching a half bow, he quizzed, "Still, a housekeeper should not be serving in the dining room. It just isn't done, you know."

"I do, my lord. It's said by some that I'm a high stickler for propriety," she replied imperiously, still holding the tray in front of her.

"Are you, ma'am? Then why are carrying what I hope is my breakfast?" he asked, a black brow rising inquisitively.

"Why, this is my special omelette, my lord. I trust it to no one's hands but my own. Of course, it's also flattering to have my Lord Castleton request something from my limited talents." Her lashes fluttered in excessive coyness over sparkling eyes.

He grinned appreciatively at her pretense of modesty. "Your talents are not limited, as you well know.

But if you don't set that tray down soon, I'm afraid I'll have to forcibly wrest it from you," he demanded in good humor.

Caroline hastened to comply. "Yes, my Lord Castleton," she mocked, obediently setting the plate before him. She bobbed pertly and backed away from the table, hands clasped before her, eyes meekly downcast, the picture of dutiful servitude.

"Minx," he teased, forgetting who and where they were.

She met his laughing eyes and their gazes held, his imparting the same message of admiration as in the garden, hers receiving it more readily than she should. "Don't forget your breakfast, my lord," she advised, to cover her confusion. "It's best while still warm."

"Perhaps you'll join me," he invited appealingly.

"You mean, share your omelette?" she asked, amazement ringing in her voice. "I'm astounded at your generosity after asserting you would eat nothing else."

"My generosity in regard to this omelette is limited," he admitted, savoring the first bite of his breakfast. "But there are many boring foods going to waste," he declared, indicating the loaded sideboard.

"Thank you, sir," she replied, her voice uneven with laughter, "But I've already broken my fast this morning."

"Coffee then, and company while I enjoy this delicious concoction," he cajoled, turning the compelling force of his eyes on her.

"I couldn't," she objected weakly, responding to his charm.

"Yes, you could," he demanded with more vigor than he would have used a week earlier. "You've already disregarded convention, so a few more moments won't hurt. Jervis, some hot coffee for Mrs. Alveston." He waved Caroline to the seat at his right as Jervis left the room.

"Really, my lord," protested Caroline, as her opposition collapsed beneath his determination. "This won't do. How will it look for me to sit at the breakfast table with you?" she asked, all the while chafing at the unfairness of her position that would not allow her to do so.

"Perfectly natural. I'm a busy man and my time is not my own. I should have thought of this earlier, but now that I have, you'll join me every morning," he commanded authoritatively.

"And what of those times after dinner?" Caroline questioned sternly.

"Why, that will continue as usual," he answered, seeming surprised she had even asked. "If you will recall, they have not been that numerous," he retorted, and Caroline understood what Jervis meant by his lordship sounding "grumpy."

"It will be strictly business, Mrs. Alveston," he said, meaning to reassure her.

"But highly unusual, Lord Castleton."

"Nonsense," he responded shortly, determined to have her company as often as possible. "Bring pen and paper," ordered the earl when Jervis returned with the coffee. "Mrs. Alveston will need to make notes."

A heavy silence hung over the breakfast table until the footman returned bearing the writing materials. "You may leave us, Jervis," Lord Castleton said.

By the end of the week the earl was pleased with his progress. Pen, ink, and paper had become part of the place setting on his right. Coffee was served as soon as Caroline joined him at the table, and each day brought a more relaxed atmosphere.

The mornings' conversations, initially dominated by the earl and sprinkled with Caroline's stilted comments as to what needed to be replaced, were now lively discussions that ofttimes went far astray of their intended objectives. The paper was seldom utilized, since conversation seemed more interesting than the scratching of a pen. If the ink dried to a crust in the bottom of the inkwell, Giles was too wily a tactician to mention it, and Jervis did not dare.

It didn't take Denton long to ferret out the earl's new eagerness for the breakfast table. He smiled knowingly as his master hurried through his morning's ablutions, dressing with an attentiveness that could only please a gentleman's valet.

Lord Castleton admitted his attraction to his housekeeper, mainly attributing it to his long stay on the Peninsula bereft of acceptable feminine companionship. Even in her black garb and with her hair pulled back, Caroline was easier on the eye than most. But now that he had seen her, dampened dress clinging intimately to her body, she invaded even his sleeping hours.

In the darkness he awakened desiring to know her in every way a man could know a woman, experiencing the ecstasy he knew they could reach. But in the light of day he pretended to a casualness he did not feel, resolved to keep his honor and hers intact.

Six

With renewed energy born of curbed emotion, Caroline threw herself into finishing the rehabilitation of Castleton. As she had promised, by the end of the week the cleaning was finished and the house was quiet again. Unable to remain indoors, she took Lucy by the hand and stepped outside to relax in the warm sunshine.

The earl came upon Caroline as she followed her daughter's meandering path through the garden. He, too, had been overly busy during the past days, seeing her only at breakfast. The evenings, devoted to adjacent landowners with a view to improving drainage, had left him yearning for her like an unlicked cub.

"Good morning, Mrs. Alveston. Since I've encountered only my own staff thus far, may I assume the cleaning is over?" He was pleased to see her looking even more lovely than ever, in a lavender dress with ruching trimming the round neckline. The high-waisted skirt flowed softly over curves to which the black bombazine could never do justice, and he silently applauded whatever flight of fancy had swayed her to discard it on these occasions.

"Yes, my lord. We finished yesterday while you were away from home," she reported with satisfaction.

"Then congratulations are in order. You've accomplished what I thought was unattainable: the righting of my household," he said with an exaggerated flourish and bow.

"Thank you," replied Caroline, her face blushing under his approving gaze. "It was a formidable task, but well worth the effort. I find I become more enamored with Castleton every day."

The earl's black riding coat lent an air of severity to his features, tantalizing Caroline's senses even more than usual. Her pulse beat rapidly at his nearness, and she moved uneasily down the path, ostensibly to keep an eye on Lucy, but in reality attempting to distance herself from his disturbing presence.

Turning to admire her profile, he noticed the faint bruising under her eyes and the unaccustomed droop to her usually squared shoulders. "You look tired," he said, concern softening his voice.

Caroline pulled herself erect as if to prove she was equal to the task of running his house. "It's of no significance. We did more than usual yesterday to finish. The fresh air will restore me."

"Then perhaps you and Lucy will accompany me to the stables," he invited, wanting to share the beauty of the day with her and the child. "I'm on my way to meet Burton."

"More yields-per-acre?" she teased with a sideways glance.

"No doubt," he agreed, returning her smile. "But since you've made life more comfortable, I find the burden lighter."

He tapped his riding crop against the side of his brilliantly polished Hessian, admitting to himself that it was not an empty compliment he paid. Their conversations relaxed his mind, while her beauty soothed his eye, and he realized he was content in her presence. A rather startling discovery for a man who had considered himself self-sufficient since being in short coats.

Feeling her questioning look, he picked up his train of thought. "Have you visited the stables yet?"

"No," she replied, following his conversational lead. "I've been far too busy to step foot beyond the gardens." Remembering their adventures there, she hurried on. "But your reputation for prime cattle is well known."

"And do you just admire good horseflesh from afar?" he asked, observing the interest in her expression.

"Oh, no," she answered with unabashed enthusiasm. "I think I rode before I walked. There's nothing I enjoy more than an early morning gallop."

"The past weeks must have seemed restricted to you, then," he said, feeling guilty he hadn't offered her a mount earlier.

"Not at all. It was just fond memories I was recounting," Caroline admitted. "Actually, I've only ridden a few times while residing with the viscountess. With her poor health, I didn't like to leave her long."

"Then I insist you take advantage of my stable

now that the grueling work is over." He was pleased he could finally do something for her.

"I appreciate your offer, but I couldn't." A firm note of refusal strengthened her voice.

"And why not, ma'am? Are my nags not worthy enough?" he teased lightly.

Caroline had spent hours mulling over her preoccupation with the earl, studying all aspects of their relationship, before regretfully accepting she must put an end to her fascination with him. There was no time like the present to establish her decision.

"It isn't that at all," she replied seriously. "I'm sure your mounts are first-rate. However, as I have brought to your attention before, I am your housekeeper, my lord, not a guest."

The earl's smile quickly turned to a frown. It irked him that she must comport herself as his inferior because of circumstance.

"There's no matter of equal standing between us," he said gruffly. Annoyance colored his reply, for he knew the beau monde would disagree.

Caroline focused her gaze solidly on Lucy, who was entranced by a yellow and black butterfly in the path ahead. "It is one thing, my lord, to converse equally in private, and quite another to go galloping over the countryside on your private stock."

Recognizing the determined tilt to her chin, he changed tactics. "Mrs. Alveston," he began in a silky voice, "consider that we're on my country estate, with servants who have known me from childhood. People are much more tolerant here than in London, as you well know." He stopped and took her elbow, forcing her to pause and face him. "Although I don't know your family, I do know Quality when I see it. You cannot deny you could grace Castleton's drawing room without apology."

Caroline concentrated on the earl's shirtfront, not daring to meet the eyes she knew would be studying her with dark intensity. "Perhaps you're right," she confessed, "but my current position precludes it. While life here at Castleton may, in truth, be less censorious than in London, our relationship cannot completely defy convention."

So much propriety in one slight figure was beginning to sorely test his patience. "Then if you will not accept on a personal level, let us extend your responsibilities," he proposed, smiling through gritted teeth.

"Again, my lord," she replied with a wealth of meaning.

"As often as it takes," he countered, his lips twitching in amusement at her pointed comment. "Now, since I do need help in exercising the horses," he continued, "and since you can certainly use the fresh air, you would be doing both of us a favor by riding. It wouldn't bode well for my reputation as an employer to have two housekeepers ill and abed at the same time," he scoffed. "Think of the discomfort I would suffer. No more secret recipes would probably upset my delicate constitution and undo all the progress I've made. Now, have I settled your doubts?"

Lord Castleton caught his breath as Caroline abandoned his shirtfront to smile up at him. Bewitching lips parted over tiny white teeth, and her green eyes glowed with a warmth he had longed to see. The prim demeanor of housekeeper slipped away, and a carefree young woman stood in her place. He envisioned the Castleton emeralds sparkling around her neck and in her hair, her body fitting snugly in his arms as they circled the gleaming oak floor of the ballroom.

"My lord. I fear you aren't attending." Caroline's voice jerked him back to the present.

"I'm sorry, I was distracted for a moment." Examining the delicate oval face lifted to his, he yearned to lower his head and consume that delectable pouting lip that filled his dreams.

"I will accept your offer," Caroline repeated, "if you truly think it's suitable. However, if I receive any indication from the staff that they feel I'm rising above myself, then I'll give it up. I must keep the respect of your servants in order to run Castleton efficiently."

His eyes revealed the satisfaction of a man accustomed to getting his way. "Agreed. Now, let's continue to the stables. After all, I promised days ago to show Lucy the horses. Then we'll choose a mount for you before I leave."

As the earl rode over the estate that morning, Caroline's face haunted his thoughts. He had always considered himself immune to a woman's lasting influence. Certainly, the insipid London misses had left no mark on him, and the muslin company was out of his thoughts as soon as he stepped through their door. Now a green-eyed housekeeper whose hand he had never lifted to his lips accompanied him on his ride.

Caroline's reluctance to discuss her past only inspired him to discover her secret. If she had problems, he was more than willing to help. A scandal would not even deter him now as plagued as he was with desire for her. In truth, a good scandal might put her exactly where he wanted, concerned enough about her future to be receptive to his advances.

As soon as he returned home, he would write his friend, Robert Barnes, in the War Office, requesting information on the late John Alveston and family. But for now, Lord Castleton urged Palisades faster, determined to shake Caroline Alveston from his mind for a time.

Caroline had been surprised by the intense wave of rebellion that had swept over her the day before, instantly obliterating her hard-won resolve. Lord Castleton's offer to ride had been too tempting to resist. Surely she deserved a small measure of happiness now and again, she rationalized.

Rising earlier than usual, she had already approved the day's menus and instructed the staff on their duties. Now, with the morning sun just lighting the window, she changed into her riding habit and stood before the mirror appraisingly, smoothing the full green skirt over her hips, unaware it emphasized her slender frame and made her appear even more fragile than usual. Although several years old, the classic simplicity she favored had not fallen out of style, and the habit looked as new as when she had ridden over Birchwood.

Tears pricked Caroline's eyes as she thought of those days but she rapidly blinked them away, determined to avoid unpleasant memories this morning.

Her spirits immediately lightened as she studied

her reflection, thinking how much more frivolous she felt wearing colors. Pleased with her decision to discontinue wearing black during her free time, she descended the back stairs to the stable yard.

Unwilling to disturb Lord Castleton so early, Caroline had left a note by his plate explaining her absence. An avid horseman himself, she felt sure he would understand the zealousness that took her from the house so early.

It also removed her from the intimacy of the breakfast table, where the familiar scent of his shaving soap mingled with the crisp aroma of fresh linen, tantalizing her senses. Unusual cravings stirred at the thought of leaning over his shoulder and pressing her cheek against his newly shaven one.

The mare was a sweet goer, and Caroline experienced the joy of having an excellent mount beneath her again. Not since the death of her father had she ridden such a fine piece of horseflesh. It was then her stepmother had sold off all the stables so carefully built up over the years. She contended the cost too dear for the benefit of one. Of course, the carriage horses were kept for her convenience, but the rest had to go.

It was not the expense, for Caroline's father had been a solicitous man, planning carefully for his family's future. She was aware of the older woman's jealousy, judging it a measure of revenge that the stables were emptied. Although her stepmother did not have complete control over her inheritance, she could make changes for the good of the estate. And that was all the excuse she had needed to deprive Caroline of the one pleasure left in her life.

81

It was a new horse, and although the memories it inspired were bittersweet, Caroline reveled in the feeling of freedom as she galloped across the river meadow, the early morning air fresh against her face.

She had admired the meadow from the top floor of Castleton, where she often paused to refresh herself with the view. The sunny, flower-filled land provided a striking contrast to the dark green ribbon of trees snaking along the riverbank. Her gaze had been drawn to it repeatedly during the arduous days of cleaning, until she could almost smell the flowers and feel the cool shade on her face. She had thought to walk there at first opportunity, but now she rode in grand style on a beautiful sorrel mare called Scarlet Lady.

A short time later, she sat her horse looking down at the profusion of wildflowers, her lovely face bright with pleasure. It was a captivating scene and Lord Castleton took his fill before speaking.

"May I offer my services? You're looking so longingly at those blossoms, I'd be remiss in my duty as a gentleman not to pick them for you."

Startled by his voice, she swung around to see the earl sitting his stallion a short distance away. His dark brown coat contrasted pleasantly with the buckskins he wore. Brown tasseled Hessians, gleaming in the early morning sunlight, gave evidence of Denton's diligence with the polish.

Caroline immediately discerned that location and proximity did not signify in her response to Lord Castleton. Her heart beat just as rapidly and her breath became just as shallow under the morning sky as it did in the manor's dining room.

"You surprised me, my lord," said Caroline, reining in her now-fidgeting mare. Palisades seemed to affect Scarlet Lady the same way his master did her. "I wasn't expecting to see you this early."

"So I learned at breakfast. You should have told me yesterday you wished to ride early. A note is so cold. Almost as if you were avoiding me." He knew he should not tease her so, but he was exasperated that she had slipped away from him. And she was so delicious-looking in her confusion.

"Of . . . of course not," she stammered, disgusted at her lack of poise. "I just didn't want to upset your routine."

"You already have, my dear," he said, guiding the stallion closer to the mare.

Seven

The endearment, uttered in an unusually husky voice, drew a cloak of intimacy around them.

"My lord, you should not call me thus," Caroline blurted out nervously, retreating to her crumbling bastion of convention.

For a few moments longer, he sat admiring her exquisite figure set off to perfection by the excellent cut of the habit. Her eyes, intensified by the emerald-green fabric, pulled him into their depths. Seated on the lively mare, the wind lifting loose curls around her face, she was at last in her proper milieu.

"Propriety before breakfast?" he asked, watching her intently. "You protest earlier every day. May I anticipate you knocking on my door in the morning, just to tell me to behave?"

Caroline turned a becoming pink, and he hoped she was imagining him in the twisted sheets of his sleepless bed. It would serve the minx right, since she was the cause of his restlessness.

Not waiting for a reply, he continued. "I'm glad to see our accident didn't put you off riding. For many women it would mean the end of the sport," he concluded, still not removing his gaze from her.

"As you say, my lord, I am a woman, not a child . . ." she began.

"I can certainly affirm that, dear lady," he acknowledged, interrupting her speech, white smile gleaming.

Ignoring the images that flashed unbidden to her mind, she continued. "I've had my share of spills, but my father always insisted I remount immediately."

"A wise man," he readily agreed. "Now that I know you're experienced, I'll be sure to mount you properly, then." Her face burned scarlet at his double entendre.

Caroline could not understand why he was baiting her. Realizing he watched with patient amusement, she responded in the most innocent of ways. "I must thank you again, my lord, for Scarlet Lady is one of the finest horses I've ridden."

Taking pity on her, he lightened his tone. "Only *one* of the finest?" he queried, with an air of highly exaggerated offense. "My dear young lady, for your information, Scarlet Lady is of impeccable lineage. Much better than many of the ton. And to say she's only *one* of the finest shows you distinctly lacking in knowledge of horseflesh."

"I'll have you know, I could judge horseflesh before I knew my letters," she retorted, laughter shining from her eyes. "Much to my mother's distress, father deemed that skill far more important than mere classroom excellence. The mare's conformation is perfection and her gait is sweet. So I suppose I must agree and apologize to both you and Scarlet Lady," she said, mimicking his overly dramatic tone. "I fear I was mistaken. She's a fine bit of blood. Absolutely the finest I've ever ridden."

He bowed from the saddle. "Then we accept your apology, ma'am. I'm sure she'll allow you to finish your ride with no hard feelings. When I saw your hair flashing in the sunlight yesterday, I knew you would complement one another beautifully."

Caroline remained quiet under his admiring gaze, unable to mistake the message his eyes were expressing.

Anticipating chastisement, the earl held up a silencing hand. "I know, I know, Caroline; I shouldn't compliment my housekeeper. But you must understand that on the battlefield, with death an imminent reality, propriety doesn't carry the same weight as in the drawing room. I fear the habit of saying what's on my mind is one I've yet to break when in polite society. You must forgive my occasional slips."

Caroline felt dizzy from the brilliance of his smile.

"I missed you at breakfast this morning," he pressed, dark eyes piercing her.

The sudden change of subject caught her off guard. "I was eager for my first ride and thought you would understand."

"I do. I'm not such a curmudgeon to begrudge you a pleasure I personally enjoy." He leaned over, placing his hand possessively over hers. "But tomorrow, we'll return to our usual routine. We'll ride out together after breakfast and I'll introduce you to the most scenic paths."

The earl took in her heightened color and all good intentions vanished. He wished for nothing more than solid ground beneath their feet, so he could take her in his arms. Tightening his grip on her hand, he endeavored to convey a fraction of his desire.

Overcoming the temptation to respond to his touch, Caroline pulled Lady's head around, forcing him to release her. "I must continue if I'm to see more than the meadow this morning, my lord. I should return soon and attend my duties."

Lord Castleton guided Palisades alongside Scarlet Lady, pulling him in to match the dainty mare's gait. He noted Caroline had been truthful about her familiarity with horses. She was as graceful on horseback as she was with both feet on the ground. "There's no need for rushing your ride this morning. The house was in perfect order when I left."

Avoiding the dark eyes turned toward her, Caroline focused on the trail ahead, exposing her lovely profile to his devouring gaze.

"I must organize the house party you're expecting, my lord. There are menus to plan, supplies to order, rooms to check, and a multitude of other items to arrange."

"I wish I'd never invited a party," he growled. "The event becomes more distasteful the nearer it draws."

"You don't mean that," she said, surprised by the vehemence in his voice.

"Yes, I do. Just when I'm feeling comfortable again, my life's going to be turned upside down by people I scarcely know."

"I'm sure you exaggerate," she protested. "It's just being away for so long that makes you feel they're strangers. A little time in their presence will right that."

"I doubt that very much, Caroline." With the feelings she engendered, he could not think of her as Mrs. Alveston any longer. "Except for Charles, the others are mere acquaintances.

"I don't know why I invited them. Perhaps disillusionment with my homecoming. Much of polite society only views the war as an inconvenience to their travels on the Continent and buying of imported goods. The dead and maimed are too distressing to discuss." Disgust for the callousness of his peers colored his voice. "Everything and everyone suddenly seemed shallow after my return. Remembering Castleton, I thought to recreate something that has disappeared forever." A note of self-ridicule entered his proud voice.

Caroline felt his pain. "Your inclination was right, my lord. While many things have changed, you can achieve happiness again," she urged with quiet conviction. "It won't be the old life you knew, but it can be just as fulfilling."

The earl studied the sincerity in the green eyes turned toward him. A current of understanding flowed between them, so strong it held both captive for a time. How long it would have gone on if Scarlet Lady had not stumbled, he did not know. Caroline looked away while seeing to her horse and the gaze was broken, but the bond was still there, uniting two people with troubled pasts.

"I think you're half right," he agreed after she settled the mare. "The part about Castleton bringing me peace again. But I'm also convinced this ill-conceived house party could shatter it. Now come ride with me to the river, where I must unfortunately leave you to meet Burton. I believe the topic this morning is crop rotation," he quipped.

Due to a slight fever Lucy acquired, it was several days before Caroline rode with the earl again. In truth she was relieved, for the increasing closeness they shared was growing disquieting to her. She did not need her upbringing to tell her their relationship was developing in a totally unconventional direction. It took only common sense to see that their attachment, whatever it was becoming, was unacceptable.

"You must take some air, Mrs. Alveston. You are looking peaked again," assessed Lord Castleton after tracking her down in the stillroom. "I'm assured by a visit to Mrs. Davies that the household and Lucy will be safe for the next few hours," he stated implacably.

The offer was so inviting that Caroline did not even endeavor to avoid it. A short time later the earl was sharing a site with her where rare flowers bloomed. Next he pointed out his favorite fishing spot, where at five years old he had caught the biggest fish in the river . . . or it had caught him. He had been stubborn even at that age, for when it pulled, he held on, ending up being towed downstream until he hooked on a hanging limb. Riding farther, he showed her a stone wall, indicating the exact spot where his pony had suddenly balked and sent him over alone. Many a tenant raised his head and smiled as their laughter intermingled on the summer breeze.

"I fear I'm causing you to neglect your business,"

Caroline protested when their ride extended to mid-day.

They were returning to the manor house for luncheon, and the earl felt only impatience at their separation for a repast he knew would be much more pleasant in her company. However, even country manners would be strained to accept their taking every meal together.

"I find I'm enjoying avoiding my newfound responsibilities, Caroline. Please don't ring a peal over my head after such a pleasant morning," he entreated boyishly.

"I can't feel right about causing inattention to your tenants," she objected vigorously, her conscience still goading her. "And I should not be whiling away the morning enjoying myself; it's not what I'm employed to do."

Seeing mutiny rear its head in the form of her pouting lower lip, the earl resolved not to let this winsome baggage elude him so easily. "You are employed to carry out my orders," he said with inborn hauteur. "We can ride and attend to business at the same time."

"Extending my responsibilities again, my lord?" asked Caroline in an ironic tone. "This is rapidly becoming a habit."

The earl chose to ignore her comments. "I am persuaded you're well acquainted with the running of an estate and assisted either your father or husband in these matters." Becoming more pleased with his idea, he expounded on it. "My tenants have long been deprived of a gentlewoman's attention and would welcome a visit from you. If you'll agree, of course."

"What? Asking my opinion," she inquired with

acerbity, "when you've just reminded me I'm employed to carry out your orders? I don't think it's my place to accompany you to the farms," she added stubbornly.

Her objection was so expected that Lord Castleton ignored the jab and continued without pause. "I know," he interrupted. "What would everyone think? I tell you, Caroline, the tenants' wives and families have been long neglected and will think nothing but kind thoughts for someone taking an interest in them again."

Giles had guessed correctly. Although Castleton was more immense than Birchwood, Caroline had performed the same duties with her father. She had followed him over the estate, first on her stub-legged pony, then on a series of increasingly frisky mounts, until her horsemanship and husbandry rivaled his.

Inevitably, Lord Castleton's will triumphed, but only partially. Caroline agreed to accompany him to the farms once a week, while drawing on every evasive skill in her small storehouse of knowledge to keep him at arm's length.

The earl rejoiced at his modest victory, seeing it as the beginning of her complete capitulation, and contentedly observed as she fell into her new role quite naturally. Becoming acquainted with the women on the estate, Caroline was soon praising needlework and accepting tea from a work-worn hand without hesitation.

Learning of her skill with salves and herbal medications, mothers began asking for help with sickly children. Each successful case further established

Caroline's reputation for having healing hands, until she gave up denying the rumor.

If the earl saw anything unusual in her rapid adjustment to her new duties, he gave no indication. To do so would send her scurrying behind her shield of secrecy again, just when they were dealing comfortably together.

Surreptitiously, he studied this woman who ran Castleton with so much assurance and wondered why she was not in a home of her own. Even with a child, any man would be proud to have her for a helpmate. Perhaps she had still not dealt with the sorrow of losing her husband. He knew instinctively that she would be a loyal person and, for the first time, felt envy for a dead man.

As he had proven on numerous occasions, Lord Castleton was not one to have his wishes easily thwarted by convention. He had been the adored heir of two loving parents, surrounded by a retinue of devoted retainers, all determined that his childhood would be exceptional.

Despite the attention lavished on him, Giles grew up to be an honorable and loyal young man, a tribute to his forbearers. His military career was distinguished by numerous deeds of courage for his country and unselfish bravery for the men who fought by his side. With this background it was only to be expected he could skillfully sidestep social custom when the situation demanded it. Thus, the matter of lunching together was not abandoned, but the approach was changed to avoid convention, not flaunt it.

The days remained unseasonably fine and on their

rides over the estate, Lord Castleton would occasionally ask Madeline to pack a basket for their lunch. He seemed to know just how often he could employ this maneuver before Caroline took him to task for lack of propriety.

Ironically, he found these luncheons did not always bring the comfort he sought. The simple act of eating had never aroused him before, but when Caroline's pink tongue darted out to remove a crumb from her lip, the tightness he felt had nothing to do with a full stomach.

The earl's desire for his housekeeper bordered on obsession. And while he knew she was aware of the tension between them, Caroline had not yet indicated he would be welcome in her bed. She played such a game that he would think her an innocent if it were not for Lucy. He had never forced himself on a woman, and taking advantage of an employee was anathema to a gentleman. Biding his time, Lord Castleton hoped Caroline's reticence would vanish before his patience.

Eight

Lord Castleton had finished another solitary luncheon and the afternoon stretched dull before him. Estate ledgers held no appeal for him after the morning's unusual activities.

He and Caroline had arrived at the Johnson's cottage in time to welcome the most recent of a long line of Johnsons into the world. The unexpectedness of the birth had left no time to summon the midwife, and unhesitantly, Caroline helped deliver the tiny baby boy. As she stood cuddling the small bundle, murmuring soft noises, the earl experienced an overwhelming desire to hold a child of his own. At that moment, he wanted no other than Caroline for his child's mother.

The sentiment astonished him, and he turned, ducking through the low doorway into the sunlight, seeking to regain his composure before she joined him for the ride home. However, the craving remained, creating a small warm spot in the pit of his stomach that stirred occasionally, reminding him of its presence. He rationalized these prods by admitting the war had emphasized his mortality and the need to set up his nursery.

It was not an heir, however, that filled his mind as he left the table and wandered purposefully into the hall, but the image of large green eyes above a softly kissable mouth, along with rich glowing hair tumbling in disarray over pearly white shoulders.

So deep was his distraction that several moments passed before the musical notes attracted his attention. Searching out the source, he experienced a sense of *déjà vu* as his mother's favorite melody drifted out of the music room. Two housemaids, listening in the hall, melted away at his approach.

Stepping noiselessly through the partially open door, Lord Castleton regarded Caroline seated at the pianoforte, oblivious to his entrance. Large west-facing windows threw sun-filled patterns on the highly polished floor, where dust motes danced through the beams, transforming the room into a scene worthy of the most skilled artist's brush.

Absorbed in her music, the haunting ballad flowed from Caroline's fingers, arousing the yearnings he had suppressed earlier in the day. He stood listening, until her hands fell quiet on the keys.

"I didn't know you played," he murmured in a subdued voice, reluctant to break the spell.

Caroline turned slowly, still held in a web of her own making. "You did not ask," came the soft, succinct reply.

"Must I ask for everything, Caroline?" he complained in frustration. "Could you not freely offer a few innocent details of your life before you came to me?" he pleaded, his desire to know her leaving him vulnerable for the first time in his adult life.

The appeal in his dark eyes wrapped around her very soul and she fought the urge to take him into her confidence. If it had been only herself, she would confess everything in a moment, but Lucy's future hung in the balance. "I'm afraid, my lord, playing the pianoforte is so innocuous that I felt it not worth mentioning." Her voice was tight with emotion as she struggled to gain control.

"And the rest of your life? What of it? Damn it, Caroline!" he burst out explosively. "What are you hiding? Do you feel it's so depraved you can't share it even with me? Am I such an ogre you think I'll condemn you out of hand? I assure you, my life is not so spotless I can sit in judgment."

The silence lengthened. He knew more forceful demands would damage the tenuous bond beginning to form between them. Sighing, he passed his hand over his face in defeat.

"If you had but known my mother and her love for that particular song, you wouldn't dismiss your talent so lightly." He took a few more steps into the room.

"I'm sorry if I brought you pain, Giles." Consternation filled her voice as she rose from the satinwood bench, facing the tall figure before her.

The earl noticed but did not remark on the familiar use of his name, fearing to shatter the intimacy of the moment. "It's a pleasant pain, my dear," he answered, reaching out to loosen the hands she clasped tightly before her. "Your playing brought my mother's image back to me." He toyed with her hands, wondering how such dainty fingers could wring so much beauty from cold ivory keys.

He was silent a moment, gathering his thoughts before continuing. "I saw more death and suffering on the Peninsula than any human should be forced to endure, Caroline." His hands tightened on hers, but she made no complaint. "When I returned home, I thought to forget the savagery of war by immersing myself in more pleasurable forms of civilized barbarity. I had just removed here from London after my abortive attempt at hell-raising." A derisive smile formed on his lips.

"Who better than you would know the level to which Castleton and I had sunk when you arrived. Everything my mother held dear was in disorder. I couldn't bear to think of her then. You've worked wonders in the weeks you've been here. So much so that when I heard you playing, I could envision her again, filled with pride in Castleton."

Caroline's hands remained captured in his. He pulled her closer, imprisoning them over his heart. "On the Peninsula," he continued pensively, "I cut myself off from feelings to survive. London and the ton did nothing to revive them. But I've felt more emotion today than I have in months. I'm beginning to come alive again, my dear, and I have you to thank for it." He looked deep into her eyes, searching for an awareness that matched his own.

"You give me too much credit," replied Caroline in a husky voice. "But I won't argue the point," she conceded quickly, as a frown drew his dark brows together.

He smiled at her swift response. "So you can be

97

perceptive when you wish. I hope you'll make it a habit in the future." He raised her hands and brushed his firm lips over her fingers.

"I'm afraid I must go," he said without removing his gaze from her face. "Burton is to wait on me this afternoon." He was puzzled to find his passion had been supplanted by a tenderness unfamiliar in his dealings with women.

"I have been gone too long myself. I'm sure Lucy thinks I have abandoned her." Caroline gave a slight tug on her hands, but not exerting enough force to free herself.

"Lucy will get enough attention today," the earl assured her. "I promised to take her to see the horses after my meeting with Burton."

"Don't feel you must cater to Lucy's whims. She's playing on your softheartedness," Caroline warned him.

Giles had never thought of himself as softhearted and didn't know whether to consider it an insult or a compliment. "It's not a burdensome obligation. She's a pleasant child and I enjoy being with her."

"I know she looks forward to seeing you also, but if you should change your mind, don't hesitate to tell me. Now, I have other duties that call, my lord."

"What happened to 'Giles'?" he questioned, daring to tease her about her indiscretion.

"That was a mistake best forgotten. It just slipped out in—"

"—the heat of the moment," he suggested, and watched a blush stain her cheeks. Such modesty in a married woman was unheard of in his circles. He did not know whether to deem it pretense or prudishness, but either way the results were charming.

"You must know, Caroline, that you are coming to mean more than a housekeeper to me," he confided, thinking she might respond to a straightforward manner. "I am in hopes that perhaps you share a small part of these feelings. I would like us to know one another better." His aspirations wavered as her rosy countenance turned pale at his words.

"We are not in a position to become better acquainted, my lord," she replied bluntly, the slight tremor in her voice effectually invalidating the harshness of her remark. "It can only bring confusion about our relationship to others' attention."

"I am not at all confused," he responded untruthfully, increasingly aware his feelings were in turmoil when he thought of their future. "As for others, they do not signify."

"Very well for you to say." Her words were cold and clipped. "Your ability to provide for a child does not rely on your reputation as does mine. I cannot see where our becoming better acquainted can cause me anything but grief," she answered honestly.

"The last thing I want, dear lady, is to harm you or Lucy in any way." The sound of Burton's arrival echoed down the hall, reminding them they were not alone in the world. "I fear we must continue this conversation later." He paused, waiting for an acknowledgment from her.

Caroline remained silent, studying his shirtfront, unable to meet his gaze and keep her emotions in check. "I shall see you after dinner," he finally said, saluting her hands before releasing them. "I hope you'll honor me with another display of your musical talent." Cupping her chin in his large hand, he tipped her face up toward his. "Consider our conversation, Caroline." Giving a slight bow, he disappeared through the door before she could form a coherent reply.

Further denial was futile; he was her weakness. It was prudent to admit it and prepare as much as possible to rebuff his advances. Caroline wondered how long she could refuse if he unleashed all his charm on her. Not long, she thought, groaning and burying her face in her hands.

In the ensuing days, the earl often hurried impatiently through an excellent dinner, hoping to enjoy Caroline's company. While they did share several evenings at the pianoforte, his voice joining hers in the simple airs they both admired, it was not nearly enough to satisfy him.

Caroline avoided all mention of their unfinished conversation from the afternoon in the music room, but it lay uneasily between them, awaiting compromise.

Madeline observed with misgivings the relationship developing between the two. It would not do for Caroline to fall in love with the earl in her present straits. But unless she was mightily mistaken, that was the way her friend was headed. She hesitantly broached the subject one evening as they left Mrs. Davies's room.

"Of course, I'm not getting too close to the earl, Madeline," answered Caroline a little too quickly.

"He's lonely and I'm just a diversion until the house party arrives. Remember, I was just such a companion to the viscountess."

"Yes, but the viscountess was an elderly woman, not a handsome man in his prime. There's a great deal of difference," pointed out Madeline unnecessarily.

"I do know, Madeline," replied Caroline patiently. "But I can't refuse him when he asks me so nicely."

"That's exactly the problem," retorted the cook. "I only hope he limits his requests to respectable pursuits."

"Why, Madeline, what can you mean?" Caroline blushed, remembering the earl's tenderness in the music room. Since then, he had been careful to keep their exchanges proper, but she could not ignore the intensity of his gaze nor the response of her heart to him.

"Only that you were raised a lady and he should know it. Be truthful with his lordship. He'll understand and respect your privacy."

"I can't share my past with anyone else, Madeline. It's too risky. Don't worry about my future. Respectability won't be a concern if I should decide to marry. My inheritance will surely bring someone up to scratch."

But will you want another after Lord Castleton? questioned Madeline silently, saying no more on the subject.

Caroline's demeanor remained composed, but she realized she would face a scandal broth once she returned home with Lucy. Openly acknowledging the child as her own, among people who knew her to be unmarried, would exile them from society.

Giles was making a cake of himself over his housekeeper, and he could not stop. He peered through windows to catch sight of her in the garden. He spent more time with Lucy, hoping Caroline would join them. When she didn't, he brooded in the library or went for solitary rides, bringing Palisades back hot and lathered.

The nearer the house party date drew, the more Giles cursed himself for his stupidity. Except for Charles, he regretted the invitations. However, it was too late to cry off and he must make the best of it.

His company would be aghast if he included his housekeeper in their circle. Yet, the thought of two weeks without Caroline's closeness made him want to ignore society's restrictions.

Damnation! In some ways, things were much simpler in war, where time was too precious to worry about birth and position.

"I wonder if you would excuse me after dinner this evening, my lord." Although Caroline had accepted his familiar address, she still kept up an attempt at formality. It had been their day to visit the tenants, and her request came as the earl reached up to help her dismount. He lifted her gently to the ground, but did not remove his capable hands from her waist.

"You know I count on your company," he said, inhaling the rose fragrance she used. "You have not joined me for several days now. Couldn't you put off whatever else demands your attention?" he asked, stretching out the moment to enjoy her nearness.

"I'm afraid not. It's Lucy's birthday, and little girls are not easily persuaded to put off their birthday presents."

Scarlet Lady suddenly sidled into Caroline, pinning her against the hard length of the earl's body. Blushing, she put her hands against his chest, looking up in mute apology. He was again lost in her eyes. Usually, he left his dalliances until the evening hours, but with Caroline his urges were with him in both bright sunlight and dark of night.

"Of course, you mustn't miss her birthday," he agreed, still holding her close. "I remember my own as the most important day of the year." Standing as they were, no one would believe the subject to be a child's birthday, and he was sorry that was all he could claim. "Couldn't you spare a few minutes after she's put to bed? I would like your opinion on a school for the estate."

"I had no idea you were thinking of such a thing," exclaimed Caroline, delighted with his interest in bettering his tenants' lot. "That is wonderful, my lord! You are to be commended."

The earl reddened beneath her praise and, for once, his eyes dropped before her admiring ones.

"It's long been on my mind," he confessed. "I thought you could help guide my good intentions."

"I should like that above all things. Perhaps we could speak of it in the morning," she suggested, feeling a twinge of disappointment. "I fear it would be too late this evening. The staff would rightfully think the worst." She remained content in his grasp, relishing his touch.

He searched the loveliness of her upturned face. "I find it increasingly unfortunate they would be wrong, ma'am. Perhaps someday soon we can change that."

Caroline wondered if the hammering of her heart was audible as he continued staring down at her with a warmth that melted the core of her femininity. It was wrong to encourage him, but she was hard put to voice an objection when he was so close.

"I doubt anything will change between us," she replied, unable to hide the regret she felt.

"Perhaps it would if you could find it in your heart to trust me," he murmured persuasively.

"I do not exactly mistrust you, my lord," she said, falling deeper under his spell. "But it would not be fair to drag you into my troubles." Anxiously, she searched his face for any sign of understanding.

He met her gaze with steady assurance. "I would deem it an honor to be privy to your confidences, if you would only consider it."

"I cannot," she cried out in an anguished voice. "We are a world apart." Her green eyes, awash with tears, pleaded silently for compassion, as she repeated in a shaky voice, "A world apart."

"Do not be so sure, Caroline. You are here with me now. We will find a way to rectify our situation." He would push her no further. She had come close to disclosing her difficulties; he would bide his time. Smiling at her innocent protestation, he bent his head and brushed his lips lightly over hers.

"Now, go plan your party. We will talk of the school tomorrow, as you suggested. It will give you time to marshal your thoughts." Releasing her, he led the horses to the stables.

Nine

Caroline stood alone in the yard, shocked by her near capitulation to the earl's pleadings. This is insanity, her head cried as her heart disregarded the warning. Her hands curled into fists as she railed against a fate that put her beyond the reach of happiness that should rightly have been hers to claim. Her stepmother's intolerance had forced her into a charade fashioned by a tissue of lies that strangled her.

Caroline knew her present position made any honorable alliance with the earl all but impossible. If they had met before Lucy had been conceived, their relationship could have been. But with Lucinda, whose birth she would never regret, Caroline had ceased to be an acceptable party for any but the most hard pressed.

While Lord Castelton had never indicated he held her in low esteem, her intuition insisted the earl was only seeking a diversion while he was rusticating. After all, he knew her as an experienced woman, a widow with a child. And although she did not hold with the practice, Caroline knew discreet lovers were acceptable with the ton. Sorrow penetrated bone deep as she acknowledged her irrevocable decision. She could not be Lord Castleton's wife, and she would not be his mistress.

"Will Mrs. Alveston be joining me, Jervis?" asked the earl, hoping she had changed her mind.

The footman set the tray down before answering. "I do not think so, my lord. She's celebrating her daughter's ... ah ... birthday, I believe."

"Yes, she mentioned that earlier today, but I thought it might have been over by now." He swirled the amber liquid around in the glass Jervis handed him.

"That had been the plan, my lord, but cook was delayed in decorating the cake. I don't think it will last long, since the hour is late for a child; however, she didn't order refreshments for herself."

Whenever Caroline joined him, the earl would insist she take tea while he enjoyed his brandy. The single bottle and glass confirmed his evening would be a lonesome one.

After Jervis left the library, Giles sat in solitary splendor for some time, thinking back over the kiss he had shared with his housekeeper. Slight though it had been, its effects were devastating for such a worldly man as the earl. He had kissed many women, from parlor maids in his callow youth to the most famous courtesans on two continents, and none had affected him as had the touch of Caroline's lips. He had not planned the kiss. In fact, he had resigned himself

107

to a lengthy seduction, but now the wall had been breached and he wanted more.

Of course, he had to admit it was not all physical need that made her desirable. Although he admired beauty, it had never before aroused more than carnal desire. The compatibility they shared was new to him. Caroline's quickness of mind, her obvious concern with the estate and its people, had engendered deeper feelings than he craved to entertain. But it was only a temporary condition, he smugly theorized, as only a man who has never been in love could do.

A second glass of brandy could not dispel the feel and taste of Caroline. Instead, the potent spirit seemed only to intensify his thoughts. Pacing did not help, either, nor did another visit to the decanter of the fine aged liquor.

"Damned if I'll let propriety stop me," he said. Tossing back the last of the brandy, the earl slammed the hand-blown glass down on the table and stalked through the door toward the back of the house.

The kitchen was empty, already cleaned from dinner and ready for the next day's meals. Dough had been set to rise near the oven, but his thoughts were on something other than food. A few weeks ago a good meal would have satisfied his needs, but now his body was on the mend and demanding sensory fulfillment, which was sadly lacking in his life. His housekeeper had satisfied one need but had ignited another in its stead.

Anger and desire, spurred on by too much brandy, stirred in his body. What kind of woman was this red-haired siren, who acted the respectable innocent while leading him on?

He pushed open the door to the servants' quarters without knocking. Madeline, Jervis, and the other house servants had congregated in Mrs. Davies's sitting room to celebrate Lucy's birthday. The little girl was a favorite with all the staff and they were pleased to be included in the small gathering.

Mrs. Davies was propped up with a multitude of pillows so she could view the proceedings. White hair curled around a face beaming with pleasure at seeing the earl.

"My lord, how good to see you." She had spoiled him when he was a child, and she always welcomed a visit from him now.

"You are looking much better, Mrs. Davies." The pink shawl drawn around her shoulders brought more color to her face and the lines of pain were all but gone.

"That I am. 'Tis Mrs. Alveston's tisanes that are helping. I feel . . . oh . . . so much better since she began mixing them for me."

"It seems that Mrs. Alveston has carved out quite a niche for herself here at Castleton," said the earl, gazing at the object of their admiration until a blush rose high on her cheeks.

Caroline had looked up in astonishment at Lord Castleton's sudden appearance. His presence momentarily stilled the gaiety in the room until he indicated they were to continue.

Thoroughly at ease with the earl after their time spent together, Lucy smiled happily and held up her new doll for him to admire.

The sight of Caroline sitting on the floor holding the child completely undid Giles, and his anger dissipated immediately. In honor of Lucy's celebration, Caroline had changed into a white dress figured with violets. Dark green ribbons encircling the high waist dropped to pool in her lap. His gaze explored the creamy expanse of skin disappearing into the low, square-cut décolletage. Auburn hair and blond were both tousled; green eyes stared at him with caution, blue with happiness.

Again, Lucy uttered a happy giggle and offered her toy for his inspection. Surprising everyone, including himself, he dropped to his knees beside Caroline and held out his arms. The child went to him with no coaxing, rewarding him with her usual pat on the face.

Much to the astonishment of the servants present, the earl entered into the festivities wholeheartedly. Discarding the role of master, along with his coat, he rolled up his shirtsleeves and joined Lucy with her new toys, feeding her cake and carrying her to bed when she fell asleep in his arms.

"I think the party was a success, don't you agree?" asked the earl quietly as he gently deposited the child in her bed.

"Judging by Lucy's face, I do," Caroline responded, noticing the dark hair curling on his forearms and feeling the intimacy of the moment. "Thank you for making it such an enjoyable one. It was a special treat to have you pay her such particular attention." She tucked the cover under the tiny chin. Caroline had often longed to share these times, but now it only served to remind her of the loneliness still ahead. "I fear she misses a father in her life."

Lord Castleton noticed the look of sadness creep

across her face. He knew it was unreasonable to be jealous of a memory, but common sense seemed to desert him when around Caroline.

"And do you still mourn him?" he asked quietly, not entirely sure he wanted to hear her answer.

"I mourn the fact that Lucy will not know both her parents, will not grow up with the happiness of a full family life. Childhood memories are the things that have made my own life bearable at times."

They moved silently from the room into the hall. Giles hid his disappointment when Caroline made no further comment about her past.

"I hope we didn't disturb your evening," she said, recollecting her duties. "Jervis did serve the proper brandy, didn't he? I personally selected it." She looked up questioningly into eyes that caught and held her captive in their mesmerizing depths.

He silenced her agitated chatter by laying a finger gently against lips she was nervously moistening. The sensual touch of her tongue to his finger struck both of them forcibly as she took the taste of him into her mouth.

"Jervis acquitted himself admirably in your absence, Caroline," he said hoarsely. "But I discovered I no longer find solitude agreeable."

"My lord, I fear . . ."

"You have nothing to fear, Caroline. I will not hurt you. Just stay a moment, thus so," he whispered huskily, drawing her into his arms. He held her gently, pressing her head to rest against his shoulder. "Let us hold one another for a moment to take away the loneliness."

His breath fanned the hair at her temple. "You

must sense the rightness of this, Caroline. I cannot be alone in my feelings."

Caroline stood quietly, drawing comfort from his solid strength. Giles was right. The loneliness that lingered, even with Lucy near her, dropped away, and she was at peace for the first time since her father's death.

Lord Castleton stroked her back from shoulder to waist. It was a touch meant to comfort, not to inflame. She instinctively burrowed deeper into his arms, until the touch of his lips against her temple forced her back to reality.

Caroline stepped out of his grasp, wanting nothing more than to remain in the secure haven of his arms. "I'm sorry, my lord," she whispered, reason slowly reasserting itself. "We have been over this before, and you know it will not do. I pray you will excuse me." She turned and disappeared quickly into her daughter's room, leaving a frustrated man staring after her.

Ten

Several hours later, Caroline sat in the shadows cast by a lone candle and watched her bedroom door open. Giles slipped through and moved silently to the bed.

Still wearing his boots, his shirt unbuttoned to the top of his breeches and his black hair curling over his forehead, he looked like a pirate ready to claim his prize.

"I'm here," she said as he stared in puzzlement at the empty sheets.

"Caroline? What are you doing there?" he asked, turning toward the dark corner.

"That sounds more like a question I should be asking," she responded, rising from her chair.

Caroline had spent the last hours considering her situation. She should never have allowed Lord Castleton to come so close. The accident in the forest had removed the initial barriers erected between strangers and forged an undeniable bond between them. From that moment, her defenses had slowly eroded in the force of his attraction, but now she had touched sanity again. There was too much at stake to abandon herself to the passion that consumed her at his touch.

Even though their compatibility went beyond a mere physical attraction, she resolved to ignore it. While the interests they shared would help bond a couple in marriage, they would mean very little in the alliance she was sure he was offering.

As the earl moved closer, his breath caught on a ragged rasp that carried clearly through the room. "You should be in bed, Caroline," he said, eyeing the thin gown.

"No, I shouldn't." She met his eyes in the dim light and saw desire still burning there. "For if I had, we would have been lost."

"I can't deny it, Caroline, but I certainly wouldn't consider it a tragedy. After all, you're not a green girl." His voice was curt with impatience at her reception. "Your husband's been gone some years now, and I have firsthand knowledge your desires didn't die with him. I didn't come to ravish you, my dear," he continued more gently. "Only to find out why you ran away tonight. You know my feelings."

"Only too well. That's what sent me from you," she said, struggling to maintain a composed facade while dealing with his blunt speech.

"I don't understand. I know you are as deeply affected as I." A tender smile curled his mouth and he reached out to stroke her cheek with his fingertip. "I do not mean to rush you. I understand and respect your hesitancy, if you haven't been with anyone since your . . . husband. I promise, we'll go as slow as you wish."

His words left no doubt as to his plans for her. There would be no proper offer for her hand, no dreams of a future life together. Only the ignoble position of paramour, until he tired of her and moved on to another. Why was she surprised? Why did this cold shard of ice penetrate to her very soul? She had known from the first a permanent alliance was impossible, but hope dies hard. Caroline steeled herself against her heart's vulnerability.

"My husband is not what stands between us," she stated flatly. "You forget. I'm here for only a short time."

"Don't say that!" he demanded, his voice rough-edged with emotion. "You're here for as long as you like."

"Or for as long as you like! Either way, I'll soon need to find another position," she said, her defiance beginning to ebb in the face of reality. "Even if I should agree to what you're suggesting, this is your home. Neither of us can afford the scandal which would accompany our being found together. You're taking a dreadful chance coming here now."

"That's unimportant," he protested, refusing to accept her decision.

"Perhaps to you. You have Castleton, wealth, generations of family behind you. Finally, as a man, it's accepted you'll find female companionship. For the time being, I must retain my good name to earn a living for Lucinda and myself. You seem bent on destroying it."

"That's the last thing I want, Caroline," he objected harshly. "I long to cherish and care for you."

Hope blazed until she realized he did not mean

marriage. He had a title to secure, and while he might treat her like his countess, she would still be only his mistress.

"I need more than what you're offering. I need security for Lucinda." She was unaware her hands were balled into fists at her side, until he reached for them.

"I promise, Caroline, you and the child shall want for nothing." He pried open her fingers and lifted them to his lips.

"For how long? Until your interest wanes? Then where will we be?" she asked, her voice distraught, anguish marring her countenance.

"Caroline, listen to me," he pleaded, attempting to pull her close.

"No, Giles." Jerking her hands from his grasp, she resolved to stand fast against his entreaties. "If I can't trust you to give up on this pursuit, I'll be gone before breakfast."

Alarm raced through him at her threat. "You can't," he pronounced emphatically. "We have an agreement, Caroline. You'll stay until Mrs. Davies is well enough to return. The house party will be arriving soon. You can't neglect your obligation."

"Then I must have your promise," she said, strain stretching her voice thin.

"We'll discuss it in the morning. I can't seem to think straight when I see you as you are." His eyes raked boldly over her body clad only in the thin white gown. Her hair, loose from its confining pins, came well below her shoulders. He did not attempt to hide his desire.

Caroline wrapped her arms around herself, seeking to shield her body from his searching gaze. She was hard put not to cover herself in the first thing that came to hand, but he would not expect an experienced woman to cringe so under his masculine admiration. With a surprising strength of will, she did not flinch beneath his regard.

"Caroline, have mercy on us," he pleaded. "Don't ignore what we both want for convention's sake."

"It's not convention that's stopping me," she replied, unbearable pain shafting through her at their impending estrangement. "It's responsibility that must come first."

Giles had never wanted to possess a woman as fiercely as he did Caroline. The uncontrolled savagery that had emerged in the forest swept over him again. If he once pulled her into his arms, he would not be able to let her go until she was completely his. He reached out, squeezing a handful of her hair in his fist, closing his eyes against a picture of life without her. Finally, he released her and she sank into the chair, knees too weak to hold her upright.

"I think it's best we postpone this talk until we're both dressed and in a more composed frame of mind."

"Yes," she choked out in agreement.

The Aubusson carpet absorbed his footsteps as he left the room, and the door closed noiselessly behind him. Caroline spent the night convincing her mind to ignore the demands of her heart.

A few hours later, Lord Castleton finished a scanty breakfast. The place at his right remained empty.

Jervis hovered over him like a mother hen, offering one dish after another to tempt his appetite.

"Don't fuss so, Jervis. I won't melt away in one morning. The cake last night lessened my usual appetite."

"Very good, my lord," replied Jervis with relief. He had spent weeks watching the earl regain his vitality and did not want him to fall into a decline.

"And please advise Mrs. Crawford that I find no fault with her cooking. I wouldn't like to lose her good will." The earl impatiently tossed his napkin beside his plate and strode quickly out the door.

"Yes, my lord," said Jervis to the empty room.

Lord Castleton settled himself in the library with the morning post, wondering how soon he could request Caroline join him without cause for speculation.

After leaving her, he had paced his room, cursing its loneliness. In his anger, he reconsidered paying a visit to the neighborhood inn, but the earl knew only Caroline could quell the fire that burned in him. His craving for her had built steadily, from that first day when she had lain before him on a bed of moss until last night's confrontation.

Now he must work through this tangle of emotions in which he was ensnared. He readily admitted to a desire more powerful than any he had felt before. That she was the only one who could sate his need left him feeling more susceptible than on the battlefield and angry that she could bring him to this point.

He was puzzled why she fought their need to be together. If she feared notoriety, theirs could be a discreet affair. More baffling, though, was her physical response to him. He was no greenhead and knew she desired him; but she exhibited a tentativeness that surprised him in an experienced woman.

Perhaps her husband had cared more about taking his pleasure than making the act of love enjoyable to his wife. Damn! He wished he could have been the one to initiate Caroline to love's mysteries. If he had, she would not have rejected him last night. Given time, he knew he could change her mind, but her tenure at Castleton was rapidly drawing to a close. He must find a way to either extend her duties or break through her stubbornness.

In the meantime, he would convince her he could keep his desires in check if she continued at Castleton.

The sound of carriage wheels jerked him abruptly out of his brown study and brought him to the window. He was hard put to recognize the pale, haggard man assisted from the black traveling coach as his childhood friend.

The last time he had seen Charles Dalton was in London, where he was recovering from his wound. Giles could not believe the emaciated figure mounting the front steps, supported on each side by a footman, was the same man.

All thoughts of the previous night's disaster fled as he hastened to the front door to greet his guest.

"Charles, my friend, welcome. I was hoping to see you soon." The men lowered Charles into a hall chair and Giles reached down to grasp the painfully thin fingers.

"I'm sure you didn't expect to see me in this condition, though." The frail voice matched Charles's body, and the earl stooped down beside the chair in order to hear him.

"Charles, what has happened to you?" he asked, meeting the feverish blue eyes. Golden hair, which usually captivated every female in sight, hung lank and dull around the pale, thin face of his formerly robust friend. "When I left London, you were assured of a speedy recovery."

"I'm afraid the prognosis was a bit premature." Charles's weak attempt at humor was cut short by a fit of coughing. "This arm wound is a devil to heal. I'm running from the doctor who says if the infection isn't controlled soon, only an amputation will save me."

Giles winced inwardly for his friend. Losing an arm would destroy Charles, as it would himself.

"You were right to come. I'm convinced that being here will put you to rights. If the country air won't do it, then the cuisine will."

"No more broth, Giles. I cannot abide the sight of it. If I'm going to die, I'm determined my last meal will be a good joint of beef."

Giles laughed, encouraged by his show of resistance. "All right, Charles, I'll see to it. Or rather, my housekeeper and cook will. Although I'd be willing to wager even their broth would tempt you. They've brought me back from my slump and you'll be another challenge to them.

"Come. I apologize for keeping you sitting in the hall. Let's get you settled in your room, then we'll talk." The earl rose and found Caroline standing nearby, compassion clearly written on her face at the sight of the ill man.

"Mrs. Alveston, will you make a room ready at once. We have welcome company." He smiled down at Charles.

Caroline moved closer and indicated the footmen should follow her upstairs. "I've kept a room ready, my lord, since you told me there might be an early arrival. I need only to add fresh flowers."

"Please don't add flowers for my benefit, ma'am." The two footmen once again lifted Charles between them. "I'm too near death's door as it is and don't need the cloying scent of blossoms to push me through."

"But you haven't seen Mrs. Alveston's arrangements, Charles. They'll change your mind completely about the feminine predilection for flowers. Before you leave I expect you'll be clipping and arranging them yourself." The earl's nonsense brought a grimace of a smile to his friend's face as he was helped up the stairs.

Lord Castleton repaired again to the library while Charles was being settled in his room. He was deeply concerned for his friend's health, but Caroline's pale face reminded him of their unfinished business from the night before. He knew the longer they avoided the issue the more difficult it would be to face.

"Jervis, please have Mrs. Alveston attend me when it's convenient." He stood staring out the window, mentally composing himself to meet Caroline with some degree of normality.

When Caroline entered a short time later, the earl was still at the window, hands clasped behind him.

121

She studied the stiff set of his broad shoulders and wide-spaced legs, realizing the interview would not be an easy one.

"You asked to see me, my lord," she said, lowering her eyes before the thrust of his dark gaze.

He felt her unease at meeting again after what had transpired between them. "Please be seated, Caroline." He indicated her usual chair by the fireplace.

Making time to gain control of her emotions, Caroline deliberately arranged her skirts around her.

Watcing her graceful movements, the earl recalled their first evening together. The intervening weeks had brought them from total strangers to near lovers. He could not let her go until he fulfilled his aspiration.

Lord Castleton took the companion chair facing her and leaned back against the leather, attempting to appear at ease. "I hope you're not overly upset about last night," he drawled calmly.

Caroline's incredulous gaze lifted to his. "I hardly think 'upset' adequately describes my feelings," she admitted with an honesty that drew a chuckle from the earl.

"Nor mine," he agreed more gently than usual. "Please don't fault me for my plain speaking, but I know I tell you nothing new when I say you're a most desirable woman." Caroline remained silent, hands clasped tightly in her lap. "I'm sure your husband made that clear to you." If anything, she turned paler than before.

Again he was perplexed by her reaction. He could understand a blush, but that she should look so stricken appalled him. Was it possible her husband

122

had gone beyond being inconsiderate and had subjected her to some deviant behavior? His hands clenched in anger at the thought.

He stopped for a moment, straightening his stiff fingers and steepling them beneath his chin before continuing. "We can't erase the happenings of last night, but since it's your wish, we can attempt to control what led to it."

Having observed his tenacity over the past weeks, Caroline was surprised at his easy concession. Concealing the lover who had pleaded so eloquently a few hours earlier, he appeared as an employer valuing her more as a housekeeper than as a potential mistress.

"Somehow I feel you're still determined to leave Castleton . . . and me." He looked inquiringly over his fingers at her.

Caroline flinched from the thought that had kept her awake after he had left. Averting her eyes, she remained silent.

"Please reconsider, Caroline." The earl dropped his hands and leaned forward in earnest supplication. He could not physically hold her, but he must delay her departure for as long as possible, in order to give him an opportunity to change her mind. "I want you to stay. I need you. We all do." The depth of his sincerity surprised them both.

He heaved a sigh and leaned back in his chair, again awaiting her reaction.

"You must realize that our relationship has been most . . ." She spent a few moments searching for an adequate word. Finding none, she finished lamely, ". . . most irregular."

Hearing another chuckle, she looked up to see a smile curving lips that had so recently begged for her favors. "If you mean it's not a pattern card of propriety according to the ton, that's probably the understatement of the Season. However, rest assured my respect for you is undiminished."

Caroline knew society demanded she be disgusted by his behavior the night before, but it was her own blazing response to him that frightened her. "I don't know whether we can regain a working relationship," she answered honestly.

"Nor do I," he replied just as candidly, "but I'd like to try. The morning's light hasn't changed your attractions. But you know you're needed here. I'll further shamelessly play on your sentiments and ask you to think of Charles." The dark eyes became solemnly retrospective again. "I fear for his very life. I've seen too many like him on the Peninsula who never came home. I know you've helped many of the tenants and their children through illnesses. They speak of your special salves and syrups, and they've told me of your healing hands. I ask you to use them on Charles." The plea came straight from his heart to Caroline's.

"I'm not sure whether I can help him, my lord."

"I only ask that you try. I've lost so many friends, Caroline, I don't want to lose another."

He felt more than a little guilt that if she agreed, her altruism would benefit his pursuit of her, but the earl quickly shrugged it aside. He couldn't lose her before consummating their relationship or she would haunt him the rest of his days.

"I'll do what I can," she promised, unable to refuse.

He rose and stood towering over her. "Then come, Mrs. Alveston," he said, taking her hand as she stood. "Let's unite our efforts in saving Charles's life. What do you say, madam?"

"I will agree, sir," replied Caroline, knowing in that instant that she loved this man with all her heart and did not want to leave him yet. Perhaps she could stay long enough to gather memories for the lifetime of loneliness she faced. After him, there could be no other in her heart.

"Thank you, my dear." He lifted her hand to his lips and bestowed a respectful salute.

Eleven

Caroline laid a restraining hand on the earl's arm as he raised it to knock on Charles's door.

"My lord, before we enter, you must realize Mr. Dalton may not be receptive to my methods. Many people call what I do quackery, you know. They have no faith in the old ways of healing."

The warmth of her touch through his coat sleeve caused his pulse to quicken, memories of the night before still fresh in his mind. "Don't worry about Charles. I think he's desperate enough to try anything to save his arm. He's had the best doctors London has to offer and they've failed him. Perhaps good old-fashioned quackery is just what he needs now." He smiled in his familiar way and her heart turned over.

Henderson, Charles's valet, answered the door. Like Denton, he had been with his master during the war and had witnessed the deaths of many men. His anxious face made Caroline even more aware of the graveness of Charles's condition. She wondered whether the small store of knowledge she had would be sufficient to save him.

Caroline began her treatment of Charles with a chamomile tisane. The relaxing herb tea enabled her to inspect his injury with as little discomfort as possible.

The wound, kept tightly wrapped on the instructions of the London physicians, was red and angry-looking. Removing the confining bandages, she cleaned the area thoroughly, then applied comfrey poultices to reduce inflammation and aid in healing.

Charles had been running a fever when he arrived at Castleton, and despite all she could do during the day, it increased. Heat ravaged the sick man's body that night and the next day. She and Henderson attended him constantly, bathing him with cool cloths and forcing live-giving liquids down his throat.

Caroline slipped away only to give necessary instructions to the staff and to reassure Lucy that everything was all right. She had mixed emotions when she found the child full of her adventure with Lord Castleton, who had taken her up with him on Palisades. Madeline and Mrs. Davies both vowed to keep a close eye on Lucy while Caroline continued her vigil.

Finally, in the evening of the second day, the fever broke and Charles lapsed into a deep sleep. Sending the faithful valet to bed, she sat with the sick man, watching his shallow breathing.

It was well past midnight when his eyes opened and focused unsteadily on Caroline. "I never thought I'd be here," he said weakly.

"And why not, Mr. Dalton?" she asked curiously.

"Since you're an angel, I must be in heaven. And believe me, my celestial being, my life hasn't been conducive toward an upward turn."

"There must be something peculiar in this house that makes all men be taken with heavenly things. But as you can see, Mr. Dalton"—she rose and, turning her back to the bed, looked over her shoulder at him—"I have not sprouted wings."

"Yet you've saved my life," he said hoarsely through parched lips.

"There's no need to be quite so dramatic, sir. I merely bathed your brow," she responded lightly.

"I'm sure there was more to it than that, angel," the sick man whispered. "But I'm too weak to argue the point now."

"Then go back to sleep, sir. It will help you recover more quickly." She gave him a cool drink of water, then smoothed the counterpane beneath his restless hands.

"Although I'm weak, the heat in my arm seems to have lessened. I have much to thank you for." His eyes were clouded and his voice still slightly slurred.

"I've contributed little to your present state, Mr. Dalton. It's been your own determination that has carried the day. Now you must rest," she insisted.

"If you'll hold my fevered hand," said Charles, proffering the pale extremity. Caroline smiled in return and took the thin fingers in her own.

"I must remind you, it is no longer feverish, sir." His regular breathing soon told her sleep was upon him. She gently laid his hand on the cover.

"Very touching, ma'am," declared a voice from behind her. "I see you've rescued another poor soul."

TAKE ADVANTAGE OF THIS SPECIAL OFFER, AVAILABLE *ONLY* TO ZEBRA REGENCY ROMANCE READERS.

You are a reader who enjoys the very special kind of love story that can only be found in Zebra Regency Romances. You adore the fashionable English settings, the sparkling wit, the captivating intrigue, and the heart-stirring romance that are the hallmarks of each Zebra Regency Romance novel.

Now, you can have these delightful novels delivered right to your door each month and never have to worry about missing a new book. Zebra has made arrangements through its Home Subscription Service for you to preview the three latest Zebra Regency Romances as soon as they are published.

3 **FREE** REGENCIES TO GET STARTED!

To get your subscription started, we will send your first 3 books ABSOLUTELY FREE, as our introductory gift to you. NO OBLIGATION. We're sure that you will enjoy these books so much that you will want to read more of the very best romantic fiction published today.

SUBSCRIBERS SAVE EACH MONTH

Zebra Regency Home Subscribers will save money each month as they enjoy their latest Regencies. As a subscriber you will receive the 3 newest titles to preview FREE for ten days. Each shipment will be at least a $11.97 value (publisher's price). But home subscribers will be billed only $9.90 for all three books. You'll save over $2.00 each month. Of course, if you're not satisfied with any book, just return it for full credit.

FREE HOME DELIVERY

Zebra Home Subscribers get free home delivery. There are never any postage, shipping or handling charges. No hidden charges. What's more, there is no minimum number to buy and you can cancel your subscription at any time. No obligation and no questions asked.

TO GET YOUR 3 FREE BOOKS
LL OUT AND MAIL THE COUPON BELOW

3 FREE BOOKS

Mail to: Zebra Regency Home Subscription Service
120 Brighton Road
P.O. Box 5214
Clifton, New Jersey 07015-5214

YES! Start my Regency Romance Home Subscription and send me my 3 FREE BOOKS as my introductory gift. Then each month, I'll receive the 3 newest Zebra Regency Romances to preview FREE for ten days. I understand that if I'm not satisfied, I may return them and owe nothing. Otherwise, I'll pay the low members' price of just $9.90 for all 3 books and save over $2.00 off the publisher's price (a $11.97 value). There are no shipping, handling or other hidden charges. I may cancel my subscription at any time and there is no minimum number to buy. In any case, the 3 FREE books are mine to keep regardless of what I decide.

NAME

ADDRESS _____ APT NO.

CITY _____ STATE _____ ZIP

(   )

TELEPHONE

SIGNATURE _____ (if under 18 parent or guardian must sign)   **RG0294**

Terms and prices subject to change. Orders subject to acceptance by Zebra Home Subscription Service, Inc.

GET
3 FREE
REGENCY
ROMANCE
NOVELS—
A $11.97
VALUE!

Not wanting to disturb his friend but anxious to know of his progress, Lord Castleton had silently entered the room while Caroline's attention was held by Charles.

She smiled, choosing to ignore the cutting edge in his tone. "I promised I would do all I could for Mr. Dalton."

The earl was ashamed of the anger he had felt seeing her holding Charles's hand. It made him seem thankless for her endeavors on his friend's behalf.

"I apologize. I didn't mean to imply any criticism. It's been a long vigil and extremely vexing for me, since I've been of no use except to pace."

"I understand you've entertained Lucy, and for that I'm grateful. As for pacing, I'm convinced it's a requisite part of the healing process," she replied, a teasing note entering her voice. "Especially when faced with a crisis. Indeed, if not for your pacing, I daresay Mr. Dalton might not have escaped the grim reaper as quickly as he did."

He would not allow her to diminish her deeds. "Few would have attempted what you have." His voice was warm with admiration. "I'm indeed grateful you've been able to help Charles. I'm sure he'll voice the same when he's able."

"He's already done so," she said, pleased with his compliments. "But I need no thanks. To see him whole again will be enough."

"Then you think he'll recuperate completely, Caroline?" He could not stick to formality with this woman. She could break down the barriers society imposed with one glance from her thickly lashed eyes. It was not lost on him that she no longer objected to his familiarity. He chose to think it indicated the possibility of a more intimate relationship in the future.

"There's a much better chance now the fever's broken. The most crucial step is curing the infection. If we can do that, then with rest and good food, he should recover."

He looked back to the still figure on the bed. "Charles is a friend of long standing, and to lose him here would have been worse than on the battlefield. I admit I wasn't hopeful when he first arrived."

"You were right to feel that way, my lord. A few more days, a week at the most, and he would have been too weak to recover," she admitted. "But I must warn you, his recuperation is still not guaranteed."

"Even so, I thank you for your effort. First for Charles," said Giles, and raised her hand to his lips. The contact revealed their need for one another had not abated in the least. Green eyes met black and their passion flickered into flame. "And then for me," he murmured. Placing her hand on his chest, his good resolve crumbled with her nearness. He bent, capturing her enticing lower lip between his teeth, worrying it gently before covering her lips with his.

Caroline clutched the earl's coat as her knees weakened from his touch. Too tired to resist the hunger burning inside, she gave herself over to his kiss.

Feeling his control slipping at her response, Giles unsteadily put her away from him, noting her bemused expression with a touch of triumph. He would woo this woman until she willingly came to him. "Surely, you won't take me to task for one small kiss,

Caroline, considering the spirit in which it was given?"

Trusting the dimly lit room concealed her disappointment when he let her go, she replied steadily, "No, I accept it as it was offered, as thanks. Now, if you wouldn't mind staying with Mr. Dalton a few minutes, I'll call Henderson to sit the rest of the night."

"Not at all." The earl turned to look down at his friend. "Go along. We'll be fine."

"Good night then, my lord."

"Good night, Caroline. Sleep well," he answered without turning.

After Henderson's arrival, Lord Castleton returned to the library and poured a brandy. Pacing before the fireplace, his blood burned brighter than any drink could fire. Regardless of his promise, he wanted nothing more than to follow Caroline to her room and accept the invitation her eyes could not hide.

Reminding himself that Caroline was not just a bit of muslin, he subdued his urge. The amiability they shared was unique in his experiences with females, and he was bent upon pursuing a long-term relationship. To that end, he was still determined she would come to him on her own, fully cognizant of her decision. He must continue to keep his desire in check until he judged her ready to capitulate to their mutual attraction.

The liquor was running low before he quit the library. Damn! He was going to have to bring the situation to a head soon or restock his cellar on a monthly basis.

* * *

Lord Castleton crossly eyed the lone bottle and glass that Jervis set beside his chair. "Am I to be solitary again this evening, Jervis?"

"It would seem so, my lord. Mrs. Alveson has sent word she's attending Mr. Dalton and will be unable to join you."

"Of course," he muttered. Caroline had proved elusive since their encounter in Charles's room. Giles saw only her skirts disappearing around corners, up stairs, or through doorways. She was very adept at vanishing when she put her mind to it, and he had run out of excuses to see her other than the obvious.

"Do you wish anything else, my lord?"

"No, Jervis." The man bowed and left the room. "Nothing you can help me with," remarked Giles to the closing door.

Caroline filled his thoughts. Awake or asleep, he could see the deep green of her eyes, could feel the silkiness of her hair between his fingers and the warmth of her body against his. Every corner of the house and estate brought an unbidden picture of her to mind. Breakfast was dull, the laughter had gone out of his rides, lunch was too solitary, and he had not heard the pianoforte for many days.

He rejoiced in his friend's improving health but found his declining contentment coincided with Charles's increased demands on Caroline's time.

The earl felt Caroline slipping away from him as the days passed. Even in war, he had not experienced this level of anxiety. Then his feelings had been numb with the excessive brutality surrounding him, and he had performed his duties with emotionless dispatch. Now he felt betrayed by his inability to remain aloof as incessant refrains ran through his mind. *"It must not happen, damn it! I will not allow it to happen!"* There had to be a way to keep her with him. He had nurtured this attraction and would not rest until he possessed her.

Recalling his discussion with Denton on Caroline's first day at Castleton, before his unreasonable obsession had begun, he found the answer. He would offer her the position of housekeeper at his London home until he could convince her to accept his protection in more than name only.

Contact in the smaller townhouse would be greatly increased, and given their physical response to one another, her seduction should be quick work once they were alone. None of his past amours had been able to reject his advances for long, he thought complacently.

Lord Castleton stretched his long legs out before him, considering the shine on his boots while congratulating himself on his excellent strategy. In the meantime, he must act a pattern card of propriety. It was now only left to get through the days and nights of this damnable house party until they could be private again.

Caroline kept herself busy by filling her days concocting healing tisanes and poultices for Charles, and spending evenings with Lucy and Madeline in Mrs. Davies's room. The two older women had become fast friends, sitting together sewing while Madeline kept the injured housekeeper up on happenings.

Caroline was going through considerable anxiety

concerning her uninhibited response to the earl. Her early life had been filled with love. But her father's death, along with the past three year's self-imposed exile, had forced her to keep her emotions in check for safety's sake.

She prided herself on being realistic, admitting her suppressed affection had found an outlet in the Earl of Castleton. From the beginning she had offered little resistance, having responded like the veriest schoolgirl to his advances. She was chagrined to find herself incapable of retaining a cool detachment with her employer. Now they were embroiled in a situation unacceptable to their stations.

Having no recourse but to stay until the end of the house party, Caroline made plans to leave shortly thereafter, even if Mrs. Davies was not completely recovered.

Until then, she must retain her self-respect and control her susceptibility to the earl. She suddenly found herself pleased about the house party, for propriety must be followed with guests in the house. There would be no more after-dinner tête-à-têtes nor rides on the estate.

In addition to tending her patient and spending time with Lucy, she would be supervising the house for the comfort of the guests. The earl's attention would also be directed to entertaining and he would certainly not expect to see her as often.

Comforted by her thoughts, Caroline breathed a sigh of relief. The solution to her problem could at least be put off for another fortnight. Until then she would remain in the background, as befitted the position of housekeeper, making it obvious by her appearance and demeanor that she aspired to no other.

Entering the library several days later, Lord Castleton came to an abrupt halt at the sight of Caroline instructing a new housemaid on the proper way to clean the bookshelves. Caroline looked up, meeting his furious expression.

"Dismiss the maid, Mrs. Alveston. I wish to speak to you in private," he ordered sharply.

"Of course, my lord. You may attend to the music room now, Sally."

They waited in thunderous silence while the girl left the room—Caroline with apprehension, for she had not missed the light of battle in his eye, he with barely concealed impatience. As soon as the door closed, he strode angrily toward her.

"And just what do you call that?" he demanded, pausing in front of her, feet widespread and hands on hips.

"What do you mean, my lord?" she asked, avoiding his gaze.

"Don't act the innocent with me, madam. It won't wash. Although our acquaintance is not long-standing, I know you're not addlepated. Now, once more," he growled, spacing his words distinctly, "what is that thing on your head?"

Twin spots of color rose on Caroline's cheeks. "It is commonly called a cap, my lord. Sometimes a widow's cap," she explained, the flush of anger spreading.

"And why are you wearing it?" he demanded.

"Because I am a widow and a housekeeper. I've told you before, I must keep the respect of your staff," she retorted, indignation ringing in her voice.

"And you think that thing will bring you respect? I don't know what possesses you, Caroline, to take pains in making yourself as dowdy as possible," he accused disgustedly, "but this is more than enough. I will tolerate it no longer." He reached forward and jerked the cap from her hair, scattering pins and loosening the tightly coiled knot.

"Lord Castleton, you need not remove my hair along with the cap," she protested, wincing as the stubborn pin finally gave way. In truth, you need not remove either. I cannot see what interest you have in my chosen mode of dress." She reached up to smooth the liberated strands.

"You're in my employ, and I'll have my staff properly dressed. If you must have a uniform, I'll furnish one, but I tell you now, it will not include a cap," he exploded, crushing the offending article in his fist before flinging it into the farthest corner.

Anger showed vividly in the slash of dark brows above stormy black eyes, and a flush rode high on his cheekbones. Pushing her arms to her sides, he attended to the wayward curls with his own hands.

"I fear you must begin again," he said, his anger dissipating as he caressingly removed the remainder of the pins from her hair one by one.

She stood silently while pins fell to the floor around them. His face registered triumph when her hair hung loose around her shoulders in a mass of tangled waves. His fingers, a warm living comb, gently sifted through it, then tightened, masterfully cupping the back of her head, before slipping to the nape of her neck and releasing her.

Her body, no longer her own, resented her stern stricture to ignore the earl's appeal. Beyond his physical attractiveness, she missed the sharing of minor incidents that would never change the history of the world but were important to their own small realm. Caroline wished with all her heart to reach out to him, but she would not give in to her desire. Denying the demands of her body and mind, she said quietly, "This will not do, my lord."

Twelve

Lord Castelton was unaccountably disturbed by the tears welling in her large green eyes. Reminding himself that she was under his protection, the honor of generations before won the battle of wills. Albeit, he was ready to acknowledge a gentleman's honor could be a tiresome thing indeed.

"You're right," he conceded, stepping away from her and making his way blindly to the brandy bottle.

Behind him, she drew a ragged breath that he could hear across the width of the room. "My lord, I think you'll agree it would be best for me to leave Castleton," she said, her voice trembling.

"I don't want you to go, Caroline." His words conveyed an acknowledgment of defeat. "Don't worry, I won't force my attentions on you again," he promised, setting the bottle down without pouring.

He turned to the slight figure standing forlornly against the bookshelves. "I can only plead that the years in service have blunted my sensibilities where gently reared ladies are concerned, and I offer my

138

apologies. But I will not allow that to drive you from here," he stated firmly.

"It seems there are a great many things you will not allow," answered Caroline with a watery quaver.

"I do have the habit of ordering people's lives, but with good intent, I assure you." A contrite smile twisted his lips as he considered his intentions regarding Caroline. "If you'll remember our bargain, you agreed to stay until after the house party is over or Mrs. Davies is ready to return to her post. Neither has happened yet. So as a gentleman of honor, I'll refrain from any further advances, and as a woman of honor, you'll then be able to complete our contract."

"I cannot agree," she argued. "It would be foolish to ignore what has passed between us. I'll leave Castleton before the house party arrives and no explanations need be given. Between Madeline and Mrs. Davies, you'll be fine."

Fury burst into an inferno as her words streaked through him, abrading nerves already rubbed raw from too many sleepless nights. So she thought to leave him, did she? Well, she could think again! He would never allow it.

"No, madam, I will not be fine, as you so graciously put it. You will keep to the letter of our terms," he demanded, his defeat turning into anger, as he advanced upon her. "If you do not, if you leave this house without my permission, I'll see you never work again." Speaking through clenched teeth, he took her upper arms in a punishing grasp. "Don't doubt I can do it. All it needs is a word from me and no one will hire you. Only the lowliest jobs will be available and you'll not tolerate those, particularly with a child to care for. No, I think you'll remain exactly where you are until our contract is fulfilled."

He released her swiftly and stomped from the room, throwing the door back against the paneling. Caroline stood motionless until the slam of the outer door echoed down the hall.

The next morning, Caroline discovered that Lord Castleton had gone to London on business for a few days. She could only be glad for time to compose herself to face him on his return.

Considering her options during the long night just past, she knew she had few choices. She felt morally bound to fulfill the terms of her agreement with the earl. Even if she had the nerve to fly in the face of his threats, she and Lucy could end up destitute. Without his reference, she would either be forced into taking a menial position or returning to Castleton.

Confident the earl would honor his word, Caroline acknowledged she needn't be concerned about his unsolicited overtures. However, it was herself she worried about. The longer she was around him the stronger her feelings grew, weakening her resolve to keep her distance. She did not want to consider the results of several more weeks in his company.

Three days later Caroline heard the bustle of Lord Castleton's return from London but did not go out of her way to greet him, certain they would meet all too soon.

After lunch, Jervis brought a message that the earl required her presence in the library. Cautiously approaching the paneled door, she tapped lightly and entered at his command. Giles sat comfortably in his leather chair, head resting against the back, observing her from beneath lowered lids.

She appeared more vulnerable today, wearing a tatted lace fichu over her long-sleeved black dress. And while her hair was drawn back tautly, stretching porcelain skin over her cheekbones, no cap hid it. Giles wisely concealed the pleasure he took in this slight victory.

"Mrs. Alveston," he intoned, surprised he could utter her name so evenly when her presence brought chaos to every fiber of his being. He indicated with a wave of his hand that she should be seated.

Ignoring his direction, Caroline stood rigidly before the desk, hands clasped at waist level. "Lord Castleton," she responded in kind, then waited for him to continue.

"Have you nothing more to say to me, ma'am?" he asked suddenly, straightening in the chair, irritated at her composure.

"We're glad to have you back, my lord. The hangings for the rose suite arrived and have improved the room immensely. I hope you'll find time to give me your opinion as to whether they're agreeable to you. Other than that, I have nothing remarkable to report," she recited mechanically, her eyes focused somewhere over his left shoulder.

"You take me back to my soldiering campaign, Mrs. Alveston. I've received many such reports from my men, but perhaps with a bit more passion." He pulled himself to his feet and paced around the desk, unsettled by her vacuous countenance. "I trust by your response you've forgotten that nonsense about leaving my employ." He paused in mid-stride, brows raised in inquiry, waiting for her answer.

"It seems I have no choice, my lord. If I were not bound by my word, then I would be by your threats," she replied bitterly, still not meeting his eyes.

"Caroline," he breathed in a soft, exasperated voice, wondering if they would ever meet on equal footing. "I wasn't threatening your well-being, only attempting to protect you."

"Then heaven help me if you ever desire to hurt me," Caroline muttered, immediately wishing she had kept her tongue between her teeth.

Why should he expect her to understand his motives, when he often couldn't fathom them himself? "Let us cry peace until after the house party, then we shall settle our differences," he suggested, thinking of his plans for her. "Perhaps by then they will no longer be important."

"Whatever pleases you, my lord." Suppressing the humiliation that threatened to engulf her, Caroline curtsied and left the room under his forbidding frown.

The household now ran smoothly with a minimum of direction, and with the exception of time spent with Lucy, Caroline was able to allot much of her day to Charles. Part of the day the wound was left unbandaged, allowing air to circulate freely. The laudanum he had been taking depressed his appetite as well as his spirits, and she gradually replaced it with the chamomile tisane. She conferred with Madeline on light dishes that wouldn't tax his weakened system yet would give him the nourishment needed to regain his strength.

The London doctors had prescribed a darkened, closed room for complete rest. Caroline pulled the curtains wide and opened the windows during the day when the weather permitted, shutting out only the damp night air.

Ignoring Charles's comment about no flowers, Caroline concentrated on wild blooms and field flowers, such as daisies, and summer phlox that he might have noticed on his rides. She hoped they would bring back pleasant memories and encourage him to strive for a healthy constitution again. Finding him asleep one afternoon with a black-eyed Susan clutched in his hand convinced her she had won him over.

Caroline's time with the earl continued to be limited. Breakfast and morning rides had ceased altogether, and their evening meetings were sporadic and brief, consisting only of the necessary exchanges of information. She and Lucy still visited the garden, but Caroline attempted to make sure their outings occurred when the earl was otherwise engaged.

Meanwhile, Charles's wound showed improvement under her nursing, and hope glimmered in his eyes. As he gained strength, Caroline arranged a retreat on the terrace, where he could relax on a comfortable chaise longue, and reap the benefit of the summer sun. Believing the mind played a significant role in bodily healing, she devoted her energy toward guiding him to a positive viewpoint.

As soon as the infection was conquered, Charles's condition improved daily. Color returned to his face, and although still weak, Caroline could see the man he had once been. It would be only a matter of time before he was at his full strength once more.

"I must commend you again, Mrs. Alveston," said Charles as they sat on the terrace late one morning.

"And what is the subject this time?" she inquired, closing the book she had been reading aloud.

An easy camaraderie had developed between them during his convalescence, and Caroline enjoyed the give-and-take of their relationship. Some might think them too familiar, but she could not be stiff with the wounded man. It seemed habitual for her to lose all sense of propriety with the men in this house.

"Why, my prodigious recovery," he quipped lightly, turning his head to smile at her. "Surely you've not so quickly forgotten the part you played?"

"How could I, when you so generously—and incessantly—remind me. Indeed, sir, I soon fear your vocabulary will shrink to two words. And how will you get on in the world saying only 'Thank you'?" she inquired innocently.

Charles gave a shout of laughter. "I will contrive, ma'am, if only to affirm it at our every meeting."

"You've already thanked me enough to last a lifetime, Mr. Dalton," she admonished good-naturedly.

A shadow darkened his blue eyes. "That's because I wouldn't have a lifetime without you."

"Nonsense, sir. I just helped speed nature's healing a bit."

"No, you saved my life and I'll not be talked out of believing it. I don't know what drove me to come to Castleton, but that I didn't want to die alone," he admitted thoughtfully.

"And you have not, sir. I trust when your time does come, you'll be surrounded by a loving family. But that will be a long time yet, unless your good health leads you into some foolishness." Caroline again opened her book, prepared to begin reading.

"I assure you this is as close to death as I want to come. I intend to stay well away from bullets from now on. I suppose by now Giles has told you who I am," he said, changing the subject.

"Yes. We spoke of you on the day he hired me. He said you are the viscountess's grandson. I'm sorry you were unable to see the viscountess before her death," she offered sympathetically. "She was extremely fond of you."

"Yes, we were very close. She raised me after my mother died. I assume you also know that Cresthill was unentailed and will come to me."

"So I understand. It's a grand old house," she said, a fond smile curving her lips, "and has been well taken care of. You need only to increase the staff when you're ready to take up residence there."

"But you've stolen my cook," he complained with mock severity.

"I do plead guilty to that," Caroline conceded. "But there are many good cooks in England."

"I hope that's true. And since it's you I have to thank for keeping Cresthill in its pristine condition for the past few years, I'll forgive you," he said, smiling.

"I'm sure most of the staff would return, Mr. Dalton. They were very fond of Cresthill and many have not yet found another place."

"And could I get you to come back to oversee them, Mrs. Alveston?" Caroline met his eyes, seeing the sincerity there. "Giles told me about Mrs. Davies. She'll be ready to come back someday soon," he added.

Caroline recoiled from the thought she kept pushing to the back of her mind.

"It would be ideal if you'd return to Cresthill," Charles continued. "You know the house and staff, and I'm assured you do an excellent job, for my grandmother was a real stickler." He grinned at the memory his words renewed.

"I have no references other than the viscountess and Lord Castleton," interjected Caroline.

"Being here at Castleton is all the proof I need as to your ability. It's as smooth running a household as I've seen, and everyone sings your praises. Even Henderson, who is a difficult man to move to compliments."

Caroline smiled fondly. "You've no need to offer me such Spanish coin, sir. I fear the staff refines too much," she objected. "I wouldn't want you to think I'm perfect."

"Enough so for me, ma'am. I ask you because I think we could deal well together, and that's important on a country estate. Needless to say, your child would be welcome."

"I don't know whether I'll stay in the neighborhood, Mr. Dalton, but I promise I'll consider your proposal."

"Thank you, Mrs. Alveston. That's all I ask."

Charles impulsively lifted her hand to his lips. "I would be proud to have you in my home again."

"I can see you're progressing rapidly, Charles."

Caroline snatched her hand away at the earl's voice, turning to see his broad shoulders filling the doorway.

Charles laughed as Giles strolled lazily onto the terrace and dropped into a chair. "Caught in the act, my friend. I was just trying to steal Mrs. Alveston away from you. After Mrs. Davies returns, of course."

"Of course," mocked the earl dryly. "And did you accept, ma'am?" he asked, dark eyes studying her intently.

"Not yet, my lord," she stated firmly, attempting to ignore his powerful presence. "I will stay until you no longer need me, as we agreed," she stressed pointedly, "then I shall make a decision."

"You might have been a bit hasty, Charles," he commented, rising from his chair. "For I also have an offer for my most creditable housekeeper."

Caroline stared apprehensively at the man towering over her, wondering just how honorable his offer would be considering the state of their relationship.

"Don't look so surprised, Mrs. Alveston. We'll discuss this later in private." He flicked an arrogant look her way. "Now, please excuse me. Denton awaits. I must wash away my dust before luncheon." Sketching a bow, he sauntered through the French doors.

Charles waited until the earl disappeared into the house before turning to Caroline. "I don't want to cross Giles since we've been friends for so long, but

147

if his proposition is not to your liking, remember there's always a place for you at Cresthill."

"Thank you, Mr. Dalton. I'll keep your offer in mind."

Caroline was truly grateful for Charles's suggestion that she return to Cresthill. When the time came, it could solve many problems. She would not have to search for a position nor uproot Lucy again, and the staff would be known to her. But mainly it would give her a quick escape from the earl. The more she thought on returning to Cresthill, the more attractive the idea became.

Unfortunately, Lord Castleton's thoughts were not taking such a pleasant course. His serene front was a far cry from the turbulence that raged within him. The little he had seen of Caroline since their confrontation in the library was totally unacceptable to the impatient earl. She was always hurrying in and out of Charles's room or snatching a few hours rest between her myriad duties. He did not have the heart to interrupt her precious time with Lucy in order to see if her anger had abated. Instead, he had focused his thoughts on the future, gritting his teeth and accepting the circumstances with his best manly fortitude. But to discover Caroline and Charles in such an intimate moment, when he desired her company, sorely tested him.

As soon as he was out of sight of the terrace, his stride lengthened and he slapped his riding crop angrily in his hand. Taking the stairs two at a time, he slammed into his room, causing Denton to start, eyes widening at the earl's unusual display of temper.

"I take it the morning did not go well, my lord?" the unflappable valet asked.

"Damnation, Denton! What is wrong with mankind, I ask you, when a person takes someone in, saves his life, and then finds he's nurtured a viper?" The earl hurled his crop across the room, exposing the valet to more unrestrained anger than he had seen in his service. Denton wisely kept quiet as the earl continued pacing the room.

"Trying to steal Caroline from under my very nose. I ask you, Denton, is that something an honorable man would do?"

Again, the valet offered no comment, knowing an answer was not required.

"Well, I'll not stand for it," raged the earl. "Even though we've been friends since our youth, it does not follow I must accept such treachery. I'll beat him at his own game, that's what I'll do." He stopped pacing and stood silently meditating. Denton breathed lightly to avoid notice.

"Yes, I will advance my time schedule. Thank you, Denton, for your usual good advice. Now I must change for luncheon."

The valet drew a relieved breath and helped Lord Castleton remove his coat.

Although personal contact had become virtually nonexistent between Caroline and the earl, even their infrequent encounters would come to an end with the house party's arrival. Their relationship would not be acceptable to his guests except when matters of necessity dictated. Now, with the additional existence of their honorable agreement between them, the gulf was becoming wider.

Lord Castleton's irritation at Charles's offer, along with Mrs. Davies's quickly approaching return to her duties, only served to exacerbate his idea that everything was conspiring to separate him from Caroline.

Giles freely admitted she was more than a housekeeper whose presence insured his physical comfort, and more than a woman who ignited his desire. He enjoyed her company and was aware that her involvement at Castleton transcended the boundaries of an ordinary housekeeper. Despite all this, he had not considered her future role in his life beyond the obvious, and he continued with his initial plan, blithely unaware of its obsolescence.

That evening after an excellent dinner not fully appreciated by the earl, he returned to the library for his usual brandy. Charles was still not up to dressing for dinner, and tonight Giles was thankful for his solitude since he had specifically requested Caroline join him.

Arriving a little late and more flushed than usual, Caroline was determined to carry off their meeting with aplomb. She would not allow him to goad her into tears or anger again.

"You seem somewhat discomposed," Lord Castleton remarked as she entered the room, his eyes eagerly consuming her.

"Just a minor crisis in the kitchen, my lord. Nothing to worry about," she replied calmly, seating herself.

"I'm sure you handled it efficiently," he agreed,

looking at her curiously. "Have you put aside your black completely?" he asked, observing that her lavender dress heightened the fairness of her skin.

"For the most part. Between attending Mr. Dalton and running the household, I have no time to change back and forth. As you pointed out, we are in the country where people are less censorious, and I believe the staff know me well enough by now not to take offense. Besides," she hesitated, pink staining her cheeks, "Mr. Dalton said black reminded him of death and asked to see me in another color for the hasty restoration of his health."

"And you were taken in by that?" he questioned skeptically.

"Of course not," she admitted with a twinkle in her eye. "But he asked so winningly, I couldn't say no. He's been so undemanding in his illness."

"I haven't noticed," grumbled the earl, thinking of the time he now rode the estate alone.

"I'm sorry if you're displeased, my lord. But you did especially ask that I humor his requests, didn't you?"

"Yes," he grudgingly agreed. Along with discarding her black, she had softened her hairstyle and was even more desirable than before. "I find no fault with your actions. I fear I, too, have been spoiled by your attentions. Maybe I'm sorry I didn't suggest the change myself and wonder if you would be as eager to accommodate me." His black eyes impaled her, asking questions she chose to ignore.

"Didn't I accept your suggestion that I not wear a widow's cap, my lord?" she purred with utter sweetness.

He looked at her suspiciously, finally deciding to ignore the comment. "Since we are talking on a personal level, I have another proposal, which I hope you will find more appealing and graciously given than my last." He sat staring at her composed face, studying the long, dark lashes fanning her cheek, the lips that now looked firm but would melt in a moment under his.

Caroline uneasily withstood his silent perusal for several minutes before venturing hesitantly, "My lord?" Her soft voice recalled him to the present.

Embarrassed by his distraction, Giles directed his attention away from her obvious charms. He was invariably caught staring like a schoolboy when she was around, dreaming of what could be. "I wanted to talk with you about your future," he declared, more abruptly than he intended.

Caroline's startled eyes met his. "I didn't know my future was your concern," she replied rigidly, indignant that he still thought to order her life so casually. "When Mrs. Davies is ready, I shall be on my way as we agreed. There's no need for you to consider my future."

Good God! He had barely said three words and already she had her back up. Surely it couldn't be entirely his fault. "I only wish to make you an offer, madam. After Mrs. Davies returns to duty, I would like you to come to London with me."

Thirteen

Caroline jumped from the chair, eyes blazing. "If you think, my lord, I will accept carte blanche from you, you've let a kiss or two lead you to entirely the wrong conclusion."

He reeled before her anger, wondering if she could read his mind. Guilt at his plans of seduction made him overreact. "Carte blanche! What the devil do you mean, Caroline? I offer nothing but a housekeeper's job in my London home."

"Housekeeper?" came the feeble reply.

"Yes, madam. Although at the moment I feel like nothing more than retracting my offer." Lord Castleton had risen in reaction to Caroline's impassioned response. He made an angry circuit of the desk before coming to rest in front of her. Her bewilderment increased the guilt that battered his conscience, but he would not back down now. Too much rode on his ability to carry off this interview successfully.

"My townhouse has also been closed while I was away," he said, speaking in a tightly controlled voice.

"I need someone to run it, as you're doing here at Castleton. The scale, while smaller, is more formal. You would need to begin from scratch, hire a complete staff, refurbish where necessary."

Caroline did not know whether to be insulted or relieved by being asked to be his housekeeper instead of paramour. "I don't think that would be wise, my lord. Our relationship is no longer a comfortable one."

He clenched his jaw, restraining himself from pulling her into his arms, defying everyone and everything that conspired to keep them apart.

"We've both been overtaxed lately with Charles's illness and then this damnable house party. As soon as it's behind us, we'll deal very well together. I don't want to lose you. As a housekeeper, of course."

"Of course," she replied, a stunned look still filling her eyes.

"Well, what do you say? Will you come to London with me?" He would not withdraw his offer, he thought with stubborn determination, even though he had been forced to disavow the very circumstances he sought. Sure she would forgive his deceit once they explored their passion together, he pushed his highly touted honor to the back of his mind.

Sensing her hesitation, he reminded her of the most important aspect of the job. "You will be able to have Lucy with you, as you do here," he said, and immediately felt guilty playing on her love for the child.

"I'll think on it, my lord," replied Caroline, remembering her pledge to retain her dignity. "You know I must give equal consideration to Mr. Dalton's offer of my old position at Cresthill. He has also welcomed Lucy, and I do prefer the country."

"Damn Charles, anyway!" exclaimed Giles, throwing himself back into his chair.

"My lord, you do not mean that!"

"Of course, I don't. But I do wish he would stop trying to lure you away. After all, he was snatched from the jaws of death by coming here. He could at least find his own housekeeper and stop trying to steal mine," he grumbled discontentedly.

"Aren't you getting a bit overly dramatic?" suggested Caroline with mild amusement. "And by the by, I was Cresthill's housekeeper long before I came to Castleton."

"So, you're saying you're accepting his offer and returning to Cresthill?" he challenged angrily, seeing his well-laid plans going awry.

"I am saying nothing," she replied with a calmness that made him want to gnash his teeth. "Only that I have promised to take into account his offer. I would not do myself justice otherwise."

"Remuneration is no object, Caroline. Whatever Charles offers you, I will double," he said, forgetting his good intentions and slamming his fist down on the arm of the chair.

"Remuneration is no object to me either, my lord. I cannot be bought no matter what you care to think," she responded cuttingly.

"I did not mean to imply anything," he protested, rubbing his reddened hand and wondering whether he had completely lost his wits over a few French sauces. "I need you. My life changed after you came here, and I cannot think of it otherwise."

155

"You mean your comfort is important to you. I'm sure Mrs. Davies will be able to step back into her place without your being aware of any difference," she said, attempting to soothe him. "And London offers many housekeepers far more experienced with the ton than I."

"Don't tell me what I mean, and I don't give a hang for the ton, as you well know," he complained. "I didn't spend my hours on the battlefield dreaming of the beau monde, but of the comfort and peace of my home. I had little of either until you brought it," he admitted with unaccustomed humbleness.

Caroline softened at his observation. Refusing his offer would be the most difficult moment in her life. "I'm truly grateful for your compliment, but any competent person can see to your needs. There are many women able to handle the job as well as I have," she reasoned.

But not with your mind and beauty, he thought silently. "We are not rushed. Take some time to reflect before you answer, Caroline."

"I will seriously consider what we've discussed this evening," she promised. "I feel Mrs. Davies will be ready to begin helping out soon, and then it will be but a short time until she's fully able to return. I'll be superfluous at that point and will make my decision," she explained with a composure that caused him to question his memory of their time together. Surely if they had been as attuned as he thought, she could not speak of leaving so casually.

Controlling the urge to take her in his arms and beg her to stay, he spoke calmly. "If you have any doubts and plan on accepting Charles, I hope you'll come to me first."

"I will, my lord. Now, if you will excuse me, Charles asked that I read to him this evening. If you don't mind?" she inquired politely.

"Of course not, Mrs. Alveston," he replied, hiding his frustration behind a congenial facade. "After all, I did ask you to look after Mr. Dalton, didn't I. Pray, hurry off before he becomes agitated."

He felt the emptiness as soon as Caroline closed the door and knew it would multiply a thousand times over if she were to leave altogether. To have her as close as Cresthill would also be torture. He cursed softly and poured more brandy, looking forward to the arrival of the house party not one whit.

Caroline hurried into the entrance hall as the rattle of carriage wheels on gravel announced the arrival of the guests.

Lord Castleton was already on the steps of the manor house, double doors standing open in welcome.

Three traveling carriages wheeled up the drive with a mounted gentleman accompanying them. Two carriages conveying servants and baggage turned to the rear of the house, while the other stopped before the marble steps leading to the entrance.

She could hear the earl welcoming the party to Castleton as he escorted them up the steps.

"I'll have my housekeeper show you to your rooms and you can refresh yourselves before tea."

As soon as he had completed his greeting, she

moved forward in answer to his unspoken command
. . . and stared directly into the malevolent eyes of her
stepmother. Hearing a gasp, she stood frozen as her
stepsister crumpled to the floor in a faint.

The earl was the first to act, scooping up the young
woman in his arms and starting toward the stairs.

Caroline jerked herself into action and accompanied him. "I've made the rose suite ready, my lord,"
she said in a shaky voice, uneasily aware her stepmother trailed closely behind.

He laid the woman on the bed and stepped back,
allowing Caroline room to untie the pink ribbons of
the gypsy bonnet.

"You may leave her to me now, my lord," said the
older woman, elbowing Caroline aside.

"Of course. Shall I send a maid to help you, Mrs.
Langdon?" Lord Castleton asked, not knowing he
had uttered Caroline's real name for the first time.

"No, that won't be necessary. Your housekeeper
will suffice. I'm sure it's just the result of a late night
and the long journey. The dust of the road was dreadful in the coach," she replied in honeyed tones.

"Then I'll leave you. If you need anything, let
Mrs. Alveston know. I've found her to be more than
adequate in stressful situations," he offered before
leaving the room.

As soon as the door closed behind him, Caroline's
stepmother viciously turned on her. "Mrs. Alveston,
is it? So you took that man's name. And just how did
you manage to worm your way into the earl's household? Are you keeping his bed warm, too? More than
adequate, I'm sure!"

Mrs. Langdon was little changed, except to have

grown a bit stouter, but then she had always enjoyed her food and wine, and scorned even the gentlest exercise. Her light hair was covered by a straw bonnet trimmed with brown silk ribbons to match her traveling dress. As usual, she was complete to a shade in a high-necked brown and cream dress with long sleeves surmounted by small puffed sleeves at the top. Caroline wondered how she managed to dress so well when she continuously bemoaned how hard pressed she was.

"You have taken no interest in me the last three years," said Caroline, staring into the small rodentlike eyes of her stepmother. "You have no business questioning my actions now."

"Don't get uppity with me. I could ruin you in an instant with the earl," she threatened, snapping her fingers in front of Caroline's pale face.

"And I you," replied the young woman with a deceptively calm front. "Don't forget the circumstances under which I was forced to leave my home, madam."

"How dare you threaten me. You were not forced to leave Birchwood. You chose to do so," Mrs. Langdon accused in righteous indignation.

Caroline squared her shoulders, resolved to stand firm in the face of such intense animosity. "You left no choice for a decent person. My conscience would have persecuted me if I had accepted your decision."

Mrs. Langdon examined her stepdaughter, noting her simple dress and hairstyle. Under different circumstances, she would have relished Caroline's altered position.

"And you think yourself a decent person now? A

single woman living with the earl at his country home," sneered the older woman, attempting to humiliate her even further.

Caroline looked with disgust at her stepmother. "The earl knows me as a widow with a small child to care for. My reputation and references were—and still are—impeccable."

"How long will they remain so once the truth gets out?" Mrs. Langdon asked scornfully, lines of discontent deepening on her face.

Caroline remained stoic under the older woman's glare. "You and Mary are the only ones who can reveal it. As long as you say nothing, my secret will be safe."

"Why should I worry about keeping your secret when you've done nothing but rebel against my decisions?" she asked resentfully.

"Your decisions were repugnant to me. I could not live with them or you any longer. I made my own choice, and it wasn't the same as yours. You won't suffer from it as long as you remain silent," warned Caroline.

"You've grown hard since I last saw you," concluded Mrs. Langdon. "Doubtless the result of your loose living," she judged, pulling off her bonnet and tossing it angrily on the dressing table. "Where's the devoted sister now?" she asked contemptuously. "Do you think so little of Mary that you'll jeopardize her chance for a comfortable life?"

Caroline drew a deep breath, willing herself to remain calm. "I have only grown up since we last met, but if you mean I'll not bend to your will, then you're right. As to Mary, of course I still care for her.

She can't be held responsible for the decision you pushed on her when she was ill. I don't know what you mean by jeopardizing her chances, but I wouldn't knowingly hurt her."

"Don't play the innocent with me. You can't believe that we were invited here just to take the country air," she jeered. "Lord Castleton has marriage in mind, and if he gets wind of your relationship with Mary, she'll lose the best chance of her life to be settled properly."

Caroline silently digested the news her stepmother had just imparted. Her heart plummeted with the thought that the earl was contemplating marriage when the closeness they shared was still fresh in her memory. Even though she was responsible for keeping them apart, knowing that soon someone else would be in his arms nearly shattered her outward calm. Her stepmother's revelation reinforced the decision to let her air-dreams die without ever seeing the light of day.

Caroline was a housekeeper to the earl and nothing more. His impending marriage to Mary was proof he harbored no serious thoughts for her. Perhaps his offer of a position in London was just that and nothing more, except in her fertile imagination. His previous attentions most probably stemmed from their isolation on the estate. Even Madeline had warned her the earl was a man in his prime. She should have adhered to propriety and never allowed their relationship to develop beyond their agreement.

Caroline once again met her stepmother's narrowed gaze. "As I said, I don't want to harm Mary and will do nothing to interfere. I'm only here until the regular housekeeper recovers from an injury. As long as you and Mary don't say anything, the secret of my background, and yours, will be safe. However, you must be strict with Mary. If she hasn't changed, she's transparent when it comes to deceiving anyone."

The older woman waved her hand dismissively. "Don't worry about Mary. She's not as you remember her. She's so docile she has all but ruined her chances of a good marriage. That's why this visit means so much. Oh, she's still lovely on the outside, but shows no interest in anything or anyone beyond the merest courtesy."

"And who's to blame for that, madam?" Caroline's eyes flashed with anger, remembering her stepmother's actions. "I would think it apparent the fault is none but yours," she accused. "If you had allowed her to follow her heart instead of putting your pride and greed first, none of us would be in this predicament. And perhaps we would at least be tolerably happy." He words were icy with contempt for the ill-advised decisions that had ruined their lives.

"Happy! A woman cannot expect happiness in this life," Mrs. Langdon replied in a sibilant hiss. Her face turned a mottled red as she paced the room, twisting her hands. "She must think of survival and getting ahead."

"But getting ahead does not insure happiness, and that I must have," Caroline replied acidly, surprised her resentment ran so deep. "I tend to think happiness is more important to Mary also, but you didn't let her make that choice, did you? And now you must again force your will on her."

"I'm through arguing," her stepmother said, waving her hands in front of her. "I warn you, Mary's mental health is precarious. It took me months to get her to go about in society again. She has finally put the past behind her, but any mention of the child could throw her into a decline from which she might never recover. If you care the least bit about Mary, you must keep away from her."

Lucy's face was clear in Caroline's mind, and she wondered how any woman could turn her back on such a child. But Mary had been crushed by the news of John's death and under tremendous pressure from her mother. It was no wonder she did not want to be reminded of that period of her life. "I will take care of what I say to her," said Caroline.

"That is not good enough!" Mrs. Langdon shrilled in a piercing voice. "Promise you will not speak to her unless absolutely necessary, and under no circumstances must she see the child."

Caroline was taken aback at her intensity. "The child isn't here," she said with a credibility that would put aside even the strongest doubt. "So there will be no chance Mary will see her, but won't she wonder why I'm ignoring her?"

"I'll take care of Mary. I assure you, neither of us will acknowledge we knew you before we came to Castleton, and I'll expect the same from you. Of course, you must leave as soon as possible, but I do realize you can't desert the earl with a house party in residence."

"So good of you, madam," Caroline replied from between clenched teeth.

"I have no need of your sarcasm, Caroline. I suggest we agree on not publically disagreeing while we're both under the same roof."

"Certainly. I'll give Lord Castleton your regrets that you cannot join him for tea," she said, turning to leave.

"Yes, but tell him I'm sure Mary will be recovered by dinner and we will see him then," she replied smugly.

Caroline closed the door behind her, sagging against the cool wood. The shock of seeing her stepmother and Mary struck her anew as she took the back stairs from the house, seeking her favorite bench in the garden.

The anguish of three years earlier was as fresh as the day it occurred, and she sat on the flower-encircled seat, her mind drifting back.

Caroline was the only daughter of the Honorable James Jared Langdon, younger son of the Earl of Rutherford, and Lady Olivia Fitzhugh, who had died when Caroline was only sixteen.

The Langdons' period of mourning had just ended when Caroline's father accompanied her to a local assembly, where they met Sarah Hudson and her daughter Mary, who were visiting relatives in the neighborhood. The widow Hudson attached herself to James Langdon with a tenacity he could not long resist. Convincing him Caroline would soon be gone and he would be left alone, Mrs. Hudson swept him into a marriage he quickly regretted.

While the gulf between the second Mrs. Langdon and her new family widened, Caroline and her father came to love Mary as their own, protecting her as best they could from the virulent tongue of her mother.

Caroline was nineteen and Mary three years younger when Mr. Langdon died suddenly. Certain that the shrewish actions of his second wife had hastened his death, Caroline marshaled her forces to ride out the storm until she would be free of the overbearing woman and could order her own life.

Even though their mourning forced them to lead a quiet life, both Caroline and Mary had been popular with the young men in the vicinity. Mary's petite blond-haired, blue-eyed beauty caught the attention of John Alveston, a young lieutenant who was visiting the local squire's son.

John's regiment was suddenly called up and the couple pleaded for permission to marry before his departure. But Mrs. Langdon had other plans for Mary, and they did not include marriage to an untitled, modestly endowed lieutenant in the army. Convinced the young couple's attachment was real, Caroline attempted to intercede for them. Unrelenting, Mrs. Langdon was not swayed, and John left without obtaining Mary's hand in marriage.

Mary remained pale and quiet after his departure, while her mother rejoiced at their separation. The air rang for days afterward with Mrs. Langdon's shrill imprecations for Mary's ridiculous fantasies and Caroline's interference.

A few months later, Mary took Caroline into her confidence and confessed she was carrying John's child. Caroline protected Mary from discovery as long as possible, but eventually her condition became evident and Mrs. Langdon's rage was renewed. In the midst of the chaos came news that John had fallen in battle at Barossa, causing Mary to collapse from shock and bringing on an early birth.

The child, though frail, had a lusty squall as Caroline took it into her arms. Still insensible with a raging fever, Mary could not even hold her newborn daughter. Immediately after the birth, Mrs. Langdon indicated a burly man waiting at the door and ordered the babe be turned over to him. When Caroline questioned her reasons, she found the man was to deliver the child to a foundling home in London. Mrs. Langdon insisted that was what Mary wanted.

Appalled, Caroline refused to hand the child over, unable to believe Mary did not want her baby. Mrs. Langdon claimed that Mary, faced with reality, had changed her mind, realizing her future would be ruined if the truth about the child came out.

Caroline would always remember the long hours, as she threatened to tell the world what was happening while her stepmother argued she would ruin Mary and bring shame on them all. And for what good to the child? It would still be a bastard. Nothing could change that.

Neither would give in, and finally, Caroline said she would take the child to raise as her own. Mrs. Langdon laughed and reminded her she had no means of support. Caroline replied she had her inheritance.

"And it's not yours until you are twenty-five or married, my girl," replied the woman in venom-filled tones.

"You could release it to me now and the two of us would bother you no more," Caroline said quietly, trying to bring some reason to their conversation.

"Never. How do I know you would honor your promise? No, the child must disappear for all time," she decreed.

Caroline fled with the infant in the dead of night. Leaving a note threatening exposure if followed, she assured her stepmother she would live quietly until she came into her inheritance. That had been their final contact until today.

Now the worst of her fears had come true. Her stepmother had discovered her with nearly two years remaining before she could claim her inheritance. She would immediately remove Lucy to the Johnsons for the duration of the party. Lucy loved to play with the Johnson children, and the extra money would be welcome to the large family. She doubted her stepmother would cause an uproar at this stage of the game, risking Mary's health and a possible alliance with the earl. Too much was at stake for Mrs. Langdon to allow revenge to overcome her matrimonial schemes.

Caroline stood and shook out her skirts. She still loved Mary, despite her decision to give up Lucy. But Caroline had promised to avoid contact with her stepsister to protect her well-being, and she would honor her word. It would be easier when the time came to part.

As for the earl, they would be employer and employee. Nothing more.

While Caroline was contemplating the flowers and her past, the earl was considering his house party and the next two weeks.

Besides Mrs. Langdon and Mary, there was a

young married couple, Harry and Georgana Grenville. Their appearance was unexceptional. Both were of average height, with light brown hair and eyes. Except for the loving tenderness apparent in their every act, they could have been taken for brother and sister rather than husband and wife. The earl and Harry had briefly served together in the war and had recently renewed their acquaintance in London, where Giles had issued his invitation to Castleton.

In addition, a longtime friend and neighbor of the family, Squire Randsall, and his niece, Eugenia, had joined the party, arriving shortly after the Langdons and the Grenvilles.

The squire was a bluff, hearty man, with a full head of white hair and a jovial manner. Eugenia had lost her parents at an early age and had grown up under her uncle's guardianship. She was an attractive brunette with lively eyes and a quick wit not yet corrupted by the boredom of a London season.

Giles was not a matchmaker but believed Eugenia and Charles would suit. He considered the squire might share the dubious honor of entertaining Mrs. Langdon, although that would be a supreme sacrifice, if he was any judge of women.

Turning his thoughts to the young blond woman he had carried up the stairs, he wondered why the widow Langdon thought there could be anything between him and her daughter. He had met Miss Langdon during parties and balls in London, where assuredly her docility seemed almost a virtue in the frenzy of the marriage mart. But away from that setting, the earl's first impression, albeit a short one, was of a pretty, blond-haired, blue-eyed, vacuous doll.

Judging her against Caroline's vivaciousness, she was sadly lacking. Caroline drew him like a magnet, and for the first time, he regretted their country retreat. Once they reached London—and he would not even consider she would reject his offer—they could easily pursue a flirtation to its logical conclusion. But to bed his housekeeper in the midst of a house party at Castleton would cause a scandal broth too hot to handle.

Mary opened her eyes to the exasperated urging of her mother. Mrs. Langdon was wafting a vinaigrette under her nose one moment and sharply shaking her shoulder the next.

"Wake up, my girl. The earl wants a woman for his countess, not a missish child who faints at every inconvenience."

"Mama?" Mary's blue eyes filled with bewilderment. "I thought for a moment I saw Caroline. It gave me quite a start."

"You did see Caroline, you idiot. And I want no more of this swooning," Mrs. Langdon ordered sharply. "It may seem romantic to be carried hither and yon by a lord, but it will not do."

"But, Mama, I don't want to be carried hither and yon by anyone. I did not even know I was being carried hither and yon, so how could I desire or enjoy it?" Puzzled blue eyes stared innocently at Mrs. Langdon.

Mary had never excelled at learning but had been

a lively, if light-headed, young woman until John Alveston's death and the loss of her child. Then she had withdrawn from the world to a place of her own. She followed her mother's instructions with good-natured mindlessness, as if by keeping her intellect unengaged, she could ignore the unhappiness that had occurred.

"Sometimes I pray that you're playing me for a fool, Mary, but it's my worst fear that you are not. Now, I have excused us from tea this afternoon. However, I fully expect, as does the earl, for you to appear at dinner. Until then, you must rest and then don one of your prettiest dresses."

"But, Mama, what of Caroline?" she asked in an agitated voice.

"Caroline is serving as the earl's temporary house-keeper," Mrs. Langdon explained briefly. "We will not acknowledge her as part of our family. Indeed, we will act as if we never knew her. We've talked and that's the way she wants it."

Mary's face turned even paler. "Then she has not forgiven me?"

"Did you think she would? I've told you she flew into the boughs when you gave birth. She wouldn't even allow the poor babe to be buried in the family cemetery. Just think of that when you begin to yearn for your dear stepsister." Scorn dripped from the woman's spiteful words.

"I still cannot credit Caroline would treat me so. She often said she loved me as a true sister, even after she knew about the child." A hint of wistfulness entered Mary's voice as a tear trickled down her cheek.

"That's what she wanted you to think at the time," her mother mocked. "Your precious stepsister thought to use you to convince me to release her funds early. When that didn't work, she took what she could and ran in the middle of the night to live the dissolute life she desired."

"Being a housekeeper doesn't seem dissolute to me," judged Mary with a rare flash of insight.

"Don't bother your head with the details," ordered Mrs. Langdon. "Just remember, ignore her. I'll do whatever talking is necessary. She'll not acknowledge you except in the line of duty. This is your last chance, Mary," she warned. "If you don't bring the earl up to scratch, we'll find ourselves in straitened circumstances very shortly. For you know the bulk of the Langdon fortune goes to Caroline."

"But I have my dowry, Mama. And Caroline always said I would never want for anything," reassured Mary, patting her mother's hand.

"Unless times have changed, a dowry is for marriage, and that is not yet in your future," Mrs. Langdon replied contemptuously, jerking away from her touch. "If Caroline will not even speak to you, why would she part with one farthing of her inheritance?"

"It will be a strain to ignore Caroline," lamented Mary.

"I'm sure she'll stay out of your way as much as possible. It's only for a fortnight. You can manage that long. Now rest. I want you looking your best this evening."

"Yes, Mama." Mary obediently closed her eyes, her breath soon becoming slow and even in sleep.

Mrs. Langdon sank into a deep rose chair and considered her most recent misfortune. With this invitation, she thought her scheming had finally paid off. She had gotten rid of Alveston with a forged note, after finding Mary's secret hoard of love letters. The missive, mailed shortly before news of his death, must have been convincing, for the chit had not received another. Of that she was sure. Mary was still recovering when the retraction of John's death was printed, and Mrs. Langdon made certain it escaped her notice. With no family of his own for Mary to contact, she regarded the connection permanently severed.

Mrs. Langdon was not one to borrow trouble, and she had not sought out Caroline and the child when she found them gone. She had counted on Mary acquiring a prospering husband, so she wouldn't have to rely on Caroline's generosity once she had control of her funds. Now, instead of relaxing, she must be even more vigilant until Mary had fixed Castleton's interest.

Fourteen

"Is this all I get?" Charles demanded, glaring at the small glass of wine near his elbow. As with most invalids, the better he got, the more demanding he became. Caroline adjusted a pillow under his arm and repositioned the disputed glass before answering.

"Don't become uppish with me, Mr. Dalton," she chided playfully. "And it will be no use to pester me for something stronger. You know it will be a while yet until you can imbibe as you once did."

"You sound as if it was my habit to empty a dozen bottles a night, which I assure you is not true," he grumbled. "But I suppose I should be thankful it's not another cup of your weed tea."

"My herb tea," replied Caroline in a righteous tone, "probably saved your life, sir. And I beg you to remember it. For the next time you're injured, I will certainly not bestir myself if this is the thanks I get." She brushed a nonexistent tear from her cheek and smiled charmingly.

"My dear Mrs. Alveston, I don't say it often enough, but surely you know I can never repay you for rescuing me." He took her hand between his and pressed it warmly.

Meeting the blue eyes that gazed at her with such warmth, Caroline realized what an attractive man Charles Dalton was. His fair hair, grown overly long during his illness, had regained its luster, and his frame was filling out nicely from Madeline's cooking. His shoulders might lack an inch or so to match the broadness of the earl's and his height might be just a trifle less, judged Caroline, but nonetheless he would attract more than his share of feminine attention.

"Sir, I fear I must request you return to your sickbed if you insist on this somber disposition," she answered sprightly.

"Please do not make light of my words," he responded seriously, still holding her hand.

Seeing she could not divert his sincerity, she placed her other hand over his. "You owe me nothing except a complete recovery. I'm happy I've been able to help, but it's not even certain I did. As you so often remind me, you might have gotten well despite my weed tea, not because of it," she said, attempting to lighten his mood.

"No, as much as I tease you, I'm sure I would have died had I not reached Castleton. Or, at the very least, lost my arm, which would be worse than death itself. Coming downstairs this evening reminds me how grateful I am to be alive. I shall forever hold you in great esteem, my lady."

"As do we all, Charles."

Caroline jerked her hands free and whirled to face the earl as he lounged in the doorway.

"My lord, we did not expect to see you so soon," she said to cover her confusion. He always seemed to come upon them at inopportune moments.

"That's obvious, Mrs. Alveston." Jealousy was a stranger to the earl, so he could not name the emotion that choked him. He only knew that seeing Charles and Caroline holding hands and totally absorbed in one another brought a red haze across his eyes, along with an aching tightness through his chest. "I excused myself early from the table to help Charles, but I see he has no need of my assistance." The earl strolled farther into the room, appearing more interested in adjusting the cuff of his fine lawn shirt than in the couple before him.

"Thank you, Giles, but Henderson and Mrs. Alveston have made me very comfortable." Charles glanced from the earl to the woman sitting quietly beside him. "I was just expressing my appreciation to her for what the staff calls her healing hands."

"Yes, I observed you were examining them closely, my friend. Did you find their secret?" Lord Castleton quirked a dark eyebrow questioningly.

Charles only laughed at the earl's sally, but Caroline's face blazed with color. Apprised of his intentions toward Mary, his thinly disguised disapproval was unbearable. He had no right to judge her behavior and find it wanting. "If you will excuse me, my lord, I shall retire," she said, keeping her eyes lowered to obscure her anger. Being purposefully rude, she turned her back on the earl and addressed Charles. "Mr. Dalton, if Henderson will advise me of your return, I'll prepare your evening drink."

175

"You cannot go, Caroline," objected Charles as she started to leave the room.

"And why not?" demanded the earl, irritated anew by the familiar appellation. "I'm sure you can survive a few hours of our company without my house-keeper."

"And I'm sure I cannot," grumbled the wounded man, unaware of his slip in propriety. "Caroline is the only one who can make me comfortable. She knows before I ask what my needs are. I never thought to say it, but she anticipates even better than Henderson." He lowered his voice conspiratorially while bestowing the ultimate compliment on the embarrassed woman.

Caroline raised her eyes to meet the earl's dark gaze, disappointed with this latest setback in their truce. She had begun to feel more relaxed in his company of late, their quarrel paling into insignificance next to that of her stepmother's arrival. In truth, she felt safe with him around, knowing Mrs. Langdon's venon would be carefully controlled under his observant eye.

"Then I suppose we must beg Caroline," he inflected her name with a wealth of meaning, "to stay in order to keep you from falling into a decline."

"I'm sure Henderson will be adequate, my lord," she protested uneasily. "He's in the hall within close call." Lord Castleton's continued pretensions of annoyance because of Charles's attention to her were puzzling, since his intended bride was in residence.

"No, Mrs. Alveston. It's my duty to see that my guests are as comfortable as possible. And it seems that your presence is the only thing that will ensure

Charles's peace of mind. Let us say no more. Now I must see to the rest of my company." He turned away from them as the full dinner party entered the drawing room, the gentlemen having declined taking their port in solitude.

The evening was interminable to Caroline. Never had she felt her change in status as she did tonight. She was constantly aware of the earl sitting closely with Mary, dark head inclined to blond, or offering his arm for a short stroll on the terrace. The reality of the two as a couple was forced on her with harsh clarity. A painful void engulfed her and she longed for the privacy of her room, away from these people whose lives were now separate from her own.

Caroline was grateful when Harry Grenville engaged Charles in a discussion of the Peninsular battles. She surreptitiously removed to a window embrasure, pushing open the casement to enjoy the evening breeze.

"Hiding, Mrs. Alveston?"

She knew without turning that the earl was standing closely behind her. "No, my lord. Mr. Dalton is preoccupied refighting the war, and I've found gentlemen do not always like women hanging over their shoulder."

"I can't imagine Charles feeling that way toward you, ma'am. Especially after his outburst earlier this evening."

The last few hours had taken their toll on Caroline. Still numb from confronting her stepmother, feeling an outsider among her peers, then watching the earl and Mary together, her endurance had been stretched to the breaking point.

She yearned to retreat to the safety of her room for the remainder of the evening and gather her resources to face the duration of the house party. Instead, she must suffer the rebuke of her employer for an event that had been no fault of her own.

"I beg you, my lord, if you have an aversion to my presence, please make it clear to Mr. Dalton." Her voice trembled with suppressed emotion. "I would be more than happy to forgo these evenings and retire to my usual place in the household. I'm sure you can convince him it isn't at all proper for the housekeeper to keep him company." Caroline stood stiffly while the silence stretched between them.

Strong hands closed upon her arms, turning her firmly to him. She was imprisoned in the small alcove by his body, broad shoulders blocking out the rest of the room, lending an intimacy to the moment. His finger tipped her chin until she was forced to meet his gaze.

"I apologize, Caroline. I shouldn't have teased you so seriously." His voice wrapped softly around her, soothing the hurt she felt. "Sometimes I take out my exasperation on those closest to me. Charles understands and takes no offense, but you don't know me well enough yet. I know you feel your position moreso since my guests arrived," he continued, giving her no time to reply. "You questioned my regret for the invitations. Now you know why I didn't want them here. My life—or perhaps I should say *our* life—was pleasant before their arrival. I knew it would be changed by outsiders."

His thumb caressed her cheek, holding her silent. "Do not tremble so. I will not break our bargain," he

178

murmured reassuringly, "at least not in front of so many witnesses." His smile took the sting from his words.

"I don't resent your service to Charles," he continued. "It's just now that he's recovering, my patience runs short with his dependency on you." He appeared surprised by the admission. "Could it be jealousy? I wonder?" he asked, searching the depths of Caroline's eyes for an answer. "Not a very admirable quality, is it, my dear?" he taunted gently.

Caroline's thoughts were in confusion. Why did he speak of their life together, and his jealousy, when he was ready to offer for Mary? Did he think to have them both? One to insure his bodily comfort and the other to provide a legitimate heir. She could not consider it now with her treacherous body responding to his overwhelming closeness, blocking out rational thought.

"I need no apology, my lord. My sensibilities this evening are too easily bruised. I'm caught between what I am and what I should be. We lived very quietly at Cresthill, and my altered social standing has not been conspicuous until this evening. I find I'm not as complacent as I thought." Caroline's introspection was obvious as she stared distractedly past his shoulder.

Lord Castleton hoped she would finally confide the secret held tight within her. Granting him her trust was of prime importance in their relationship. Without that her capitulation to his will would be a hollow victory. Laughter from the room behind them intruded, and he knew he would learn no more that evening.

"In a fortnight all this will be over and we can settle back into our pleasant routine," he said, as if nothing untoward had occurred. "In my callow youth, I never thought I'd settle for routine, much less yearn for it." He gave a self-deprecating chuckle. "And remember, we have London before us, for I decree our discord is resolved as of this moment. If you will consent," he amended hastily.

Her bones turned to warm liquid and she nodded silently in agreement.

"Good." He nodded with satisfaction. "Until then, I'll try to be patient with Charles's demands on you and the other guests' demands on me. But I'm not convinced I can persist with good grace." One corner of his mouth lifted in a wry smile.

"I'm sure you can accomplish whatever you set your mind to, my lord," Caroline replied, regaining her composure, while he fervently hoped she was right. "Now, if you will excuse me, I suspect Charles grows tired."

"It seems our private moments are fated to be interrupted by someone else's needs, my dear." His teasing words and endearment renewed the memory of their kisses, and her feelings spun into disorder again. She mumbled an apology and squeezed by him into the room.

"That was very close indeed, Caroline," his amused voice murmured in her ear as she passed.

Lord Castleton took her place in the embrasure, inhaling the cool night air. He considered their conversation as he waited for the effects of her nearness to wear off. Tonight was a time of firsts in their relationship. It was the first time she had acknowledged her actual station in life and her unhappiness toward her present position. And he surprised even himself in admitting the possibility of being jealous of his housekeeper.

His past experiences with women had involved only a physical need, which was quickly sated before he moved on to another. With Caroline, while his present condition was proof positive she stirred him physically, he found he desired her company as well as her body. He experienced more satisfaction conversing and riding the estate with her than spending a night in any lightskirt's bed.

Since he had never craved complete possession of a woman before, his thoughts proved unsettling to him. For once, he welcomed a bid for his attention from Mrs. Langdon, and the earl finished the evening the very epitome of a gracious host.

Caroline helped Henderson settle Charles comfortably for the night, brewed his weed tea, then retired to her room.

At the beginning of Charles's stay, Lord Castleton had insisted she move to the second floor to avoid traversing the halls at night. She had to admit it was much more convenient, and with Lucinda staying at the Johnsons, Caroline had no objections. Tonight she was especially grateful to avoid further encounters with the guests, and she closed the door behind her with a sigh of relief.

Thoughts of strong hands, dark eyes, and broad

shoulders dominated her mind. Remembering the solid wall of Lord Castleton's chest as she slipped by him brought heat to her face, and his words created confusion in her mind. He had spoken of settling into their routine again as if he expected her to always be there, and he had invited her to remove with him to London. ·

It was unthinkable for her to accept the earl's offer with Mary as his prospective bride. But think of it she did. He offered no more than a housekeeper's position, but in such an intimate setting as the townhouse her defenses would quickly crumble if he continued his overtures. Caroline's vulnerability to his charms might cause her to reveal the secret she had struggled so long to keep successfully hidden. Although her stepmother had discovered her, Mary's aspirations were a compelling reason for keeping her identity concealed.

Denying the physical attraction of Lord Castleton would be foolish. But she was not so green as to assume desire meant anything more, especially between a housekeeper and a master.

She must avoid the situations that put her in contact with the earl. He had brought his future bride, her stepsister, to Castleton, and Caroline had given her word not to interfere. She shuddered to think how he would react to find his intended had already borne a child, but that was her stepmother's problem. Her thoughts still spinning, she fell into a fretful doze.

Caroline's nursing duties lightened considerably during the blossoming acquaintance of Eugenia and

Charles. The welcome reprieve allowed her time to visit Lucy, whose loving distraction she sorely missed. She adjusted to the house party's presence, and once again appeared completely composed as she attended Charles.

A few days later the company repaired to the music room after dinner. Discovering a mutual affinity for the pianoforte, Eugenia joined Mary on the bench picking out familiar tunes.

"It's a shame no one is talented with the harp," commented Eugenia, nodding toward the neglected instrument in the corner. "There's so much music here for duets."

"Yes, my mother played," said the earl, flipping through the pages. "And my father, though not usual practice for a man, was proficient on the pianoforte. I remember many pleasant hours spent in this room."

He also reflected on more recent occasions when Caroline had graced the bench. Evenings spent leaning over her shoulder turning pages, breathing in her fragrance, her hair tickling his face as she turned to laugh up at him.

"What wonderful memories to treasure," said Eugenia, drawing him back to the present.

"Yes," he said fervently, and received a look of commiseration from the softhearted girl for being such a devoted son.

"It's unfortunate you didn't follow in your mother's footsteps," declared the young woman."

"I fear, Miss Randall, that one strum from my clumsy hand would wreak more damage to the harp than all its previous years. And, believe me, it would not be pleasant to your ears, either."

"But Caroline can play beautifully," remarked Mary without thinking. She shot a quick look toward Mrs. Langdon as the enormity of her mistake sunk in.

Curious why Caroline had not mentioned her skill at the harp, the earl turned toward her. Intrigued even more by Mary's informal address and familiarity with his housekeeper's ability to play, he looked for some sign from her, but Caroline remained silent.

"And how do you come by such knowledge?" queried the earl in a deceptively mild tone, his gaze still fixed on Caroline.

"Why, we discussed it just this morning," interjected Mrs. Langdon nervously. "I asked Mrs. Alveston if she played an instrument and she admitted to a slight talent on the harp. But nothing to speak of, she said, and I'm sure we wouldn't want to embarrass her."

As she well knew, Caroline's talent was more than slight, and Mrs. Langdon did not want her to be shown to such an advantage over Mary. The chit's ability to run the manor house was more than enough to overcome.

Not for a moment did Giles believe Mrs. Langdon's explanation, and he wondered what was between the women. "I'm sure Mrs. Alveston would not be embarrassed in front of such an intimate gathering. Would you, Mrs. Alveston?" he asked, approaching Caroline and extending his hand. "After all, we should attempt to accommodate our guests, shouldn't we, ma'am?"

During the past weeks, Caroline had learned it was far easier to accept the inevitable when it came to the earl's requests. He would have his way, and it was easier to get it over with and move on.

"Of course, my lord. Whatever you wish," she replied submissively. Placing her hand in his, she rose and made her way to the harp.

Giles was suspicious of Caroline's affability and attempted to read its significance. But she kept her eyes demurely lowered as she seated herself at the instrument.

The two women presented a delightful picture. Eugenia with her brunette curls and primrose gown sat at the pianoforte. Caroline, in blue, plucked at the strings of the harp, candlelight catching the burnished highlights of her hair and reflecting from the gilded instrument. As soon as the harp was tuned to her satisfaction, she began playing. Eugenia joined in as she grew accustomed to Caroline's interpretation. If there had been any doubt as to Caroline's background, it would have been immediately expunged. Only a treasured daughter of the Quality would have had the opportunity to play as she did on both harp and pianoforte.

When Mary was urged to take Eugenia's place, she did so in the face of Mrs. Langdon's disapprobation. "We have had enough music this evening, Mary. I'm sure the gentlemen are bored with this feminine pursuit."

"Normally, I would hesitate to disagree with a guest, Mrs. Langdon, but it has been many years since I've enjoyed a musical evening such as this," observed the earl, curious to see the two play together.

Finally, the older woman acknowledged defeat.

Further objections would only cast undue interest toward her daughter and stepdaughter, the very situation she was endeavoring to avoid.

After the first tentative notes, Mary and Caroline thought no more of the tension surrounding them and became engrossed in the music. An excellent blend of fortissimos and obbligatos flowed from their fingers, weaving a spell around the audience.

Lord Castleton's eyes narrowed in concentration at the degree of unity their performance displayed. Something havey-cavey was going on. Mrs. Langdon had protested too much. Mary was overly nonplussed and Caroline too silently agreeable.

The two women finally pleaded exhaustion before they were allowed to escape, and shortly thereafter the company dispersed for the evening. Caroline trailed behind Charles and Henderson, when the earl drew her aside.

"Mrs. Alveston, a word if you please." He guided her into the library, holding his impatience in check until the door closed firmly behind them.

Fifteen

"I gather tonight answered my question of some weeks ago," said Lord Castleton, eyes shining icy black with anger.

"I don't understand, my lord."

"Strange." The coldness spread to his voice. "I distinctly remember inquiring whether I had to ask you for everything. It now seems I must. Damn, Caroline! Do you know how I feel when a virtual stranger knows more about you than I do?" His eyes grew hot with frustration and rage.

Caroline kept a tight hold on her emotions. "I'm sorry, my lord. I didn't realize my harp playing was of prime importance to you."

"Everything you do is important to me. You must know that by now." He prayed she would raise those impossibly green eyes and confess he meant as much to her. He wanted to cradle her in his arms while she disclosed a past no longer important but for the trust manifest in the telling.

Caroline hardened her heart against the appeal in his voice. "You already know most of my accom-

187

plishments, my lord. Although I'm told my needle-work is commendable and my chess playing tolerable, I am disgustingly inadequate at cards. I must also admit to a secret propensity for novel reading over uplifting moral works. I think that is all." Caroline's voice dwindled away. She could not meet his gaze, taking refuge instead in studying the elegance of his cravat.

His broad chest heaved a sigh that moved the diamond stickpin to shoot sparks of fire. "Caroline, what shall happen to us?"

It was a question she had asked herself countless times without resolution. "I hope you're not displeased with the evening," she ventured, choosing to ignore his question. "I could not easily refuse to play, particularly when you added your voice to their entreaties."

"Of course not. I was pleased you joined in," he answered, ceding the encounter to her obstinacy, an event heretofore unknown. It was not the first change he had undergone since meeting Caroline. Before he realized it, she had slipped beneath his protective shell and turned his life upside down. He could no longer distance himself from emotional entanglements. She had made him feel tenderness again, had made him burn with desire. And now she had weakened his resolve, a feeling he wasn't sure he relished.

"I hope it was as enjoyable for you as for those of us listening," he replied, accepting his inability to press her further.

"Yes, it's been some time since I played the harp," she said, wondering how much longer she must mouth such banalities before excusing herself.

He poured a snifter of brandy, not willing to yield too easily. "Your parents must have been music lovers to see their daughter trained so expertly in two instruments."

"My parents were like yours in that respect. My mother preferred the harp and my father the pianoforte. Being the dutiful daughter, I attempted to please them both."

"I'm sure they would have been content had you been tone deaf."

"Probably. But it was much more pleasant to find I had a slight musical talent." She smiled, regaining a modicum of confidence.

"Well, no matter who taught you nor what the reason, I look forward to more evenings such as these," he said, thinking of when the house party removed.

If she had not known his intentions toward Mary, she would have been falling into his arms by now. Self-loathing spread through her at her weakness. "No doubt you will be more than entertained with Miss Langdon's talents at your disposal. You'll find them especially welcome during the long winter months." Jealousy overwhelmed her with a fierce white heat at the thought.

"Of a certainty she plays well, but not with your expertise," he replied, perplexed by her illogical outburst.

"If you will excuse me, I must see to Charles," Caroline announced abruptly.

"Of course," said the earl, unable to execute a bow in the speed of her departure. He leaned an arm along the mantelpiece and stared into the empty fireplace.

The desire for knowledge simply to manipulate

Caroline into his arms had disappeared. Although his need for her had not abated, he was now motivated by an acute interest to know her better. He did not completely understand the unfamiliar impulses driving their relationship, but he meant to tread warily until he straightened out his feelings.

Giles finished his brandy, puzzlement still clouding his face. What had happened to the accord they recently shared? And what in damnation was that nonsense about Miss Langdon and winter? Good God! The house party was for a fortnight only, not an invitation to take up permanent residence.

"Mr. Dalton seems strongly attached to your housekeeper," observed Mrs. Langdon when the men joined the ladies in the drawing room the next evening. She covertly attempted to gauge the effect of her remark on the earl.

Lord Castleton had not taken his eyes from the two since the moment they had entered the room. Caroline's gown of Devonshire brown was a color not many could wear successfully, but the reddish tint of the material complemented her hair and set off the porcelain quality of her complexion.

Charles was also looking well in light breeches, blue kerseymere coat, white waistcoat, and a flawlessly tied cravat. He smiled at Caroline in a way that made the earl's hands involuntarily clench. Observing their closeness, a moody countenance replaced his normally impassive expression.

"He credits her with saving his life," Giles replied

shortly, restlessly crossing his legs. "She's talented in helping those who are ill."

"You're fortunate to have her, my lord, even on a temporary basis."

"Indeed I am," he agreed, black brows lowering at the reminder of Caroline's short tenure.

"Well, she certainly seems to have made a conquest. Though Mr. Dalton appears to be on the road to recovery, he keeps her close by his side. Perhaps there will be a match in the offing. Without a title to secure he could marry where he chooses, and they seem well suited."

"I've known Charles since we were in short coats, madam, and I assure you they're not at all suited," he replied stiffly.

Mrs. Langdon judged Lord Castleton's forbidding looks and sudden silence as adequate proof he had his own plans for Caroline. She would have to introduce enough doubt to cause a disgust of the chit in the earl. She had broken up Mary and the Alveston man; now it seemed she must do the same with her uncooperative stepdaughter.

"I'm happy Mr. Dalton could join us after his setback last night," continued Lady Langdon casually.

"I've heard of no setback. Although he's a little tired after his unusual activity, it's no more than to be expected. His strength still isn't at full force and he should rest more than he does."

"I'm relieved to hear it. When I saw Mrs. Alveston enter his room last evening, I feared the worst. I didn't hear her return, so I only assumed she was sitting with him. Although I would expect his man to do the honors overnight." Mrs. Langdon calmly fanned herself, watching the seeds of mistrust take root.

The earl was now looking daggers at the couple engrossed in conversation at the end of the room.

Earlier in the afternoon, Caroline had returned from visiting Lucy and found Charles strolling about the garden with Eugenia. After his excessive activity, Caroline suggested he dedicate an evening to rest, but feeling euphoric with success, he insisted on joining the party.

That evening, Charles leaned heavily on his valet, as Henderson helped him to the wingback chair. Despite his protestations, Caroline knew the injured man's energy was sorely taxed. She spread a light blanket over his legs, while Jervis and Henderson hovered solicitously in the background.

"Good lord, I'm on the mend, not at the brink of death as you all must think," he complained peevishly.

"We have no fear for your demise, Mr. Dalton, only your comfort," Caroline replied soothingly. "We've invested a great deal in your recovery and don't want you to slip backward. You'll not admit it, but you've overdone yourself. Since you demanded to join the party, I must insist on taking precautions."

"As usual you're right," he admitted, regaining his even temper. "Not long ago, I would have rejoiced to have been this well; now that I actually am, I fear I want something more."

"You wouldn't be recovering if you weren't weary

of being an invalid," acquiesced Caroline. "A man of your activity must chafe under the restriction. But I assure you, if you follow our instructions, you'll soon be your old self."

"I bow to your superior knowledge, ma'am," he agreed good-naturedly.

She tucked the blanket around his legs and instructed Jervis to bring some broth and tea.

Charles groaned, raising his hand to his forehead in mock distress.

"So soon after you promised to follow my instructions, Mr. Dalton?" she requested forbiddingly.

"I apologize again, Mrs. Alveston. I also promise to do better if you will call me Charles. I cannot abide another Mr. Dalton." His blue eyes glinted with deviltry.

"And I cannot consent to be on such familiar terms with one of Lord Castleton's guests," she replied sternly. "I must set an example for the rest of the household."

"Please agree we may be less formal," he begged. "I swear I cannot think of my angel as Mrs. Alveston any longer. Can we not be Caroline and Charles in our private moments?"

"Perhaps. But only if you undertake to follow my instructions, sir," she coaxed.

"That is blackmail, madam, but charmingly done. I give you my pledge, Mrs. Alveston. Caroline, if I may?"

Smiling at his undisguised manipulation, she looked up directly into the earl's dark scowl.

* * *

Lord Castleton cut short his morning ride the next day and approached the house from the rose garden, certain he would find Charles relaxing on the terrace.

The earl had spent much of his evening speculating on Mrs. Langdon's information. If Caroline had instigated the visit to her patient's room, it would be the last. Assuming she had been lured with a bogus illness, it was likely Charles was contemplating another of his discreet affairs, which marked him a successful lady's man. If his friend's thoughts lay in that quarter, he would soon put him straight. Lord Castleton had not suffered through the past weeks to have the prize stolen from beneath his nose, he concluded indignantly.

Bounding up the stone steps to the terrace, he found the lean body of his friend stretched out on a chaise, positioned to accommodate his comfort.

"All alone this morning, Charles? How did you escape Mrs. Alveston's web of solicitude?" he asked, unaware his anger was obvious.

Charles examined his friend's stiff features. He had watched Giles cut off all feeling on the Peninsula as his men died around him and the news of his parents' deaths reached him. The scars of those losses were now crippling him in a way that could ruin his life. He knew Giles denied anything but a physical attraction to his housekeeper. To do so would make him vulnerable to more loss and pain. Well, it was time to prod his recalcitrant friend toward his inevitable destination.

"It's such a comfortable web, I haven't even tried to escape," Charles admitted cheerfully. "In fact, I'm

194

endeavoring to enmesh myself even further in its silken strands."

At the mention of silken strands, the earl's thoughts went immediately to Caroline's hair. The idea of fingers other than his own tangling in the luxurious mass sent him striding to the terrace wall. He turned his back to the man whose throat he greatly desired to squeeze, sick though he was, and gazed blindly out over the gardens. Anger engulfed him at the thought of Charles giving Caroline a slip on the shoulder, and his knuckles whitened on the riding crop he held.

"Don't tell me you relish your role as invalid, Charles. I cannot believe that," he scoffed.

"I never thought to. But now that the worst is over, I find I enjoy being cosseted to a certain extent. Especially when the cosseter is so attractive." Charles chuckled at his wit as the crop in Giles's hand began to tap the stone parapet.

"I did not think you would play on an innocent woman's sensibilities, my friend," came the tense reply.

"But I'm not playing," replied Charles seriously.

Giles sent the riding crop crashing against the stone wall and turned lazily toward his friend, eyes ablaze. "And what do you mean by that?" he asked coolly.

"Just that Caroline is a very attractive and intelligent woman. I don't know about you, but our recent sojourn on the Peninsula and this damnable wound have reminded me how brief life can be. The honorable state of matrimony is more appealing to me daily." Charles's conscience was eased by the fact that he was indeed contemplating marriage, but early on he had discovered which way the wind blew with Caroline, and now the object of his intent was dark-haired Eugenia.

"Ha! You? Leg shackled? The very thought of you stepping into the parson's mousetrap makes me want to ring for Henderson and have you conveyed to your sick bed, for I'm sure your fever has returned," Giles mocked derisively. "Surely you don't envision sharing the experience with my housekeeper?" he snarled.

"And why not?" questioned Charles innocently. "Living under the cat's paw with a feline such as Caroline doesn't seem too arduous a chore."

"She has a child, you know," replied Lord Castleton, hoping to pose an obstacle for his stubborn friend.

"That doesn't lessen her charms. She'd be much better off as mistress of Cresthill than as another man's servant, or worse." He watched Giles's strong reaction to his statement before continuing. "She wouldn't have to worry about providing for the child, and she could enjoy the social status to which she's so obviously born. I'm sure no one would object to such an advantageous alliance."

Giles couldn't refute the argument, but to lose Caroline before having her was too much to ask even for his best friend. Excusing himself, he withdrew without issuing the setdown he had intended. His need for Caroline was intense, leaving him torn between desire and his honor as a gentleman not to impede her in bettering her life.

* * *

196

With the exception of Charles, the men rode early every morning. Being a considerate host, Lord Castleton suggested an afternoon ride for any of the ladies who wished to see the estate's picturesque views.

Mrs. Langdon, who could only tolerate horses harnessed to a carriage, pleaded a fictitious back injury. Blushing, Georgana and Henry announced they were expecting their first child in December, and she was being overly cautious. Since Mary was in her room with a headache, this left only Eugenia, who thoroughly enjoyed riding over the countryside but elected to forgo the pleasure to entertain Charles.

Relieved, the earl was expressing the requisite sorrow that none of the lovely ladies could join him, when Mrs. Langdon declared she was sure Mary had recovered and would be delighted to accompany him.

"I'll go up and instruct her to change into her habit immediately," Mrs. Langdon said, rising.

"There's no hurry, ma'am," protested Giles.

"Nonsense. Since it will be only the two of you, you can leave right away and have more time together," she replied coyly, rushing out the door.

"Mama, you know I'm terrified of those beasts and cannot join Lord Castleton." Mary sat in a pink striped chair, her pale face dominated by large frightened eyes.

"You have no choice. Men are absolute fools over their cattle, and you must indicate an interest in them. I'm' sure he will mount you on a gentle mare. You

197

can go slowly and spend time admiring the views. Don't be so fainthearted," she ordered callously.

Caroline overheard the conversation from the hall. She knew Mary's fear of horses ran deep and could hear the terror in her stepsister's voice.

"You should not force her, ma'am," she advised, stepping over the threshold of Mary's room.

Mrs. Langdon rounded quickly at her voice. "No one asked for your interference," she replied viciously.

"You've told me that before and it didn't stop me," remarked Caroline, a subtle threat strengthening her words.

Mrs. Langdon changed the subject before old ghosts rose up to haunt her. "Forget the past. We're talking of the present, and Mary must ride with the earl today."

"It would be far worse for him to have his ride interrupted with hysterics. Perhaps a carriage ride would be better," Caroline suggested reasonably.

"Mary will not have hysterics," her stepmother insisted stubbornly. "She will conduct herself as the countess she will be."

"Oh, Mama, you know I cannot," wailed Mary from the corner. "Ever since that nasty pony threw me, I haven't been able to get on a horse. I know I shall perish if you insist." Her sobs became louder as she buried her face in her hands.

"Forget that foolishness. Too much depends on this for you to become so missish," her mother demanded.

Caroline had heard enough. "You will not force her on a horse, madam," she commanded decisively.

"And you do not order our lives," her stepmother spat out. "Now leave this room immediately!" she ordered, pointing to the door with a shaking hand.

"You won't make her suffer unnecessarily for your ambitions," Caroline insisted stubbornly. "I assure you, Lord Castleton does not require his guests ride unless they desire it."

The two women glared at one another, both weighing the chances they were taking in the confrontation.

"Mrs. Alveston, I thought I heard your voice. Is there a problem?" The earl filled the doorway, looking inquiringly at the tableau before him. Mary sat pale and withdrawn, dressed in a fetching blue riding habit. Caroline and Mrs. Langdon confronted one another in the middle of the room, poised for battle.

Their raised voices were clearly discernible through the open door, and he had quickly grasped the situation. Disgust filled him at Mrs. Langdon's actually risking her daughter's well-being to fix his interest.

"It's nothing, my lord. Miss Langdon still isn't feeling well and regrets she cannot accompany you this afternoon," explained Caroline.

"That's true, your lordship," agreed Mrs. Langdon, wisely giving ground. "I'm afraid I offered my daughter's company too readily. I was just sending Mrs. Alveston to advise you. I know you're disappointed, but perhaps Mary can join you another day."

"I certainly wouldn't want Miss Langdon to attempt anything upsetting. Her stay should be pleasant," he added smoothly, smiling at the distraught young woman. "Mrs. Alveston, a word with you, please."

199

"Of course, my lord," agreed Caroline pleasantly, for her stepmother's benefit, all the while dreading the interview.

"Ladies, I'll see you at dinner." He bowed to the two women and stepped aside for Caroline to precede him from the room.

Sixteen

Giles took Caroline's elbow and guided her to a nearby sitting room. The small, cozy room had always imparted a feeling of safety, cocooned with flowered chintz and graceful Queen Anne furniture. Now, dominated by the earl's imposing figure, it afforded her no protection at all.

"You were quite defensive, Caroline. What brought it on?" he asked, piercing eyes watching her closely.

"Miss Langdon is terrified of horses, but her mother insisted she ride. I couldn't see her suffer," she replied, straightening a Dresden figurine to avoid his gaze.

"An admirable stance," he pronounced solemnly. "Most housekeepers wouldn't consider interfering in a family dispute for fear of their job."

"Perhaps my temporary position gives me more nerve than most. You've so often reminded me of our bargain, I'm sure you wouldn't dare turn me off," she taunted, finally meeting his gaze.

"Are you trying to force me to release you, ma'am?" he asked, amused at her challenge.

"The country air must have made me mutton-headed, for I confess it didn't cross my mind," she said ingenuously. "But if it will do the trick, I'll certainly be more outrageous." She tilted her head, awaiting his reaction.

"You would be wasting your time," he said, lifting her chin with his finger, wondering again what secrets her eyes hid. "I think I've made it clear you'll not escape me so easily."

"We shall see, my lord. Our bargain does have its limits." She left him before the frown could fully gather on his face.

While irritated with her rebellious attitude, Lord Castleton was increasingly curious about the relationship between the Langdon women and Caroline. He would keep a close watch on the situation.

The weather held perfect, with mild days and cool evenings. The earl devoted his time to entertaining the men, which was not too demanding since Squire Ransdall considered himself a crack shot and the river lured Harry Grenville to its banks.

Charles became a favorite with the ladies and they lightheartedly vied for the opportunity of entertaining him.

Luncheon was often served on the terrace or in the summer house near the lake. Cards, billiards, or music usually followed Madeline's excellent dinners. Georgana was heard to tell Harry he would die of gluttony if they stayed much longer.

Giles conceded Caroline was correct. He was proud of Castleton and the ability to entertain without

202

apology. He knew she had made it possible and accepted numerous compliments in her stead. Obviously, she could have her pick of positions if Charles's suit was not successful.

Thoughts of Caroline and Charles together ate at Giles, and he wondered if the others could hear his teeth grinding. If the situation was not resolved soon, Madeline need only cook gruel three times a day, for he would have nothing left with which to chew.

True to his word, Lord Castleton exerted considerable effort to maintain the facade of congenial host. What it cost, however, was known only to Denton, who removed one ruined cravat after another while Giles cursed in frustration at his plight.

Giles sought Caroline out as she sat in the garden at the back of the house. He had lost patience with the passive Mary and the overbearing Mrs. Langdon, excusing himself on the pretense of inspecting the progress of an injured horse in his stable.

"Mrs. Alveston," he exclaimed, feigning surprise. "I'm glad to see you taking some leisure time. You've outdone yourself for the company."

Caroline had often felt his eyes on her during the past days and was cautious in her reply. "No more than would be expected, my lord. But I'm glad you're pleased with the results."

"I am, exceedingly so. But why isn't Lucy outside in this beautiful weather?" He looked around, puzzled at not seeing the tiny figure. "She isn't ailing, is she?" he asked with some anxiety.

Giles felt guilty for not having seen the child since

the guests' arrival but thought Caroline had purposely kept her out of sight. He had missed the little minx and had hoped to catch her with her mother today.

"Indeed not. She's probably frolicking with the Johnson children at the moment, thoroughly enjoying herself." Caroline smiled at the thought.

"She's visiting for the day, then?" he asked, relief evident in his voice.

"No, I removed her there for the duration of the house party," Caroline stated casually, feigning an unnatural interest in the rose she held.

"What! I told you there was no need for that!" he exclaimed.

"There's no reason to be overset, my lord. It really is for the best; she enjoys the novelty of other children's company."

The familiar frown returned to his face. "It's not beneficial to remove a child from her family."

"It's just for a fortnight, not forever," replied Caroline, making light of the move.

"Still, I will not have my house disturbed so for strangers. We will collect her this afternoon," he insisted, tapping his crop against his boot.

"To do that now would probably upset her even more. She's looking forward to the visit, and now that she's comfortably settled in, I think it would be best to leave her until next week," Caroline stated with an uncompromising air. "I see her every afternoon, and Mrs. Johnson promised to send for me immediately if there's a problem."

"I still cannot countenance it," grumbled Giles, somewhat subdued but still affronted. "I wish you had advised me. I would certainly have discouraged this action."

"It didn't cross my mind to confer with you on Lucy's whereabouts," she replied abruptly.

He stiffened at her rebuke. "I apologize. It isn't my place to tell you what to do with your child, but I've become fond of her and wouldn't want her to be unhappy."

"I appreciate your concern, but believe me, there's no harm done. In fact, I'm convinced that Lucinda looks on this as a great adventure," she remarked lightly.

There was a space of silence while he reconciled himself to a situation he did not relish. "Since you're free, then, will you come ride with me?" he asked with a winning smile. "We'll ride by the Johnsons and visit Lucy."

"I really shouldn't. Dinner preparations are in progress and—"

"And Mrs. Crawford is more than adequate to handle any crisis, unless you have misled me on her qualifications."

"Of course not."

"Then hurry. I'll have the horses saddled and ready by the time you get back, and we'll make our getaway."

Caroline ran up the back stairs and changed quickly into her green habit. She had not been riding with the earl since Charles had arrived, and the blood pounded excitedly in her veins.

Caroline was breathless by the time she reached the stable yard. Scarlet Lady pranced skittishly as Giles tossed her easily into the saddle. The warmth of his touch made her breath come even shorter and she arranged her skirt over the saddle while her confusion abated.

"Lady will need a brisk workout today to subdue her spirit," said the earl as they took the path toward the river meadow.

"I'm surprised she's not already worn down with all the riding this past week."

"Lady has not been ridden since you were last mounted. My orders are that she's for your use exclusively." The arrogant lord-of-the-manor tone entered his voice and Caroline smiled at his unawareness of the inborn hauteur.

"That wasn't necessary, my lord. Although I do confess to being taken with her," she said, fondly patting the mare's neck.

"It's my decision," he declared sternly, "and I won't be talked out of it. You and Scarlet Lady make a perfect match. I will not allow her to be ruined by a heavy-handed guest. If you choose not to ride her, then she'll remain idle."

Caroline studied his profile in the bright afternoon sun. The blend of aristocratic features gave him an aloof, untouchable look, yet she was convinced his concern for Lucy and herself was genuine. She thought it sad he found it necessary to hide his feelings so often.

As if reading her thoughts, he sent her a sharp look. "Now, no more of this. We came out to ride." He loosened the reins on Palisades and broke into a canter. Scarlet Lady, fresh and eager for a sprint, matched his stride.

"Oh, how wonderful to be out again," cried Caroline joyfully as they reached the riverbank. She turned toward Giles, wind-tossed hair curling around her flushed face.

"Yes, I feel ten years younger myself," he replied, grinning back at her. "Let's give the horses a breather." He dismounted and tethered Palisades to a low hanging limb.

Giles reached up and lifted her from the saddle, letting her slide down his body as though by accident rather than by design. He had to feel her next to him again, and if this subterfuge was necessary, then so be it. There was a moment of stillness between them as he held her. "We'll take the mare with us to London so you'll have a proper mount," he murmured, bending to nuzzle the shell of her ear.

"I have not agreed to go," she whispered. "Do not forget Charles." His warm breath in her sensitive ear removed all rational thought, and Caroline could do no more than cling breathlessly to his broad shoulders.

"How can I forget him?" he growled. "Every time I see him he is hanging on to you. If he were not sick, I would take him to task."

A shiver ran down Caroline's spine as the implication of his words struck her. He was jealous! Lord Giles Anthony Griffin, seventh Earl of Castleton, a man whose suit would be welcomed by any family of the beau monde, was jealous of her attention to his friend.

Unable to pass up the opportunity to get back a little of her own, Caroline allowed her natural mischievousness to surface. "But he is such a wonderful person," she cooed sweetly, "I do not mind at all."

207

"Well, I mind!" he ground out, a quick flare of anger rushing through him. Stepping back, he secured Lady next to the stallion. "You will come to London with me," he commanded. "I cannot let you do otherwise."

"But I believe it is Charles's intent to offer more than a housekeeper's position, my lord," she continued in her gushing tone. "You must admit, it would be to my advantage to accept. Think of what it would mean to Lucy, and I must consider her first."

Giles could not dispute her reasoning and his anger grew. Nor would he countenance her in anyone else's arms. "I will not discuss such a ridiculous idea, and I will not spend our time together discussing Charles," he stated emphatically. "Come, the river's too inviting to ignore."

Caroline placed her hand lightly on his arm, her fingers warming from the contact as they strolled along the shady bank. She attempted to pull away from the impact his closeness had on her, but Giles would not allow it, pinning her hand to his side and covering it with his own.

Aware of her agitation, the earl was pleased he could cause such an effect even while she was considering another man's offer. Giles guided her to a rock and slipped off his coat, spreading it over the surface.

"I assure you, my habit is no stranger to a little dirt," objected Caroline at his action.

"You would be granting a favor by allowing me to play the gallant. Besides, Denton would be desolate if he could not find a little dust somewhere," he explained, seating himself at her feet.

The day was warm and Caroline was overwhelmingly conscious of the fine lawn fabric clinging damply to his muscular shoulders. Conversation was sporadic, but comfortably so, and the week's tensions seeped away with the river's flow. A chuckle broke the silence and she stared inquiringly at the earl.

"I was just thinking," said Giles. "This is exactly how I felt when I escaped from the schoolroom. I remember being totally bored by my tutor and slipping out, knowing eventually I would have to pay but at the time not caring. There was always that incredible sense of freedom, perhaps enhanced because I knew it would be short-lived."

"I know exactly how you feel," agreed Caroline, drawn into his reminiscence.

"You mean you escaped from your tutor?" he asked, turning toward her.

He looked as if he had just awakened, hair slightly disheveled and eyes filled with a sensuous inertia. She pulled herself back to the subject at hand.

"I did not have a tutor but a governess. And while we are confessing, I will admit the unthinkable for a female. I beg you will not condemn me as a bluestocking, but I liked most of my studies."

"Your secret is safe with me," he assured her. "But what caused you to hide away?"

"Drawing," she pronounced solemnly

"Drawing?"

"Yes. While I readily admit a propensity for studies, and even an inordinate fondness for music and dance, art was my downfall. I could not even render a crooked line crooked, or so said my drawing master."

Lord Castleton's chuckle grew louder as he lounged back against the rock on which she sat.

"It is not funny, my lord," she said, looking stern. "I drove the poor man to distraction. I fear I was the only failure of his career, which I'm sure ended as soon as he left our home. He said that while my sense of color was good, he could not distinguish at all between animals and people in my feeble attempts."

"And so you bid him a fond farewell, I presume?"

"Yes, my lord," she replied demurely. "But not before I completed his portrait as a remembrance of his stay. You see, I wanted to make sure he would not change his mind at the last instant," she finished innocently.

Giles had given up all attempts at stifling his laughter. "Minx. You were probably a terror when you wanted to be," he said, pulling her down beside him.

"Only when pushed, my lord. I could also be very good, as my papa would tell you." Resigned to his closeness, she remained quiet in his grasp, relishing their intimacy.

"I'm sure you could," he answered, looking into her eyes.

His breath fanned her cheek, and she inhaled the masculine scent of him mingled with leather and fresh linen.

"Are there any other confessions you wish to make?" he asked, holding her gaze. "They say it's good for the soul."

"No, my lord. I've confessed too much as it is," she admitted lightly, fearing it was true.

"Nay. Too little to give me a hold on you," he replied, noting her anxiety and attempting to mitigate it. "I had thought to be able to wrest your secret recipes from you, but an inability to draw is not enough."

The shadows left her eyes and he was glad he had not pressed her. "Come," he invited, rising suddenly and pulling her up with him. "Our mounts are rested. We were going to visit Lucy, so let's be on our way."

The Johnson farm was their next stop, where they found Lucy and a swarm of Johnson children playing under the oak trees in the yard. Lucy was happy to see her mother, and when the earl placed her on Palisades for a few moments, she gave him her usual affectionate pat on the face. After a lengthy visit, Caroline and Giles continued their ride.

They visited an empty cottage to judge its suitability for the school, then spent the remainder of the afternoon in a carefree romp over the countryside. They stopped at several of the farms for a drink of cool cider and caught up on the local gossip. Caroline and Giles were welcomed everywhere, the people's eyes full of hope, for the master's happiness followed them.

"You know we must return," Caroline reluctantly suggested some time later. "We have been gone far too long already."

His sigh could be heard over the hoofbeats. "I know. I just want to prolong this time as much as possible. But you're right, we must turn back."

The silence deepened the nearer they drew to Castleton.

"This is the first time in weeks that I've not looked

211

forward to returning home," he remarked unexpectedly.

Caroline nodded in agreement.

He allowed the silence to grow, thinking of the changes that had occurred over the past weeks. If Caroline knew what she had accomplished, she would not be so eager to leave. Perhaps he had not expressed himself well enough.

"I think I've told you before, but it bears repeating," he began. "When I first arrived in England, I couldn't consider returning to Castleton with my parents gone. I cut a swath through London before realizing nothing would change their deaths or the carnage I had seen on the Peninsula. So I came here with few expectations, and my fears became reality. Not only was my family gone, but the home I longed for was in disarray."

Caroline rode quietly at his side, attentive but allowing him to express his thoughts uninterrupted.

"I even considered returning to the Continent to avoid the emptiness surrounding me. I had no incentive to make matters right and did not even know if the results would be worth the trouble."

Giles paused, dark eyes sweeping over the surrounding countryside. Rich pastures spread green and lush on either side of the road, meeting golden cornfields or the cool dim shadows of forest. It was this he had dreamed of while shivering in the penetrating dampness of Spain. This, and something more. Something then indefinable but now ever so real, he thought, his gaze returning to touch the woman by his side. Only the creak of saddle leather and jingle of bridles broke the silence.

Lord Castleton would not admit his motive, but it was imperative she realize the place she held in his life. "But it became worthwhile again, Caroline, and you were the catalyst."

"I did no more than any other would do in my place," she protested.

"No one else could take your place, my dear," he replied sincerely. "You brought the house to life and gave me a reason for remaining." He abruptly checked his speech, realizing where his words were leading. It was the emotion of the moment, he rashly concluded, that brought him to the point of offering more than his protection to the lady. He shook the words from his mind and continued with forced humor.

"Of course, Denton credits you with helping me fill out my clothes again properly, and the staff is thrilled that I've regained my boyish spirits. Definitely, you've been my savior. I seem to recall voicing that opinion on your first evening."

"And I recall reminding you I am not of another world but of this one." Caroline was grateful the seriousness of the moment had passed. She needed no reminder of the weeks spent at Castleton. Each one was burned into her memory and would remain so long after she left. Encouraging him would be too easy, accepting what he offered too sweet to contemplate, despite the inherent danger to her and Lucy, as well the accompanying social condemnation. "It is these worldly things, my lord, including your newly acquired reputation as a successful host, that recalls me to my duty." She urged Lady into a canter that brought them back to Castleton in record time.

In the stable yard, he reached up to lift her down. "I remember another memorable parting here, Caroline. The first time I sampled this," he said, tracing his finger across her lower lip.

Seventeen

"You know you should not," she answered, eyes closed in pleasure at his touch.

"It's much too late to tell me that now," he murmured in her ear, seeming to have found a favorite spot for his lips to rest. "We've come too far. But I am resolved to emulate Charles and behave as a gentleman should." He released her and stepped back. "Although not completely to my liking, I feel I've acquitted myself admirably today."

He stood like a young boy awaiting praise for the ultimate sacrifice. Caroline had been aware of a difference in his attitude toward her. The attraction was still there, but it was tempered by a gentler element. A spark of hope surged through her, quickly extinguished by the thought of Mary.

"Thank you, my lord. It makes my existence here much easier, you know. Soon you will have Mrs. Davies back and need no longer worry about remembering your best behavior, but I vow she will tolerate nothing untoward from you."

Lord Castleton's ride with Caroline had shaken him from his complacency. He could not view her only as an object of desire, when he had come so close to offering for her. Yet, he was not ready to admit that she was necessary to make his life complete in all respects. It was not easy for a man who had pledged never to leave himself vulnerable to emotional pain to admit he was wrong; to realize that in order to live life to its fullest, he must take that chance again and entrust his soul to another's care.

Instead, he viewed it as unhealthy to dwell on the woman so, and the earl was determined to remove her from his mind as well as from his body. Since Charles had indicated his intentions toward Caroline, Giles would play the noble and give his friend a clear field, while proving to himself another woman could successfully take her place.

The earl set out on his quest the next day at luncheon. Mary was seated on his left, and putting aside his initial impression of her, he spent the meal trying to draw her into conversation. Despite his attempts, he could extract but the barest civilities from the girl, and those boringly commonplace. Perhaps he was being unfair expecting her to be interested in an estate she had not seen. He would remedy that on the morrow by showing her around. She might be just as engrossed as Caroline once she was familiar with Castleton.

Late the next afternoon Giles slammed into the library, causing Charles to drop the book he was examining.

"Sorry, my friend. I'll just choose something and get out of your way. You don't look in the mood for casual conversation this afternoon."

"Damn right," growled the earl. He had slammed in and out of more rooms, thrown his crop, pounded his fist, and drunk more in the last sennight than during the entire Peninsula campaign. Where had his hard-won peace gone? It had flown along with the arrival of the house party, as he had known it would.

"Maybe you should take your book and find Miss Langdon; teach her to read, so she'll have more conversation than 'Yes, my lord' and 'No, my lord.' " Giles filled a glass with brandy, swallowed it down, and splashed it full again.

"That bad, eh?" Charles offered sympathetically.

"Worse. Not only is she the worse milk-and-water miss I've ever known, but she has no interest in anything on the estate. She was as responsive to the tenants as a lump of clay," he answered with disgust.

"Does this mean I cannot wish you happy, Lord Castleton?" the blond man teased.

"I'm in no mood for your wit, Charles. And no, you may not wish me happy, for that was never my intention," he protested.

Charles pulled several books from the shelves. "Somehow, I feel Mrs. Langdon has a different opinion," he observed blandly, flipping through the pages.

"The woman will misconstrue anything to fit her ideas," snapped Giles. "She happened to be near when I invited the Grenvilles to Castleton and wormed her inclusion in the invitation. She's unsuccessfully tried to match her daughter with every available man in town. Since I was newly returned, she thought to hoodwink me before I knew what was happening."

"Well, since I have no advice to offer and you deserve some peace, I'll toddle along. Caroline's waiting to begin our reading," Charles informed him, uttering the final affront of the day.

As the door closed, Giles's glass shattered in the fireplace, adding another offense to his rapidly expanding list.

Caroline had observed Mary and Giles depart in the landau, and her heart plunged to the nether regions of her stomach. Shortly thereafter, she was summoned to Mrs. Langdon's room.

"There you are, girl. You certainly took your time," she complained.

"I came as quickly as I could, madam," Caroline replied shortly. "I do have household duties and a convalescing guest."

"Yes, I've seen very well how you care for Mr. Dalton. Thinking to sink your claws into him now the earl has escaped you?" she asked maliciously.

"The earl has not escaped me, since I never thought to trap him, as you do. Now, if you have only brought me here for insults, I shall leave you." Caroline turned angrily toward the door.

"Don't get on your high horse with me," warned Mrs. Langdon. "Remember what I know."

"Let's not go through this again, stepmother." The emphasis on the familiar appellation was self-explanatory and the older woman beat a hasty retreat.

"Well, yes. That is to say, I wish a tour of the house," she demanded bluntly.

"Why on earth would you want to see Castleton?" asked Caroline, surprised.

"Because Mary obviously cannot stand the strain of your company while showing her around. Naturally, we must know the house we . . . she's to live in after her marriage and the changes that we . . . she might wish to make. I'm looking it over in her stead." The victorious expression on her face was unmistakable.

Caroline steeled herself and guided Mrs. Langdon through the manor house. She introduced her to the staff and was forced to listen while her stepmother blithely reeled off who must go and who could stay, as easily as she had dispensed with the heirloom silver, the green furnishings in the countess's suite, and the earl's favorite wingback chair.

"I assume you know his lordship took Mary out this morning?" the older woman gloated, watching for her reaction.

"Yes. I saw them from the upstairs window," Caroline answered, remaining outwardly calm. She would not expose her unhappiness at the situation.

"No doubt wanting to show her off to the tenants," Mrs. Langdon continued, bent on punishing Caroline for her interferences.

Caroline could offer no more than a brief rejoinder through clenched teeth. "No doubt."

"You see," Mrs. Langdon declared triumphantly, "I was right in not allowing Mary to marry that upstart Alveston. She would now be an impoverished widow saddled with a squalling brat instead of being courted by an earl."

"And I still say she would have had a period of happiness versus a lifetime of sorrow," shot back Caroline, unable to allow her to rejoice in victory.

"Would that put food on her table?" demanded Mrs. Langdon viciously.

"You know I would have provided for Mary as I have for her child these years," Caroline replied, weary of having the same quarrel again.

"For as long as it amused you," Mrs. Langdon said, seeing her dejection and thinking she had finally won. "Then she would have been in the street, most likely."

Caroline would never be able to sway her stepmother's stance and, in truth, it was no longer important. The past could not be changed and it seemed the future had been decided. She would endure the next few days with the poise she had acquired over the past years. Withdrawing to the sanctuary of her hard-won composure, Caroline met the hostile scrutiny of her stepmother's stare. Mrs. Langdon's elation faltered before her steady gaze.

"I think you've seen everything there is to see, madam," stated Caroline in a steady voice. "Now I must attend to my duties."

An unspoken truce fell between Caroline and Mrs. Langdon after the ill-fated tour. The older woman had indicated the only decision left was when the betrothal would be announced.

Accepting that Giles was truly lost to her, Caroline

attempted to conceal her pain. Unable to lavish care on Lucy, she redoubled her attentions on her recovering patient.

Lord Castleton's lips twisted into a bitter smile as he observed Caroline's renewed dedication to Charles. He avoided the two as much as possible without seeming inhospitable.

Charles was dissatisfied that his ruse was no closer to success, but he could think of no other way to bring Giles to his senses.

Lord Castleton scheduled a ball for two days before his guests' departure, intending it to serve as his reentry to neighborhood society.

Aware of Castleton's reputation, the entire staff threw themselves into the preparation, determined to live up to the past. The floor of the long-neglected ballroom was waxed and rewaxed. In addition to refreshments a late dinner would be served, and Caroline and Madeline worked diligently to contrive an acceptable menu.

When the earl inspected the room on the afternoon of the ball, he voiced his amazement that there were any flowers at all left in the gardens. His aloofness of the past week vanished, as he turned to Caroline and grasped her hands.

"I cannot thank you enough, my lady," he said warmly, forgetting for the moment his vow to remain distant, leaving the field clear for Charles.

Caroline blushed becomingly at his obvious sincerity, rendered silent by his touch.

The address had been spontaneous on the earl's

part, but he was quick to note she did not demur at its use.

"It is your staff you should thank, my lord," replied Caroline, finally regaining her speech. "They have devoted their entire energies to resurrecting the pride of Castleton."

"And you may be sure I'll let them know my sentiments," promised Giles. "But without your guidance, I fear the result would not have been the same no matter how sincere the effort."

"Thank you, my lord."

"Come, Caroline, our relationship seems to be regressing. There have been times when you have addressed me other than 'my lord.'" Her color intensified, and he knew she remembered as well as he. "Even Charles is granted more familiarity than I," he continued, wondering how his friend's suit was coming. "Could you not call me Giles this evening, if for no longer?"

"I will try, my lo . . . Giles," she stammered. "Although it will be difficult. I hope you will allow a few slips on my part."

Lord Castleton studied the features he had denied himself the past days. Her faultless complexion, which still held a hint of blush, the small determined chin that could raise so rebelliously, and the tip-tilted nose, which he had yet to discover how she could look down from at her height. His gaze moved to brows delicately arched over eyes that haunted him day and night. His lips curved in tender amusement at the tendrils of hair escaping its hotly contested confinement to wisp around the translucent skin of her temples and the graceful column of her neck.

Saving the best until last, the earl's insatiable eyes paid homage to her lips.

Dear God, those lips would drive him mad with the want of tasting them! His nostrils flared with the effort of controlling the need to cover them with his own.

"My dear, I would allow you much more than that," he promised, hands tightening on hers, suddenly blindingly aware he could not give her up, even to his best friend's honorable intentions.

"I must check on Charles," she uttered reluctantly, yet remaining in his grasp.

"Of course, you must," he agreed, happy to have gained a small victory. "He's coming down this evening, isn't he?"

"I couldn't force him to miss it. He's so much improved, he's a different man." The earl's touch emboldened her and she brazenly curled her fingers around his.

"Not in everything. I understand he's still urging you to accept your previous position at Cresthill," he grumbled, distracted by the response of her fingers entwined in his.

"Yes, but he knows I'll make no decision until Mrs. Davies returns."

"And do you plan on taking Madeline with you if you go and leave me starving once again?" he teased, now more confident she had feelings for him.

"Madeline is able to make up her own mind, but I feel she's well satisfied here. Mr. Dalton is also aware you've offered me a position in London."

So Charles had not proposed yet, he mused. A glimmer of hope began to flicker. Eugenia and

Charles had been in one another's pocket of late, and he wondered if the object of Charles's pursuit had changed.

Abruptly releasing his hold on Caroline, Giles ran agitated fingers through his black locks as he absorbed her words. An increasing sense of distaste arose when he considered his plans of seducing Caroline. He wanted more from her than mere physical release; he wanted to share each day with her, to see her heavy with his child, to grow old with her by his side.

"Ah, Caroline, we need to discuss that matter." He faltered, not knowing how to continue.

"You mean you want to retract your offer?" She had been preparing herself for this moment but was still not ready to hear him declare his intentions toward Mary. "I can understand you and your bride would not want a child about in the close confines of your London home," she said, rushing into speech before he could frame an appropriate reply. "I'm sure I'll have no problem in finding another position if I should decide against returning to Cresthill."

"Caroline, that is not at all what I meant," he said, cutting in on her nervous chatter with exasperation, wondering where in the damnation a bride, other than herself, entered the picture.

A kitchen maid appeared almost magically and bobbed a curtsey. "Ma'am, cook would like to see you immediately." She turned quickly and disappeared into the hall.

"My God, Caroline. Do you always keep people lurking around corners to summon you at crucial points in our dealings with one another?"

"No, my lord. Perhaps it's just fate and we should bow to it."

"Never!" he protested strongly to her retreating back. "And we are not finished with this yet!

Eighteen

Charles had insisted Caroline attend the ball and solicited Giles to add his weight to the argument. Yielding to their combined entreaties, a sense of defiance dominated her spirit. She would dispense with Mrs. Alveston for the night and become Caroline Langdon again: an attractive young woman, dressing for the man she loved for the first and last time.

Leaving his suite early, Giles made his way toward Caroline's room to right the misunderstanding his words had caused earlier that day. He could not allow his bumbling to mar the evening. He tapped lightly on her door and, when it opened, was hypnotized by the graceful figure before him. His breath caught as she stepped back into a pool of candlelight, more beautiful than ever envisioned in his dreams.

A willow-green dress bared her shoulders and arms, while narrow puffed sleeves cradled an expanse of creamy skin above the revealing décolletage. The skirt fell straight from beneath her breasts, the filmy material clinging sensually to her figure with every move.

Caroline had dressed her hair high on her head, letting the shining tresses fall in curls, with wispy tendrils around her vivid face. No artificial color was needed on her cheeks as she returned his look with a proudly lifted chin.

"My lord," she acknowledged a little stiffly, the afternoon's conversation still between them. "Is there something I can help you with?"

Her beauty wiped the original purpose of his visit from his mind. "Yes, there is, Caroline. I will return in a moment. Please wait here for me."

A few minutes later the earl stepped through the door again, carrying a velvet case. "I would ask a favor of you, ma'am."

"Of course, my lord," she said with restraint.

"I would like you to wear this tonight." He opened the box exposing a large square-cut emerald surrounded by diamonds, suspended on a delicately wrought gold chain.

"I cannot," she said with a gasp, one hand pressed to her breast in consternation.

"What? Are you not going to say it isn't proper?" he teased, feigning amazement.

"I'm unable to even say that," she confessed faintly. "I'm overwhelmed with the honor, but I could not do it."

"Caroline, it's more than a whim that I ask. This was the bride gift from my father to my mother. She wore it at our ball before I left for the Peninsula. It's the last picture I hold of her. It would make her spirit live again if you would consent to wear it tonight."

"Your own bride should wear it," she protested, thinking of Mary.

"Since I do not yet have a bride, I would be honored if you would agree. You will bring it to life again, and it needs that as much as I did when we met."

Tears glistened in Caroline's eyes, producing a luminous quality to rival the gems. "You play shamelessly on my feelings, my lord, and I see you will not allow me to say no. I doubt even the most hard-hearted person could refuse your plea."

She turned and lifted the gleaming curls, baring her neck to him. He fastened the necklace around her throat with unsteady hands. He yearned to press his lips to her soft skin but controlled his desires. Emotions stretched tight between them, and he knew it would take very little for them to explode. He wanted more time when that happened than was now available.

Caroline moved to sit in front of the satinwood dressing table. The earl's powerful body filled the mirror as he followed, coming to stand close behind her. The emerald and diamonds sparkled with life against the creaminess of her skin.

Caroline had heard whispers that courtesans installed mirrors over their beds and she now understood why. Her senses flared as she watched his hands possessively caress her shoulders, then trace the line of her neck, until his fingers lightly framed her delicate jawline on either side.

His reflection showed only to mid-chest in the mirror as his husky voice flowed, disembodied, from above her. "Now you are a princess," he pronounced seductively. "No, more regal. A queen."

"And which queen shall I say I am, my lord?" she asked, failing in a lightheartedness she did not feel.

"Giles, my lady. Remember, it is Giles for tonight." His voice was husky with desire.

"Giles," she repeated mechanically as his hands moved back to her shoulders, again gripping them possessively.

"Why, mine, of course." He bent and met her gaze in the mirror, the promise in his eyes unmistakable.

Caroline said not a word as he bowed, touched his lips to her bare shoulder, and strode from the room.

Standing outside the closed door, Giles summoned every trace of his precarious forbearance to resist the demands of his heart. Clenching his fists to keep from reaching out to open the door again, he moved unsteadily down the hall toward the sounds of the first carriage arriving.

Inside the candlelit room, Caroline sat staring at her reflection, feeling her heart thud heavily against the wall of her chest. What had she done by agreeing to wear the necklace? Lord Castleton could only infer that she was ready to grant him whatever favors he asked. The holy state of matrimony was reserved for Mary, leaving only the shadows of his life for her to occupy. A bitter taste filled Caroline's mouth as the irony of the situation touched her. She had given up respectability for Mary's child; now, because of that, Mary would have the man she loved.

The earl was at the door greeting his guests when Caroline and Charles descended the stairs to the ballroom, sparing her the immediate necessity of facing the consequences of her actions. She made her patient comfortable near the terrace doors, where a breath of fresh air would prove welcome in the crowded room.

Some time later, Mrs. Langdon and Mary entered, escorted by the earl. The older woman took it as a sign he was finally coming up to scratch, thinking perhaps the house party would end successfully despite Caroline's presence.

Lord Castleton seated the bedizened Mrs. Langdon with the matrons and led Mary onto the dance floor. He would perform his duty before seeking out Caroline, for once he held her in his arms, he would want no other.

As the dance ended, he returned Mary to her mother's side and allowed his glance to survey the room. His eyes locked with Caroline's and held.

Aware of his inattention, Mrs. Langdon followed his direction and was alarmed to see Caroline looking more beautiful than ever.

Since she had left Birchwood, the chit had matured and acquired a sense of composure that unsettled the older woman. Mrs. Langdon found her independence alarming, and her approaching majority threatened the tenuous hold the older woman had over her. It was only Caroline's ridiculous loyalty to Mary that allowed her any advantage at all.

Mrs. Langdon kept track of the earl during the evening. He performed his duty dances with a pleasing demeanor, but his attention returned repeatedly to Caroline.

Knowing the necklace her stepdaughter wore did not come from the Langdon family, Mrs. Langdon had one other explanation. The earl had furnished it.

If he and Caroline were not yet lovers, they would be soon. Their mutual desire was palpable tonight, and Mrs. Langdon did not want it consummated before the earl offered for Mary. After that, his life was his own.

Lord Castleton acquitted himself as benefited his station, then made his way across the room.

"Caroline. Charles," he acknowledged, executing a formal bow. "You may have noticed I've been an exemplary host this evening, dancing with every ablebodied female in the room. Now I have come to claim a reward."

Charles grinned warmly at his friend. Before the ball, Giles had knocked at his door and stiffly demanded an explanation of his intentions toward Caroline. Unable to make him suffer any longer, Charles admitted he had reconsidered asking for her hand in marriage. Relief filled the earl's voice as he thanked his friend and hurriedly left the room. If Charles was not mistaken, Giles was ready to make Caroline his own.

"I will say I never thought to see it, my friend. The best reward I can offer is the use of my chair and a footstool for your bruised toes."

"Thank you for your generosity, Charles. But I deserve to enjoy at least one dance this evening. I'm here to spirit away your nurse, if you can spare her for the space of a waltz."

"I couldn't leave Mr. Dalton. It's been a long night and I'm sure he's tired," objected Caroline. Being held in the earl's arms again would only make the break more unbearable when it came.

"I would be a poor testimonial to your healing if I couldn't abide a short time alone," Charles assured her. "Eugenia will be back as soon as this dance is over. It will do me good to see you enjoy yourself."

Giles raised an inquiring eyebrow. "Well, ma'am, what other excuses can you come up with quickly?"

"None, sir," she said truthfully.

A devilish grin lit his face. "Then I suggest you take your advice of this afternoon and bow to your fate, my lady."

"No, my lord, I believe I will curtsey," she replied pertly, suiting actions to her words.

With a youthful laugh, he captured her hand and led her onto the floor.

Giles pulled Caroline closer than was acceptable and guided her smoothly over the polished oak boards. Their bodies dipped and swirled in concert, until they were aware only of one another. He stared into the green pools of her eyes, rejoicing in the love he had been reluctant to admit these past weeks. He did not want Caroline as his mistress but as his wife. He knew with a certainty he loved her. Whether she was lowborn or highborn did not matter. The weeks before the house party were the happiest he had ever known. Since their forced separation and the threat of losing her, he had felt incomplete. With her in his arms he was whole again, dissatisfaction a thing of the past. He wanted to spend the rest of his life with this bewitching woman. When the music ended he grudgingly returned her to Charles, oblivious of the knowing smiles directed his way.

The guests had departed and the house settled down for the night. Servants removed the food, leaving the remainder of the cleaning until morning. Caroline made one last inventory of the rooms, said good night to the staff, and turned toward the stairs.

She caught a glimpse of herself in the hall mirror and realized she still wore the emerald necklace. Thinking she had seen Jervis convey a decanter to the library, she knocked on the heavy paneled door, pushing it open when she heard the familiar voice bid her enter.

"My lord, I'm sorry to interrupt . . ."

The earl silenced her with an uplifted hand. "The night is not yet over, Caroline. Remember our agreement."

"I came to return this, Giles," she said, softly touching the emerald lying warm against her skin. She had experienced many emotions this day toward the tall, dark man facing her and waited serenely for the final outcome of the evening.

Making no comment, he set down his glass and stepped forward as she lifted her arms to remove the necklace.

"Allow me, please," he said, staying her hands. She felt his gentle touch at the nape of her neck, and a rush of pleasure washed through her.

The earl's desire for Caroline was at a fever pitch, fueled by his newly realized emotions and their contact that evening. Her closeness, the scent of her, the warmth from her body, all taxed his control to the limit. He must tread carefully or he could not answer for the results.

Helping a woman remove her jewelry was an intimate service to perform and brought memories of the boudoir to his inflamed senses. He placed the necklace on the table without breaking their gaze, lifting first one hand and then the other, touching the inside of each wrist with his lips. Her fingers tentatively grazed his face as he held her hands captured, placing another kiss in each palm.

"We have much to talk about when we are once again private, my love." He gave her a smoldering look before adding, with a rueful grin, "The first being not to have another house party for a long time. Don't you agree?"

"Whatever you say, Giles," she murmured, still enthralled by his touch.

"And now I think you should retire while I'm able to allow it. Remember, there are only two more days before Castleton belongs to us again."

He turned her gently toward the door, then pulled her back into the circle of his arms. How could he have ever considered Caroline a passing fancy, to be used for a time then pensioned off? At this moment, he could not imagine life without her. He felt full of love and wanted to bathe her in it. Burying his face in her rose-fragrant hair, he held her for a long moment before loosening his grip.

"You must go, Caroline." His voice was hoarse with passion. "I hope you sleep better than I will."

"I doubt that I will," she confessed softly.

After she left the library, Giles prowled the room,

too restless to retire. Picking up his glass again, he sipped the fiery liquid, reviewing an evening that had been quite momentous for him. Admitting his love for Caroline was long overdue. He was anxious for them to be alone and smiled as he thought of their idyllic life. As soon as the house party removed, he would seek a special license. He was impatient to wed her and could not let her go now, no matter what her rules of propriety dictated. For her, he could solve any problem. For her, he could slay dragons.

Nineteen

The day after the ball had been deliberately left free from any planned activity. After a late luncheon, the ladies decided a short drive to river and a stroll along the shady banks might prove a pleasant and undemanding diversion.

Mrs. Langdon, Mary, Eugenia, and Georgana led the procession in an open carriage. Greatly fatigued from the previous evening, Charles followed in a second carriage with Caroline and Henderson in attendance, while Giles, Harry, and Squire Ransdall accompanied them on horseback.

Upon arriving at the river, Henderson selected a shady spot in a fragrant patch of grass and spread a blanket for his master to rest on. Caroline hovered solicitously around Charles, plumping pillows and offering refreshments, until Lord Castleton growled in discontent and stalked away.

He was immensely unhappy to see his lady's attention occupied by another so soon after he discovered himself in love. Love had never struck the earl, but having opened himself to it, he felt it a singular episode occurring only once in eternity. Furthermore, he deemed it highly irresponsible that whoever managed eternity had the poor taste to allow love to occur under such awkward auspices.

The party returned to the house to rest before dinner. Caroline's attention was claimed first by Charles and then by dinner preparations, before slipping away for a short visit with Lucy. Unusually impatient with his guests now that their visit was drawing to an end, Giles retired to the library to catch up on his correspondence. As he flipped through the accumulated letters, he found one from Robert Barnes at the War Ministry.

The events of last evening had supplanted his need for information on John Alveston. After admitting his love for Caroline, his curiosity about her background could wait until she chose to tell him. With little enthusiasm, he broke the seal.

Barnes wrote that John Alveston did indeed serve in the Peninsular War and had been reported killed in action at Barossa on March 5, 1811. However, there had been over twelve hundred British casualties alone, and the report of Lieutenant Alverston's death had proved to be in error. He was pleased to inform Lord Castleton that Lieutenant Alveston was now Captain Alveston and doing well in Canada. He hoped his news relieved the earl's mind. At the end of the letter, Barnes had scribbled a hasty postscript.

"By the way, unless Captain Alveston has married since he left England, your information concerning his wife and child is in error. He is still a single man."

Giles looked down to find the letter crumpled

tightly in a ball. What kind of game was Caroline playing?

He remembered the glaze of passion in her eyes the evening before, the heat of her skin beneath his hands. Was she playing him for a fool? Did she burn for everyone like that? Had she indulged Alveston without benefit of marriage? The letter was compressed even tighter as thoughts raced through his mind.

He imagined a younger Caroline, increasing and unmarried, with nowhere to turn. Society was a cruel and censorious world. A man could satisfy his most depraved inclinations with seldom a repercussion, while only a slight faux pas could ruin a woman. An unwanted pregnancy would mean ostracism for both mother and child.

His clenched fist slammed the desktop as he thought the worst. Had Caroline actually shared a loving relationship with Alveston and taken his name for the child's sake when she thought him dead? Or was the child even his? Although he now knew about Alveston, Caroline's past was still shrouded in secrecy.

His thoughts grew increasing chaotic. He had been out of the country and did not know the on-dits from three years ago. Perhaps Caroline had been a Fashionably Impure and had chosen a name at random from the casualty list during her pregnancy. It was not unknown for poverty-stricken ladies to join the muslin set. Caroline was beautiful enough to attract any man's attention and could command a high price for her charms. Anger and disgust rose to choke him.

The Earl of Castleton sat in his library until the afternoon sun quit the windows, asking question but getting no answers.

It was fortunate the staff could go about their chores without strict supervision, for Caroline was totally distracted the day following the ball. Giles had been very tender the night before, not forcing himself on her even when the opportunity was ripe. Was he softening her up for the final assault on her virtue? He was a man of the world and, without a doubt, knew her feelings toward him.

Watching Mary and Lord Castleton together over the past few days, Caroline could find no indication of affection on either side. In fact, many times she felt they avoided one another's company. If Mary and the earl were not contemplating marriage, she owed nothing more to her stepmother.

If Giles offered marriage, instead of the carte blanche he had so vehemently denied, she could accept, then reveal the truth about Lucy. After their marriage, she would provide a settlement for Mary and remove her from her mother's influence. Caroline's inheritance was made to her alone, and she could dispose of it any way she wished. But first she must know what was in the earl's heart and mind.

The outing that day had further tired Charles, and he took dinner in his room that evening. Giles assumed Caroline was with him, cajoling him to eat the sustaining food Madeline had prepared. Closeted in the library, ruminating on Caroline's transgressions, had brought Lord Castleton to a tightly controlled frenzy.

Barely able to keep his attention on polite conversation during a meal he did not taste, Giles paired his guests off for an evening of cards, then hastily excused himself pleading business. He beckoned Jervis into the library and sent him to request Mrs. Alveston join him at her convenience. He would give Caroline a chance to explain her past before condemning her actions. If she cared for him, she'd give him her trust and confidences.

Giles leisurely rose to his feet behind the pedestaled mahogany desk when Caroline entered the room a half hour later. He indicated her usual chair and settled into the opposite one, as he had done on numerous occasions over the past weeks.

"Would you care for some refreshment, Mrs. Alveston?" he asked lifting his snifter.

"No, thank you, my lord," said Caroline, surprised by his formality after the previous evening. "I must return to Charles soon. He's rather restless tonight."

"As am I, ma'am. As am I," muttered the earl. From beneath hooded eyes, he examined this woman who had almost brought him to his knees.

Caroline was puzzled by his summons, thinking at first they would talk about the future he had hinted at last night. But his face remained impassive and filled with a coldness that chilled her to the bone.

The earl reached for the crystal decanter and poured with a lavish hand. "I'm also weary of Mrs. Langdon's unpleasant voice praising her daughter's accomplishments. I wonder she doesn't realize that true proficiency need not be touted but is apparent. Such as yours, Mrs. Alveston."

The last was said with an acrid sneer that caught

Caroline unawares. "Have I done something to upset you, my lord?" she asked, leaning toward him anxiously.

"Do not heed me, ma'am. As I indicated, I need some pleasing tones to soothe my injured sensibilities. Something I thought you might be able to furnish." He tossed back the remaining brandy and once again filled his glass with the amber liquid.

"Would you like Jervis to bring some coffee?" she asked, eyeing the rapidly declining level in the bottle.

"Ah. Do not worry, my very correct lady. The Earl of Castleton can hold his liquor. If I can survive war and the rigors of London's marriage mart, I will certainly not buckle under a little drink." The hastily consumed brandy arrived in the earl's empty stomach with a jolt. Stormy eyes regarded Caroline over the glass rim in leisurely contemplation.

"Have I told you how well you look out of that infernal black, Caroline?" His voice was soft and intimate, but a core of hardness contradicted his tone.

"I believe you have mentioned it on occasion, my lord," replied Caroline. She did not understand the mixture of contempt and anger she heard in his voice.

"But it deserves more than just a mention, my dear."

Caroline stiffened at his cold endearment. The violence emanating from him was not imagined, and a chill ran down her spine.

"It is not noteworthy, my lord. Women dress in colors other than black every day," she replied carefully, endeavoring to keep her voice even.

"But not women such as you, Caroline, after such a long time hiding your attributes. I wonder what re-

241

ally changed your mind?" he asked with a twisted smile that did not warm his eyes.

"I told you, it was more than time, my lord." She paused. "And Mr. Dalton requested it."

"Ah, yes. Charles. And will you give him everything he requests, Mrs. Alveston?" His voice was all hard cutting edges.

"I do not know what you mean, my lord. I've attempted to make his stay comfortable. I hope he has no complaints," she replied, making a concerned effort to hide the agitation she felt.

"I'm sure Charles has no criticism, my dear, other than not having your company enough. He's made no secret of his admiration for you," Giles mocked.

Caroline remained silent, wondering where this was leading but not daring to ask.

"And your late husband, madam, would he be happy to see you put off your mourning and resume a normal life again?" The black eyes pinned her to the chair, seeming to strip away every secret she held.

"I . . . John was a lighthearted person. He wanted everyone to enjoy life to its fullest," stammered Caroline, feeling her fingernails bite into her palms.

"So he would give you his blessings?" inquired the earl. "I'm sure you're happy you married before he left," Lord Castleton continued without giving her time to answer. "It's very uplifting for a man to know he has a devoted wife at home. Did you have much time together before he left, Mrs. Alveston? Or was he snatched away immediately after the wedding?" *Dear God*, he thought behind the cold facade. *Let her tell me and put an end to this punishment for us both.*

"I cannot understand your interest in past history, my lord," said Caroline, not knowing the relief with which her confession would be greeted.

"I tell you I'm weary of this house party and its insipid women," he declared impatiently. "I'm only trying to escape by living vicariously through your experiences. Surely there's nothing to be ashamed of in your marriage. After all, you have a lovely child and fond memories." His anguished thoughts raced again. *Please, Caroline, tell me. Make it right.*

Caroline could not deal with his innuendoes any longer. "Yes. I do have Lucinda, and every day I am grateful for her," she burst out, anger battling for the upper hand. "Now, if there's nothing else, my lord, I must return to my patient," she continued, hastily rising and swirling out of the room to escape his inquisition.

Defeat washed over the earl as Caroline's last words reached him. If her love had matched his, she would have taken the opportunity to explain her past. Finishing off the brandy, he ordered Jervis to bring another bottle. The footman reluctantly obeyed the command and was dismissed as soon as the cork was drawn.

Giles sat brooding, consuming a goodly portion of the new bottle, until the house was silent. His anger had turned to cold rage, and he desired nothing more than to punish the woman who he believed had played him false.

He no longer thought of her with pity. A helpless female taken advantage of by a thoughtless soldier and left behind to pay the price. John Alveston had been erased completely from his mind, replaced by a

243

long succession of lovers who had enjoyed seeing her dressed only in her glorious hair.

That she should have been nothing more than a housekeeper and owed him only an honest day's work did not enter his brandy-ladened mind. He had conveniently forgotten his machinations to put her in his company and ultimately in his bed. No, she had led him on, or had misled him and played him for a fool. Had demanded respect when she was no better than any lightskirt. Even worse, for at least they plied their trade forthrightly, while she played him and his best friend against one another.

Well, he would be put off no longer. If she was for sale to the highest bidder, he could certainly offer her more than any other. By the time he finished with her, she would beg him to stay.

The earl rose slowly, moving carefully toward the door. He had drunk more than he had in many a day, but he could still negotiate the stairs. The entire household was abed except for Denton, who would be napping in his dressing room, waiting for him to retire. Even Jervis had finally deserted his post, Giles noticed as he made his way deliberately up the stairs, holding on securely to the smooth oak banister.

The upper floor was quiet, with all the doors closed. He passed his own chambers and stopped outside the door at the end of the hall.

Resting his ear against the wooden panel, he could hear no movement from inside. The earl guessed that by now Caroline was asleep, and he carefully turned the doorknob.

A candle guttered out on the table and dimly lit the figure lying on the bed. Caroline's hair spread in disarray over the pillow, framing her delicate face. Lord Castleton stood admiring what would soon be his.

She awoke suddenly with a gasp, seeing the figure standing over her.

"Don't be frightened, my dear," he said in carefully enunciated tones. "I'm not here to hurt you. Indeed, I hope to bring pleasure to us both."

She immediately recognized the liquor-induced anger from earlier in the evening. "My lord, it's late to be visiting. I'm sure whatever you want can wait until morning."

"It cannot wait until morning, Caroline," he disputed. "It has, in fact, waited far too long already, and I'm unwilling to be put off any further." He swayed slightly on unsteady legs.

"I don't understand, my lord," she said, pulling herself to a sitting position.

"Of course you do, my lovely one. You understand better than anyone. But just in case you've forgotten, let me read something to you." Giles fumbled in his pocket and removed the crumpled letter from the War Office. He frowned at the writing in the dim light.

"Well, suffice it to say the game's over. My considerate friend at the War Office has written to say that your dear departed husband is not so departed after all."

He heard another gasp from Caroline and watched as dismay spread across her face.

"That's right, my dear. Lieutenant Alveston is now Captain Alveston, and the news of his death has been highly overstated. In fact, the good captain is even now enjoying good health—and probably Indian maidens—in Canada."

245

Giles's anger and indignation escalated as he spoke. "Mr. Barnes goes on to inform me that not only is Captain Alveston not dead, but he is not now, and has never been, married."

Caroline sat up, her hand clutched convulsively at her breast, still silent.

"Nothing to say, Caroline? Have I rendered you speechless? I understand the malady very well. I spent several hours this afternoon in the same state, wondering how I could have been taken in so easily. By God!" he exclaimed in a pain-racked voice, incensed by his gullibility. "The war must have weakened me more than just physically. To have been so idiotic as to have thought you exactly what you seemed!

"To think, even after reading this," he raged, crushing the letter in his fist, "I was eager to understand and forgive your indiscretion. To have been so besotted as to give you an opportunity to explain and to have it thrown back into my face with a mask of innocence."

Caroline recoiled from his fury, now understanding the interview in the library.

"I find it no longer matters whether you actually knew Alveston," he continued as he loomed over her, "or merely borrowed his name for the convenience of a respectable front. He could have been one of the numerous others who I am sure have tasted your sweetness," he charged, needing to completely debase her.

"Now that I'm fully apprised of the situation, I think we can draw things to a speedy conclusion. I have a new offer, which you will accept if you value your privacy.

"As soon as the house is emptied of this everlasting company, we shall travel to London," he announced. "Rest assured, I will be more generous than any of your previous acquaintances. You need not turn a hand, only direct the servants. You will be able to keep your child with you, which is more than many would agree to.

"In short, you will have everything you want, madam, except freedom to indulge your passion with anyone else but me, until I tire of your delights. I first thought to set you up in a separate residence; however, I find I want you with me. Did all your admirers want more than a short frolic in bed, my dear? I can't wait to taste the attractions that engenders such devotion."

Caroline could find no response to this stranger.

"You see, I can be as coldhearted as you when I want something badly enough. And I do want you badly. Never doubt it. So much so that I will flout your highly touted propriety under my ancestral roof and not wait until we reach London to consummate our union. I want you here and now, and I shall have you," he vowed, determined her humiliation would be complete.

"Do not appeal to my honor as a gentleman," he sneered. "That has kept you safe thus far, my dear, but soon we shall be two of a kind, and neither of us will have any."

Taking another step toward the bed, the earl caught his boot in the rug and fell headfirst into the bedside table. Caroline heard a crack and looked down to see a trickle of blood seep from beneath the black hair across his forehead.

She slipped from beneath the covers to check his pulse, finding it slow and steady. Silently, she traversed the hall to the earl's suite, where Denton waited for his master. She explained in a hushed voice that Lord Castleton had mistaken her room for his and had hit his head in the unfamiliar territory. Denton nodded gravely, and between the two of them, they managed to get the earl into his own bed without being discovered.

Returning to her room, Caroline pulled the wrinkled paper from under her pillow and found herself caught in a nightmare of her own making.

The earl's discovery had made it impossible for her to remain at Castleton. She would leave a message for Mary telling her of John's escape from death and urging her to immediately travel to Birchwood. After she explained the situation to her stepsister, they would search for John if that was her wish. If John Alveston was the man she thought him to be, he would willingly accept Lucy as his daughter. And what of Mary? Once she knew John was alive, would she change her mind about her daughter? Must Caroline give up Lucy, too? It was too much to think about now, for Caroline knew she must be gone by morning.

Twenty

Mrs. Langdon was a heavy sleeper, and it took Caroline some time to shake the older woman awake.

"Good Lord, girl. What is it?" her stepmother protested. "Why are you waking me in the middle of the night? You know I must have an uninterrupted evening of sleep."

"Then I fear you will be discommoded tonight, madam," replied Caroline calmly. "I need your help if you want Mary to make her match."

The older woman pulled herself quickly from beneath the bedcovers and reached for her robe. "What has happened, Caroline? You do not overset easily, so tell me all."

"There is naught to tell," answered Caroline, wisely keeping her counsel. "Other than you have no choice but to release my inheritance now. You must give me a letter for the solicitor tonight and I shall leave before first light."

"I will do nothing of the sort. What kind of fool do you take me for?" objected Mrs. Langdon, her nightcap bobbing in indignation.

"The worst kind if you think I'm trying to put something over on you." Caroline looked down at the woman, seeing a similar scene some three years before. "When I left Birchwood," she continued firmly, "I walked out with no demands. I was naive and eager to right what I perceived as a great wrong single-handedly. Since then, the circumstances have changed and so have I. Now I must disappear from sight, or I fear your grand plans for Mary's match will be washed away." Caroline did not add they would be anyway, after Mary found out John was alive.

Mrs. Langdon stared at the composed young woman standing before her, quickly weighing her chances of wedding Mary to the earl without giving in to Caroline's demands. Something of import had occurred between the earl and her stepdaughter. If their desire had been happily consummated, the last thing Caroline would want to do would be run away. Caroline certainly did not seem overcome by joy, and Mrs. Langdon decided to gamble that her absence would push the lonely earl into Mary's cold little arms.

"All right. I'll give you a sum of money. Enough to see you and the child through modestly," she agreed, still unwilling to admit total defeat.

"No, madam, that will not do," replied Caroline in a hard voice. "I will have my inheritance and my home. You've kept me from it too long. I have kept my side of the bargain, bypassing an opportunity to reveal everything to Lord Castleton with complete forgiveness. Now you will keep to yours," she continued dispassionately, "or I will create a scandal that will ruin any chance you ever have for Mary to marry riches. And do not doubt I will do it."

"This is blackmail, you wretched girl!" cried Mrs. Langdon.

"How can I blackmail you for my own property? I'm merely stating facts," Caroline returned placidly, concealing the turmoil churning within her breast.

Mrs. Langdon studied her stepdaughter and finally acknowledged defeat. Caroline's steely composure convinced her that the young woman would do exactly as she threatened. Now was the time to cut her losses and seize the only possibility left. She sat down at the small rosewood desk and began to write.

Settled in her bed again, Mrs. Langdon realized Caroline's disappearance must be kept from the earl for as long as possible. Although the older woman had never believed in the silly conventions of love, she knew those who did were prone to unorthodox starts. The more distance and time between her stepdaughter and Lord Castleton, the better chance Mary would have to snare him. Her treacherous mind became busy with delaying tactics for the morrow.

The earl groaned and opened his eyes to bright sunlight filtering into his bedroom. Denton dozed, slumped fully dressed in a nearby chair.

"Denton, what has happened?" he croaked, waking the valet from his light slumber.

Rising stiffly from his cramped position, the valet replied, "You fell last night, my lord." He moved to the bed, plumping up the pillows behind Lord Castleton's throbbing head, as the earl inched upward to lean back against the headboard. "Just a slight bump," Denton assured him. "Nothing more serious than a bad headache, I'll wager."

"You had best be right, for it feels as if the whole 95th is marching from ear to ear right now. It must have been more than a bump," he insisted argumentatively, "since my memory is so clouded." Shaking hands began a hesitant ascent toward the offending object setting on his shoulders, decided the end result was not worth the effort, and returned to grip the counterpane.

"Well, you had a bit too much brandy, my lord, so you might not remember it all clearly," the valet answered circumspectly.

"Nonsense. I haven't been that cup-shot since my youth. As I remember, I fell coming up the stairs last night." Giles looked inquiringly at the silent man, hoping he would volunteer information about the blank space in his memory. Denton busied himself straightening the bedcovers.

"Come, now, Denton. We haven't been together these many years for you to grow missish with me. Tell me the worst. And stop jerking me around so," he commanded, grabbing each side of the bed as if caught in a hurricane at sea.

"Well, my lord," Denton began slowly, his words gaining momentum as he spoke, wishing to get them out as soon as possible. "Actually, you were in Mrs. Alveston's bedchamber when you fell, hitting your head on a table," he ended in a rush.

Giles closed his eyes and lay back once again. Pieces of the last evening began filtering into his shattered consciousness. He groaned again, this time with remembrance instead of pain.

"Do you wish some coffee, my lord?" asked Denton, relieved the worst was over.

"Yes, Denton, that's as good a place as any to begin."

It was almost luncheon before the earl descended to greet his guests. He again pleaded business to excuse his absence, and they went amicably in to the dining room. Making a show of pushing food around on his plate, he consumed large quantities of strong black coffee, ignoring the wineglass at his place setting.

"You're not touching your wine, my lord. An excellent vintage, I must say," said Mrs. Langdon, recognizing the signs of overindulgence and sadistically relishing his pallor as she raised her glass toward him.

He swallowed, answering with difficulty. "Thank you, ma'am. I find I prefer coffee after I'm closeted with estate duties, but don't let my abstinence diminish your enjoyment. Have you decided on an entertainment for the afternoon?" he asked, shifting the attention from himself.

"We saw a wonderful old church near the village upon our arrival and thought to view it," responded Mrs. Langdon. "As you know this is our last day, and dear Mary has expressed a wish to spend it at a local sight."

Giles glanced at the young woman toying with her food, much as he was, not looking at all interested in the conversation, let alone the local church. Obligated to accommodate his guests, he smiled considerately and agreed a visit to the vicarage would indeed be pleasant.

While the ladies readied themselves for the trip, the earl sent Jervis to request Mrs. Alveston join him in the small saloon, thinking it best not to meet in the ill-fated library again. After some delay Jervis returned, saying Mrs. Alveston was visiting her daughter.

Lord Castleton scowled, unhappy to put off the interview, but the arrival of the party in the front hall kept him from pursuing it. Advising Jervis he would see Mrs. Alveston when he returned, he once again forcefully reminded himself of his duties as host and escorted his guests on what he sincerely hoped would be their last outing together.

The afternoon moved on leaden feet for the earl. Mrs. Langdon inspected every nook and cranny of the old stone church, insisting on a tour of the nearby cemetery. By the time her curiosity was appeased, the entire party heaved a collective sigh of relief.

Upon their return the earl once again occupied the small saloon and rang for Jervis to bid Mrs. Alveston join him. After a wait that seemed interminable, the elderly footman hesitantly opened the door and approached the earl. "I regret to inform you, my lord, that Mrs. Alveston is no longer here."

"What do you mean, no longer here? Of course she's here. Where else would she be?" he questioned, black brows drawing together ominously.

"I do not know exactly where she is, my lord. I only know where she isn't. And she is no longer in the house," related the servant, stepping nimbly aside as the earl charged toward the door.

Giles strode angrily through the hall and took the stairs two at a time. He threw open the door to Caroline's room, slamming it back against the wall and startling a maid who was stripping the bed.

"Where is Mrs. Alveston?" he demanded of the white-faced girl.

"I don't know, my lord. I was just told to turn out the room." She stood frozen to the spot by the enraged man before her.

Furious, he jerked open the dressing room door and pulled out bureau drawers. He was reminded of their first encounter, for every trace of Caroline had been removed as if she had never been. But he well knew she had been there, having left more emptiness than just in her room.

He descended to the kitchen and drew Madeline out into the garden. "Where is she, Mrs. Crawford? She wouldn't leave without telling you."

"I know she's gone, my lord, but that's all. She wouldn't leave her direction. She didn't want your anger to fall on me or any other of the staff. A stable hand took her to the posting inn. I tried to talk her into staying, to right what was bothering her, but she would have none of it. Said things had gone too far to solve. I'll miss her terribly," wailed Madeline, tears starting in her eyes.

"So will I, Mrs. Crawford," he said, patting her heaving shoulder. "But try not to worry. I'll find her and bring her back. Your position here is secure, for I blame no one but myself for this coil."

He left the tearful woman crying into her apron

and interviewed the groom, with little more results. After picking up the child at the Johnsons', he had deposited them at the inn before daylight that morning.

Lord Castleton called for Palisades and rode to the inn, which was a busy posting house on the main road. The owner only slightly remembered a woman and child who might have taken a coach to London, but could not swear to it.

Giles returned to Castleton in a thunderous temper. Pushing his way into Charles's room, past a startled Henderson, he ordered him out. Charles nodded and the valet made his escape.

"Where is she, Charles? Have you hidden her away at Cresthill? I swear, if you have, I'll call you out as soon as you're able," he stormed.

Unruffled, Charles regarded the pillar of outrage that confronted him. Over the years, he had seen Giles in many moods, but none as dark as this. "Perhaps you should tell me what's happened. I assume it involves Caroline."

"Of course, it involves Caroline. And if you know nothing of it, then I'm lost." The anger drained away and Charles saw his shoulders slump, defeat washing over him.

"It can't be all that bad, Giles. If you two have had a quarrel, I'm sure you can persuade her to come around," he reasoned.

It was a measure of his despair that the earl did not question Charles's knowledge of his love for Caroline. "It's too late for that, my friend. She's disappeared, and no one knows where."

"What! You let her leave and didn't try to stop

her?" Amazement flooded Charles's face. "If you allowed her to slip away from you, Giles, you're a fool," he stated flatly.

"I had no chance to stop her. She left in the middle of the night while I, a disciplined ex-officer of the Crown, was lying in a drunken and unconscious state." He paced to the window and stared blindly out over the park.

A low whistle came from Charles. Only in their early years, when they were first introduced to drink, had he seen the earl completely disguised. Whatever had occurred between the two was more than just a lover's skirmish. "What happened, Giles?"

"Too much to tell. Suffice it to say I accused her of despicable acts and tried to force my attentions on her. You were my last chance. If she's not at Cresthill, she's left the vicinity and I may never find her."

"Yes, you will. As soon as I'm able, I'll help you. In the meantime, you must go to London and engage the Bow Street Runners. They've been very successful with matters such as these. There's still hope, my friend."

"And what if I do find her, Charles? She'll only reject me again, and I can't blame her." He turned and met his friend's gaze with desperate eyes.

"You have high powers of persuasion, Giles. I know you'll be able to convince her of your mistake. For you know that's what your accusations must be. Caroline could never be anything other than what she is—an honorable lady to the tips of her lovely fingers."

"I still don't know who she is," admitted Giles.

"But it doesn't matter. Our troops survived on the Peninsula in ways we wouldn't consider here in England. If I condemned her for providing for herself and her child, I would be condemning my own existence."

Silence reigned for a time while both men pursued their thoughts. "Do you love her?" asked Giles, breaking the stillness.

"If she had let me," Charles admitted truthfully. "However, it was obvious early on that the two of you struck sparks I could never hope to equal. But she's a good friend and I'd like to help if I can."

"You're also a good friend to me," Giles said, reaching out to his faithful crony. "I don't deserve you or Caroline, and after last night, I fear she'll never want to hear my name again."

"Come, it couldn't be that bad. I'm confident you can change her mind," Charles said, returning the grasp.

"I'm going to try, but I must find her first. You know, I feel emptier now than when I returned home." Both men considered his words for a moment. "I must wait until the house is cleared tomorrow morning. I can't risk bringing scandal down on her head by abandoning members of the ton to pursue her. That will be an endless wait for me." He left the room, determined to be an unexceptional host until he could bid his guests goodbye.

Mrs. Langdon was extremely vexed as she was handed into the coach. She had barely been in time to keep Mary from discovering the note Caroline had left, telling her John was alive and to travel to Birch-wood, where they would initiate action to find him. She had been crazy to even think about trusting the deceiving chit.

And what had she gained? Lord Castleton had not offered for Mary after all. In fact, he seemed anxious for them to be on their way, and she knew exactly at whose door to lay the blame. She was sorry now that she had released Caroline's inheritance, but perhaps all was not forfeit. When the earl accepted Caroline was irretrievably lost, he might still offer for Mary. Forever hopeful, she charmingly thanked him with a sugarcoated tongue and invited him to call when he returned to town.

As soon as the coach cleared the gates, Giles was astride Palisades in search of Caroline. He could find no trace of her locally. She had told the servants at Castleton nothing of her destination, and the John-sons knew only that she was called to a sick relative. Nor had the innkeeper's memory improved with time.

Returning to the manor house, he ordered Denton to pack for London. Early the next morning, the valet oversaw the loading of the carriage and stepped aboard for a comfortable ride to town. The earl had left at sunup on Palisades, too restless to suffer through a carriage ride.

Giles reviewed his allegations continuously while searching for Caroline. With his jealousy under con-trol, he knew instinctively she was not the woman he accused her of being. Whatever had happened three years before had gone into the making of the woman he loved and could not lose.

An illegitimate child did not mean her character was marred. Emotions ran high, particularly during the war, and he couldn't blame lovers for giving in to desire if confronted by a final separation. He was prepared to protect her from society's scorn once he found her.

When he did, he would beg her forgiveness and begin their relationship anew. If she rejected his proposal, then she and Lucy would have his protection without scandal. She could return to Castleton and he would remain in London if that was her wish.

Fear and despair engulfed him as time passed. It had been four weeks since Caroline and Lucy had vanished in the early morning light. Lord Castleton and his agents had scoured the countryside searching for a clue to her whereabouts. He had engaged runners in London to check all the lodgings for a hint of where she might have gone, but to no avail. The city was filled to overflowing with people eager to catch sight of the recently returned Duke of Wellington and to join in the victory celebrations. A woman dressed in black, as Giles was sure Caroline had been, together with a child, would have been swallowed up without a trace.

The earl could not rest without knowing they were safe. With no references, her chance of getting a position as a governess or a housekeeper was negligible. Knowing she would provide for Lucinda at any cost frightened him most, for her options were limited. When recriminations overcame him, he would curse himself again for his actions and fling himself outdoors, walking briskly, eyes moving continuously over the crowd, looking for a flash of auburn hair, knowing it hopeless but unwilling to admit defeat.

It was on one of these walks that he heard his name called. "Lord Castleton. I say, Lord Castleton, over here."

He turned to see Robert Barnes approaching. "Hello, Robert," he said, endeavoring to raise a smile for the short, rotund man.

"Giles. It's good to see you again, but not looking much better than I last saw you. I thought the country air was good for the constitution."

Giles had suffered from the weeks of continuous travel and worry, but did not know it was readily apparent to others. That Denton was unhappy with his clothes again did not signify any longer. There were more important things than the fit of his coat.

"I'm afraid I've been under somewhat of a strain lately, my friend, which has undone the beneficial effects of my rustication." He attempted another smile without success.

"Then perhaps I can bring you some cheer. Look who's just arrived."

Barnes stepped aside, indicating a figure behind him, and Giles looked into the face of Lucinda's father.

261

Twenty-One

"You must be John Alveston," said Lord Castleton. A band tightened across his chest as he confronted Caroline's lover. He could be no other, for Lucinda's hair and eyes were hauntingly familiar in the handsome face of the man standing before him.

"You have the advantage of me, my lord," replied the military man.

"But, Giles, I thought you knew Captain Alveston. Indeed, was concerned for him and his family," said Barnes with confusion.

"Robert, could you spare the captain for a short time? There are things that need to be said between us which are private." Lord Castleton's face confirmed the seriousness of his tone.

"Of course. Captain, I'll see you back at the office when you and his lordship are finished. We'll need to go over a few things before you depart." Giving one last curious look, Barnes walked away.

Alveston waited for Lord Castleton to speak. "Captain, shall we walk into the park where we may be private? What I have to say is for no other ears than your own."

"Of course, my lord. But I admit I'm thoroughly puzzled as to why you desire a confidential conversation with me. To my knowledge we've never met before, though I understand you served on the Peninsula."

"I did, sir. However, my military career has nothing to do with the topic I wish to pursue," he replied as they reached a bench off the main path.

After the two men sat, Giles hesitated before speaking. "Captain, forgive me for seeming overly inquisitive, and believe that what I am about to ask is not merely idle curiosity. Truth in our conversation could mean a change in both our destinies."

Alveston was struck by the earnest demeanor of the dark man beside him. "I will answer your queries to the best of my ability, my lord."

"Good," replied the earl, directing his stiff-faced gaze across the park. Then, without preamble, "Have you ever been involved with a woman named Caroline, Captain?"

There was silence. Then, just as shortly, "No."

"You have never been married?"

"No again, my lord."

"Have you ever been close?"

Alveston scrutinized the earl and judged the man was not aimlessly exploring his private life. After another moment of silence, the tight-lipped captain replied. "Before the war, I had hoped to marry, but the lady's mother felt me too far below her with no money or title." Giles heard the bitterness in his voice and felt sympathy for another who had lost his dream.

"Captain, I will apologize to you and your lady before I even ask this question. But I must know the truth. It is extremely important to us both," stressed Lord Castleton.

"Ask away," instructed the blond officer. "I promise I will not take offense."

"Is it possible that you and your lady have a child?" He felt the man stiffen beside him. "Captain, on my honor as a fellow officer," he swore, meeting his eyes, "I assure you whatever you say will go no further."

"It is that important?" Captain Alveston asked, holding his attention.

"More than you can ever know." Lord Castleton decided to encourage him with plain speaking. "The woman I'm searching for goes by the name of Caroline Alveston and has a child. They've been missing for a month and could be in want. I must find them."

He felt the tension go out of the captain. "And what did your Caroline Alveston look like?"

The earl described Caroline's appearance so vividly that there was no doubt he was deeply in love with the woman.

"I'm sorry to say, my lord, that your Caroline Alveston bears no resemblance to my Lucy." He bit his tongue at revealing his lady's name.

Giles jerked around. "Lucy? That's the child's name. Are you sure they are not one and the same?" he inquired anxiously. "She could have changed her appearance, you know. It's done all the time in the theatre."

"Perhaps she could have changed her hair color easily, which was blond, but her eyes were a beautiful shade of blue, definitely not green. And she was more petite than your description. Besides, Lucy was just a nickname her stepsister called her," he said, thinking one more indiscretion would do no damage. "Her real name was Mary Lucinda."

Lord Castleton's hands gripped his cane-head convulsively as the pieces began to fall into place. The strange relationship between the Langdons and his housekeeper. Caroline never actually referring to John Alveston as her husband. Her inexperienced, yet totally spontaneous responses to his advances. A surge of triumph shot through him when he realized she had never borne a child, let alone known a man. He would have his wish of introducing Caroline to the joys of love, if only he could find her.

"And do you know her stepsister? The one who called her Lucy?" he asked tensely.

"Well, of course, my lord. They lived together when I courted Lucy," Captain Alveston answered easily.

"What did she look like?" he questioned, his voice intent.

"Caroline? Why, she was slim but shapely, with vivid reddish hair and great green eyes, but she could never appeal to me as did ..." Alveston's voice ground to a halt, as the intelligence he uttered penetrated his own consciousness. "My lord, you do not believe that Caroline and I ... that we ... I assure you ..." he stammered, his face going red.

"No, I do not, Captain," he said, smiling at the embarrassed man. "But I do believe there is a child, bearing a striking resemblance to you, who would be pleased to meet her father."

Realizing the topic under discussion required time and privacy, the two men returned to the earl's townhouse. Closeting themselves in the library, each related his part of the story.

Lord Castleton heard a more detailed account of Mary and John's love, along with Mrs. Langdon's scorn for such an unworthy suitor. At their last meeting, knowing they might never see one another again, passion overrode good sense. The captain received only one letter from Mary after his departure, saying she was taking her mother's advice and wanted no more to do with him. In his despair, he had volunteered for service as far from England as possible.

John's grief turned to anger that Mary had concealed the news of their child. He had the same burning ambition as Giles to find Caroline and Lucy, but first he must deal with Mary.

"I cannot say why Caroline has your child, but I do know that Mary is extremely unhappy," offered the earl, empathizing with the officer's agony. "Initially, I thought Mary was worn down by such a harridan as her mother; now I recognize she no longer cared about her destiny. Don't suffer from the same mistake I made," he warned. "Listen to her explanations before you censure her actions."

Obtaining directions to the Langdons' rented townhouse, the two men reached the residence at an opportune moment. The door was opened to them just as the ladies were departing for a ride in the park.

Lord Castleton's broad form momentarily blocked their vision of the officer that stood close behind. Mrs. Langdon offered a welcoming smile, which froze in place as the earl stepped aside to reveal John Alveston. Mary gave a gasp of alarm, crumbling to the floor again as she had at Castleton.

"Good God, madam. Does she make a habit of this?" asked Lord Castleton as John bent to her side.

"My Lord, how dare you bring this man into my home!" sputtered Mrs. Langdon.

"I dare, madam, because it seems you are being less than honest with those around you, myself included. And I am not one to take that lightly," he said menacingly.

Mrs. Langdon blanched, backing away from his anger.

"John?" Mary's voice was weak and filled with despair. "It cannot be you; I am losing my mind," she sobbed dryly. "Mama said I would if I did not get hold of myself, and it is finally happening."

"My darling girl," responded John fervently, "you are perfectly sane." Lifting Mary in his arms, he carried her into the drawing room, settling his precious burden on a silk-covered sofa. Taking a seat beside her, he untied her bonnet and eased it from her blond hair. The sight of her tear-streaked face swept away any lingering belief she had played him false. Dropping her bonnet to the floor, he captured her hands and brought them to his lips.

"Oh, John," Mary sighed, reaching up to touch his

face. "Is it really you? This is not just another dream, is it? If it is, it has never been so real before."

"I am real, my darling. Feel, I am flesh and blood," he said, holding her hands to his face until they cupped the warmth of his cheeks of their own volition.

Tears of joy dampened the radiant smile lighting her face. "Yes! Yes, you are alive! And, finally, so am I!" Mary exclaimed, throwing her arms around his neck.

"Mary. Mary," he whispered, chanting her name like a prayer. "I thought I would die when I received your letter severing our relationship, but I never completely gave up hope. Now I'm glad I did not." He pulled the young woman closer, holding her steadily in strong arms, breathing in the sweet scent of her.

"My letter? What letter?" Mary asked, shaking her head in disbelief. "I wrote no letter like that to you."

Their joy was interrupted by the harsh voice of Mrs. Langdon. "You will leave this house immediately, sir," she demanded of the military man.

"No, he will not, Mama," spoke up Mary, her hands clutching John's broad shoulders.

The earl could scarcely believe the change in her. There was red in her cheeks and fire in her eyes.

"I will not lose John again, no matter what you say, no matter how we must live." Her voice gained strength as she spoke. "For living in poverty is far better than what I have called living these past three years."

"I don't believe poverty will be called for, my love," replied the smiling captain. "But you're right," he said, looking toward Mrs. Langdon. "I will not leave, madam, until I have found out the truth." He turned to Mary again, still clasping her tightly in his arms. "Tell me, my love, did we have a child?"

"Oh, John. Yes, we did have a baby," she cried, heartbroken. "But she was born early, only a short time after I learned of your death, and died a few hours after birth. I did not even see her. I was delirious with fever for several days and by that time she was already buried."

He held the sobbing woman in his arms, attempting to soothe her.

"And what of Caroline's child?" asked the earl, unable to keep quiet any longer.

"Caroline's child, my lord?" A confused expression appeared on Mary's face. "Caroline does not have a child."

"The earl tells me Caroline has in her keeping a child who looks like me, Mary. Could it be true?" asked John.

"Of course not," she began staunchly, defending her sister's virtue before remembering her own fall from grace. "At least not that I know of. But we have been out of touch for some time now. Even so, I would never rebuke her for honest feelings."

Looking into her face, John could not believe Mary was conspiring to keep his child from him. "After talking to Lord Castleton, I believe the child to be ours, Mary. Could there be no way it could have survived? Remember, you did not see her."

"No, I didn't, but I know what happened. Mama explained everything to me . . ." Her voice trailed off as she met her beloved's gaze. "Oh, no, John, do not even think it," she whispered, disbelief betraying her vulnerability. "No one could be that cruel."

"You are thinking it yourself, my love. She kept us apart, didn't she?" answered John, regretting she must suffer more pain.

Mary turned to her mother, standing stiffly by the door. "Mama? You would not . . . could not do this to me," she pleaded.

The older woman said not a word but stared out the window. Mary looked again to the two men, her pale face a mask of shock and confusion.

"Caroline brought a child with her to Castleton," explained the earl. "A small blond-haired, blue-eyed beauty of approximately three years. Her name is Lucinda; she called her Lucy."

Mary's face went white again and she leaned heavily against the uniformed man. "That was Caroline's favorite name for me. But she could have named her child after me, if she had one. I know she loved me even though Mama said she did not." She tried with a last desperate attempt not to believe ill of her mother.

"Yes, that's probably what happened," agreed Mrs. Langdon, breaking her silence. "She was always uncontrollable."

"Caroline is still an innocent in intimate matters, madam," replied the earl curtly.

"And what do you know of it, my lord?" she sneered. "The chit is a consummate actress. I should know."

"And I should know of what I speak. I have had a little experience in that line myself."

Mrs. Langdon turned back to the window. "Believe

270

what you will. What I have done, I have done only for the good of my daughter," she contended righteously.

"Mama, are you saying my child lived and is with Caroline?" Silence greeted her query. "How could you?" she asked, the enormity of her mother's treachery devastating her. "I know you hold my idea of love in contempt, but I never knew you hated me. Please, Mama, tell me this is untrue." Again, silence met her plea. Finally accepting the irrefutable truth, Mary appealed to her love. "Oh, John, take me away. Let us go to our child. I must see her, and I must see Caroline."

"Have your maid pack as quickly as possible. Just enough for a few days. We'll get what you need later."

"Please don't leave, John. Not now, not for a moment," she pleaded.

"Don't fear, my love. I'll not leave you again. I don't trust your mother after all she's done. We'll await you here. And don't worry. Your mother won't interfere," he reassured her. "She'll keep us company while you prepare for your journey."

Mary hurried from the room and the two men settled down to wait. Mrs. Langdon kept her back to the room, never once removing her gaze from the window or breaking the heavy pall of silence that hung over the occupants. A short time later Mary reappeared, a footman carrying her portmanteau. The three left the house without speaking again to the tight-lipped woman at the window.

* * *

Arrayed in a lovely new pearl-hued morning dress, embellished with dark green leaves embroidered around the neck and hem, Caroline bent to clip another rose for the basket she carried. The weather had been perfect this summer, so her gardener said, and the profusion of blooms attested to the truth of his claims. However, it was only now, some five weeks after her return to Birchwood, that she was able to appreciate her surroundings again.

After leaving Castleton, she had disappeared with ease in the crowds that had flocked to London for the victory celebrations ordered by Prinny. Caroline had always revered Wellington, and she found it ironic his return helped her escape the notice of one of his most valued men. Mrs. Langdon's letter was readily accepted by her father's man of business, and she was soon on her way out of the crowded city, traveling anonymously in a closed carriage.

Since her arrival at Birchwood, she had executed the everyday motions of living a life irrevocably changed by her experience with Lord Castleton. The happiness she thought to experience on her return had not materialized, and she knew it would always be supplanted by the memory of a tall, dark-haired man.

Caroline was further distressed by the continuing absence of Mary. She had expected her stepsister to have arrived some weeks before and wondered if her mother had interfered once again. She would wait one more week, and if Mary had not shown up by then, she would attempt to contact her.

Her basket full, she turned to see three people approaching over the short clipped grass but, facing into the sun, could not recognize them.

Unprepared for his intense response to seeing Caroline, Giles drank in the sight of her in huge, hungry gulps. Her hair was banded with a ribbon and hung loose, blazing in the sun. She was thinner and her extraordinary eyes dominated the delicate face she turned toward her visitors. Only years of strict military training kept him from breaking into a run and sweeping her into his arms.

Mary was not so hesitant, running toward Caroline as fast as her skirts would allow, throwing herself into her stepsister's arms. Giles and John slowed their approach to give the sisters a few moments of privacy. Neither could ask for a more pleasant picture than the two young women's embrace, blond curls next to auburn, flowers strewn around their feet from the discarded basket.

But Giles could not be denied his love's presence for long, and soon Caroline looked up into his dark, stormy eyes. She lost all color when she saw him and the blond man by his side.

"John," she said unsteadily, choosing to ignore the earl. "I thought you dead for so long. Even though I've known the truth these past weeks, it's still a shock seeing you."

"It seems you were not the only one." He smiled, meeting Mary's tearful gaze. "It took some time to convince your sister I was real. I hope you'll accept the fact of my presence more readily."

"I am more than happy to be able to grant your wish and welcome you home," Caroline vowed, tiptoeing up to place an affectionate kiss on his cheek.

"Thank you. You're going to be a wonderful sister-in-law," he continued, smiling at her surprised look.

"You're getting married?" she asked, happiness lighting her face.

"We already are," answered Mary, shyly extending her hand where a gold wedding band with small diamonds glittered. "Lord Castleton arranged a special license before we left London."

"Oh, Mary, I'm so pleased." She hugged her sister again, then stepped back, laughing while they both mopped tears from their eyes.

"Caroline, please don't think it rude if I interrupt to ask about the child you have." John put his arm around his new wife and drew her to his side. "Is she ours? Mine and Mary's?"

"Please tell us," begged Mary. "I did not want to hope, but I have. The last days have been endless, and I cannot bear to wait any longer."

"Yes, Mary, Lucy is your child, and I have taken very good care of her," Caroline assured her. Although she loved Mary and knew the strain she had been under, there was still a corner of Caroline's heart that could not reconcile her sister's willingness to reject her child. For Lucy's well-being, she had to be sure Mary's unexpected solicitude was not inspired by John's return. Caroline steeled her heart against Mary's distress. "But it has taken some time for you to become concerned about her," she pointed out.

"I only found out a few days ago that she was alive. If it hadn't been for Lord Castleton, I still would not have known, nor would John and I be reunited." The misery of the past three years was reflected in her face. "Oh, Caroline," she sobbed in abandonment, "Mama told me she died at birth and that she was buried in an unmarked grave, because you wouldn't allow her to be buried in the family cemetery. My anguish has never healed, with no remembrance of her birth or death, and not even a plot of ground over which to grieve."

There was no disputing the evidence of her stepsister's sincerity. "Mary, how could you have thought that of me?" appealed Caroline, shocked by her revelations. "And how could I have believed it of you?" she demanded of herself, ashamed by her lack of faith.

Giving in to John's and Mary's urgings, Caroline described the scene leading to her departure from Birchwood Hall. Briefly, she recounted her and Lucy's life to present, promising to go into more detail later.

At its telling, Mary again dissolved into heart-wrenching sobs. John enfolded her in his arms, wet traces also marking the soldier's face. "I must see her. Please, I must see her now," Mary pleaded, her face against John's chest.

"And you shall, my love. We both shall, just as soon as you gain control," promised John. "We don't want to frighten her, do we?" He placed a kiss on the golden curls and looked appealing at Caroline.

"That's right, Mary," agreed Caroline. "She's very kindhearted, and it would upset her to see you in so much distress. Besides, she's having her nap now. By the time you stop being such a watering pot, she'll be awake and I'll take you up to her."

"Oh, Caroline, thank you," cried Mary, mopping the tears from her face. "Our baby would have been lost to us if you hadn't saved her. I don't know how we can ever repay you."

"Shush, Lucy. I ask for nothing except your forgiveness for keeping your child from you. No matter how good my intentions, I should have believed in you and found a way to let you know what had happened. But it's time to put all that behind us. Now stop your crying or you'll never see little Lucy. I'll tell you everything when you're composed, but know that I never stopped loving you." She hugged her stepsister tightly.

"Come now, love," said John, seeing the earl waited impatiently for a word with Caroline. "Let's prepare to meet our daughter." The captain guided Mary toward a garden bench and settled there, pulling the weeping woman against his broad chest.

"You can no longer ignore me, Caroline," Lord Castleton said quietly.

"I'm surprised you chose to seek me out, my lord. I would think it beneath your station to pursue a Cyprian to offer carte blanche again. Surely there are many women ready to throw themselves into your bed for much less effort." Caroline's words were brittle with anger.

Twenty-Two

"There is no carte blanche. There never should have been. I've come to apologize. And you will listen to me since I've finally run you to earth."

"Still demanding, my lord? I see nothing has changed at all," she replied coldly.

"No, damn it! I'm not demanding," he asserted angrily, forgetting his vow to remain calm. "I'm just trying to untangle this coil. It would have been easier if you had trusted me to begin with."

With no secrets demanding complete discretion, Lord Castleton felt the full import of Caroline's temper. "So now it's my fault," she shot back, green fire sparking in her eyes. "My life—even more important, Lucy's existence—depended upon our secrecy. She could have been taken from me and thrown into an orphan's home, or worse. You were a stranger. How could I confide in you?" she demanded, her anger matching his.

"Caroline," he murmured, finally understanding her actions but more determined than ever to make her listen. "You know as well as I, we were more than strangers from the first day we met. It was there, unexplainable but real. Tell me you know it."

Caroline stared into his dark eyes. For the first time she could speak frankly without fear for Lucy. "Yes, I know it now and I knew it then. I was just hiding, not dead," she said with a flash of her old humor. "But don't you see that was even more reason to keep quiet? How could I trust my feelings? They were so new, I thought them a product of my loneliness." She was unaware her voice pleaded for understanding. "I had never felt anything like I did for you. But you spoke only of desire, and as little as you may think of me, I must have more than physical fulfillment."

His spirit soared. She had just admitted in so many words she loved him. Hope sprang to life again. Surely when she knew how much he loved her, she would forgive him.

"Caroline, my dear, I—"

"Caroline, I think I'm ready to meet Lucy now," interrupted Mary.

Alveston read the frustration in the earl's face and felt a stab of pity for the man. He understood the need to straighten out matters with Caroline, but Lucy had waited three years to meet her parents. The earl could suffer a bit longer. He might be more appreciative when he laid his heart at Caroline's feet.

"I'll take you to the nursery immediately," replied Caroline. "Let me tell you a little about Lucy; it might help you become acquainted." Taking one on each arm, she continued to talk as they strolled toward the house.

The earl followed impatiently, reminded of her preoccupation with Charles on the riverbank after he first discovered his love for her. Would he never have her to himself?

It was some time later that Caroline returned to the drawing room, where Giles waited. He had been provided with refreshments but did not want even a whiff of liquor on his breath when he spoke to her.

"How did the introductions go?" he asked as she entered the room.

"Very well," Caroline answered with her old familiar smile. "Lucy is taken with Mary's blond hair and John's medals. She seems to be enjoying herself hugely." Caroline felt as light as a breeze with the weight of the last three years lifted from her shoulders. Even though she could no longer claim Lucy as her daughter, the child was at last in her rightful place with her parents.

"Then that leaves only our situation to be straightened out," he said with determination.

"Our situation, my lord? I didn't realize we had one," she remarked, looking down her finely molded nose at him. "You no longer need me now that Mrs. Davies is well. You can readily hire a London housekeeper who is more in keeping with the duties you so graciously outlined to me, and I have Birchwood again as my home. It seems we are free of any obligation to one another."

Giles felt shame rise in remembrance of a night he would rather forget, but he could not retreat if he wanted this woman for his own.

"You must listen and know my sincerity," he pleaded, moving closer. "I would give anything to undo that last night at Castleton. I was consumed with jealousy. I had finally admitted my desire for you was love, not lust." His voice dropped to a husky rasp, which set off sparks of excitement in Caroline. "I had never loved before, and it was a new and exhilarating experience. To be immediately confronted with what seemed your perfidy was more than I could bear."

He passed a hand across his eyes before he continued. Remembering he had made the same gesture on the day they met, Caroline recognized the frustration it indicated, but she would not let herself weaken now.

"I couldn't bear the thought that someone else had lain with you, possessed you, other than in the honorable estate of matrimony. I convinced myself I could accept that, but anything else enraged me."

"Even when your intentions were not so honorable, my lord?" she asked, still insulted he had, however temporarily, thought so little of her.

"Even so, my lady." The rueful smile did not reach his shadowed eyes. "There was no doubt in my mind you were a lady, from the moment I rescued you from that infamous scrub bucket," he continued, his lips curving in a gentle smile of remembrance. "But I was determined not to become attached to anyone whose eventual loss would bring me pain. Evidently, I perceived a threat in you from the first, because I denied my true feelings, replacing them with the basest intent." Red tinged the ridge of his cheekbones at his confession.

"Caroline, I would ask you to forget that night, but the things I said to you were unforgivable. I hope that time and your generous spirit will allow those memories to fade. I know it makes no sense at all to you now, but that despicable scene rose from my love for you. If you wanted retribution, you could have chosen no harsher punishment than the past weeks. I've searched continuously since your disappearance, hoping to bring you back to Castleton where you belong."

"To become your doxy, my lord?" she inquired bitterly.

"No, first to become my wife," he admitted humbly. "Then, if you wouldn't agree to that, I had determined to stay in London and insist you and Lucinda remain at Castleton for as long as you needed. You'd mentioned being able to take your place in society again. I thought to wait until you were ready to disclose your secret to me, although I was not at all sure of my patience. Denton and I had even discussed a trip to the Continent in order to remove me from temptation."

Caroline did not know what to say. While Mary played with her daughter, John had told her of the earl's frantic search for her. His offer to give up Castleton was proof enough he loved her. She studied him from beneath her lashes. He had lost weight again, and the haunted look had returned to his eyes.

Despite the insult of his offer that last night at Castleton, her love for him had not changed. He had attempted to hide his generous nature behind an exterior of indifference, but his concern for Charles and those on the estate betrayed him. More than once she had glimpsed the man he would be once he dropped his protective facade. It was this man she had come to love and wanted to live with for the rest of her life.

"And how does Castleton fare?" she inquired, playing for time.

He mulled over his answer, deciding it was too late for pride. "It's no longer a home without you, Caroline. The plans for the school have gone begging. The servants are discontent, Mrs. Crawford's cooking lacks its flair, and I swear, I heard the door hinges squeak on my last visit. I can't ride out without the tenants beleaguering me about when you're returning, and each day brings someone to the doorstep wanting a syrup or a salve from your weeds."

"You're as bad as Charles," she responded vigorously. "They are not weeds, but perfectly acceptable healing herbs for certain maladies. I left particular instructions with Madeline for their preparation. Don't tell me she hasn't made them up." Concern sharpened her voice.

"Let's say she's tried but has been less than successful. However, I must admit to some interesting odors emanating from the stillroom." He was heartened by her look of misgiving and continued. "But I've forgotten the most important thing, Caroline."

"And what is that, my lord?" She could not break his ardent gaze.

"Myself," he replied, his voice again husky with emotion. "I've missed you with every fiber of my being." He stepped close enough for his breath to stir her hair. "I've returned once to Castleton since you've been gone. The music room was too still, your chair in the library too empty. I couldn't even sit at the breakfast table without seeing you beside me." Her rose fragrance brought back vivid memories, and his senses stirred.

Taking her hands, he pressed a kiss in each palm. "Even so near you as now, I miss that part of you that is not yet mine." Caroline colored more from the excitement his words conjured up than from embarrassment.

"Caroline, I don't even anticipate a positive reply but I must try, for I love you more than life itself. The prospect of a future without you is one I cannot bear to contemplate. I want to waste no more time in making you completely mine. I've had a special license waiting since your disappearance. If you'll only say the words, we can be married immediately."

A rumble from the earl's stomach for once made him color in embarrassment, and he wished he had partaken of the refreshments. "As you can plainly and unromantically hear, my stomach misses you, too."

"And how, my lord," asked Caroline with the old twinkle returning to her green eyes, "do I know it's not just my mother's recipes you desire?"

"I'll admit they're a great inducement, my love. But say yes, and you'll find my appetite for something other than food is just as insatiable for being kept waiting so long."

"How could I refuse such a proposal, my lord?" she said as his lips claimed hers for his own.

Summer was again in the river meadow when Lord Castleton and his countess rode admiringly through the wildflowers. They made a handsome couple, the earl's broad shoulders encased in a green riding coat from the expert hand of Weston, topped buff breeches, and gleaming black Hessians. Caroline was radiant in a green velvet habit, a small hat perched atop her head, where a green dyed ostrich plume curved enchantingly against her cheek before coming to rest on her shining curls.

"It was only last year I saw you here, Caro, looking more beautiful than the blossoms themselves."

"But not as fashionable as I am now," she teased. "My new habit is perfection, Giles, but you are completely spoiling me."

He waved a dismissing hand at her thanks, though secretly pleased she liked his gift. "You had best become used to it, Countess, for I intend to continue spoiling you, even though you are beautiful in anything you wear.

"You need not flatter me so, my Lord Castleton. I've already instructed Madeline to prepare your favorite dinner this evening," she answered pertly.

"Here I'm trying to lure you to the riverbank for a bit of debauchery and you mention food. How gauche, Countess," he reprimanded her.

"Just what is your definition of *gauche*, my lord?" she asked, smiling. "We left our bed only a short time ago, and now it appears you're attempting to seduce me again."

"Your omelette has given me strength. You didn't by chance toss in a few erotic herbs, did you, my lady? I do feel particularly restless this morning," he said, giving her a lecherous look.

Caroline laughed. "Giles, you're shameless."

"I just want to catch up with our friends," he explained, wondering which of them their first child would resemble.

"I'm so happy for Charles and Eugenia," enthused Caroline, recalling the announcement they had recently received from the newlywed couple. "They're perfectly matched, and to be setting up their nursery so soon is wonderful."

"A man can't wait forever to insure his line," Giles replied, remembering a particularly private place by the river.

"Did I tell you Mary is increasing again?" she asked, ignoring the innuendo of his comment. "She and John are making up for lost time."

"An admirable quality . . . perhaps one we should emulate," he suggested, deciding to abandon subtlety.

"And have you noticed how quickly Lucy has taken to Mary?" asked Caroline, still following her own train of though. "Why, she barely cried the last time we parted. I haven't wanted to complain," she continued wistfully, "for I am quite happy being an aunt to Lucy, but I must admit I miss being a mother."

Caroline's eyes looked soft and warm and slightly out of focus. Giles was determined to begin fulfilling her heart's desire as soon as they dismounted.

"Allowing them to live at Birchwood was very unselfish, Caroline. I know what the estate means to you."

"It was my childhood home, Giles," answered Caroline, changing the course of her thoughts before she became maudlin. "I'm more than fond of it for my father's memory, but it needs a loving family in it, and John and Mary will do nicely. After all, I have you and Castleton now," she said affectionately.

"Yes, you do, my dear," he replied, reaching out for her hand and bringing it to his lips.

"Giles," Caroline said with a warning note in her voice, "I become suspicious when you call me 'my dear' in broad daylight in the middle of a meadow."

"But we've reached the riverbank, love." He quickly dismounted and turned to lift her down. "Now let's see if we can work up an appetite for that special dinner you planned, and perhaps accommodate your maternal wish at the same time." His lips met hers in a kiss that never failed to make him forget his stomach.

A Memorable Collection of Regency Romances

BY ANTHEA MALCOLM AND VALERIE KING